SENTINEL
IN THE MOORS

BOOKS BY SHIRLEY BURTON

HISTORICAL FICTION

Homage: Chronicles of a Habitant

THRILLERS

Red Jackal

THOMAS YORK SERIES:

Under the Ashes - Book One

The Frizon - Book Two

Rogue Courier - Book Three

Secret Cache - Book Four

The Paris Network - Book Five

MYSTERY

Sentinel in the Moors

INSPECTOR FURNACE MYSTERIES:

Mystery at Grey Stokes

Swindle: Mystery at Sea

CHRISTMAS

Clockmaker's Christmas

Christmas Treasure Box

FANTASY

Boy from Saint-Malo

shirleyburtonbooks.com

SENTINEL IN THE MOORS

SHIRLEY BURTON

HIGH STREET PRESS

HIGH STREET PRESS
Calgary, AB
www.highstreetpress.com
First printing 2016

Printed in the United States of America and worldwide under license.
Available in eBook formats.
Cover photo licensed Shutterstock.com.
Design and edit Bruce Burton

Library and Archives Canada Cataloguing in Publication.

Burton, Shirley, 1950-, author
Sentinel in the moors / Shirley Burton

ISBN 978-1-927839-06-5 (pbk.). —ISBN 978-1-927839-11-9 (bound)
ISBN 978-1-927839-07-2 (ebook)

STAITHES
North Yorkshire, England

The charming seaside village of Staithes in North Yorkshire is the location of the fiction SENTINEL IN THE MOORS. *Roxby Beck is a stream running through Staithes, the border between the Borough of Scarborough and Redcar and Cleveland.*

Enjoy the fictional characters and the pretty setting of this wonderful town.

SENTINEL
IN THE MOORS

1

Viking Longboat - North Sea Coast of England, 1066

THE DRAGON HEAD, carved into the breast of the boat, rose above the crest of the wave, then plunged under the ocean's swell. Rolling in the murky water, the wooden longboat was spat out to come apart against rocks under the surface. The boulders should have been a forewarning that this was not to be a landing cove.

The angry wave jolted and swamped the gunwales, as the men's long oars fought the tempest. Thunder and lightning bolts cracked across the sky while the sea pounded its fury.

With battle as their mission, the Viking clinker schooner was sailing under a lone square mast, to bring Scandinavian warriors to the northeastern coast of England.

Built with overlapping planks, the double-ended hull was now failing against the beast that the crew feared had been sent by Thor, the god of thunder. As the frame split, the crew spilt out into the ten meter surf.

The pilot gripped a broken crosspiece from the bow, and yelled to Har, "O'er thar . . . the Peninsula and harbor." His voice was devoured by the wind, and he waved an arm to the shore, then was gone.

Har, the Norwegian King, had a full height of seven feet, with giant hands and feet—an intimidating appearance that created fear even across his own land. His reputation was further exaggerated by a legendary feature of one eyebrow inches higher than the other. With flowing golden hair, he prided himself for the length and beauty of his beard and mustache.

"Land Ho," Har yelled back. His head was barely above water, and an iron helmet and nose guard obstructed his vision, with the weight restricting his breathing. Fearing imminent drowning, he let his crown drop to the bottom of the sea.

The savagery of the North Sea pulled half his oarsmen into the deep, and the remaining Norsemen were catapulted against the cliffs, with survivors clamoring for land and life.

Har, the son of Sigurd Syr, struggled to tread water, constricted by his clothing and boots, and kept his head above the frothy surf, hiding his panic from the men.

He flailed for any buoyant debris, and wrapped his arms around a split plank. With its security, he raised his head for a full gulp of the sea air, filling the ache in his lungs.

I hear the chaos of my men—I'm not the lone survivor. For the sake of my people and the loyal crew, I will survive. My destiny is to reclaim England as my father intended. My quest, to lead my men into battle even to my death, will prepare my way to Valhalla.

Grasping the longboard from the helm, he cried out, "Surely one of the gods will save me. Balder, God of Peace and Goodness, have mercy on my soul and spare my crew."

Before long the sea was calm as he willed.

Over the surface, he viewed the jutting land within reach. Exhausted, he rested on the board and allowed the tide to propel him to the rocky shore.

Yielding his remaining strength to the strong arms of two surviving crew, he was pulled, bleeding and with feet dragging, over the rocks to a moorland plateau. The beleaguered crew went about burying their dead in a pagan ritual of cremation, then set a roaring campfire of split yew.

A skinned, woolly sheep was roasting on a huge spit, with milk salvaged from the unfortunate beast to strengthen Har, barely strong enough to sit. The hide would be cured to make clean clothing and blankets, and the sheep's head made into a King's helmet, fit for royalty. Meanwhile, wild boars were hunted for their tusks, essential for the battle cry, and ironstone from the rocks was crafted into hammers and swords replacing those on the ocean floor.

Scavengers were sent to gather broken shards of wood to build new shields for the battlefield. Residue from an iron bog was cooked into a pliable mush and baked into iron sabers and nails.

Nothing in life would be wasted by the indigenous people of the North Sea.

Sven, one of Har's scouts, returned with maidens borrowed from a nearby Viking homestead, with pots and a clay oven and libations for a feast. The local women would be their luxury as cooking servants, to bake flat iron bread to feed the army, then serve wines until the wee hours of the morning when the crew was fully intoxicated and asleep. A few of Har's crewmen had frequented the Viking village on earlier travels, bearing children and building stone houses.

A mile inland, the advance party of Har's Norwegian raiders awaited his arrival by a monolith, their arrows hewed and swords sharpened in preparation for the impending war.

"Honorable leader, the scouts have returned to tell us that Edwin of Mercia and Morcar of Northumbria are rallying north of the moors. They're camped at Stamford Brigg, at least seven days journey. We can follow the Derwent from the coast. Tostig has barricaded the bridge and would prevent our advancement."

"My brother Tostig—is he there now?" Har asked, wearing his new headdress. It was suitable for the King of Norway, his title earned after his victorious invasion of Northumbria.

"My Royal Highness. Ye Tostig awaits thar with the English flag. They will obstruct your rightful path to the throne of England too, at all costs. We can pass at night in the Derwent. The river flows all the way from the sea to the brigg of Stamford."

"Salvage a boat, and divide the men—some to boats and others on land. They will not expect both. I know the conniving of my brother."

The day of advance on Stamford took until dusk, setting up camp in the misty moors, not far from Tostig's camp at Riccall. Their encampment was stalked with scouts sent by Tostig, perched in holes to survey the approach of any Englishmen. The intention of a surprised ambush had leaked its way to Stamford, and the English lay in wait.

By the light of a campfire, Har's men simulated the Viking raid on a piece of wooden board. Stones created Hnefatafl, a chess-like game with twelve red pawns and twelve white of walrus teeth, a king carved from whalebone, and a spiked die cube. The bold who dared to challenge their comrades would meet the ultimate enduring decision in a single moment. A loss would be a disgrace, and winning was either victorious or deceitful, depending on the status of the opponent.

When the board was reduced to two Kings, the opponents were in painful mental debate. It would not be viewed well to succeed over Hardrada's son, and the defender's temple pulsed with sweat—not pleading for his life, but in a battle to the end like roulette, a precursor of September 28, 1066, the end of a Viking era.

Feasting on wild boar preceded their attack on the Saxons. The warriors' spirits were raised to frenzied levels with games of wrestling and bone tossing, until blood was shed, encouraging the barbarians' rise to ferociousness. These were preliminary exercises to heighten the taste for battle.

In the veil of night, Hardrada's men were ready, attacking with vengeance, with the forewarned English prepared to retaliate with sights to take their leader.

Har's brother, Tostig Godwinson, was determined at all costs to eliminate Har's claim to the British throne. A bloody battle raged for hours, with Hardrada's men finally chased into retreat, pursued by swords, spears, and arrows. When caught, they were bludgeoned and some beheaded.

The brothers, Tostig and Hardrada had quarreled viciously over the brewing rebellion.

Har wanted unity for England, with Tostig preventing him. The brothers had come to a standstill, glaring with opposing vengeance on the threshold to determine England's destiny.

In Har's final battle, Tostig chased him down, shooting at him with poison arrows. At last, with the finest sight, Godwinson pulled back on the poison tipped golden arrow he carried in his sack.

Hardrada saw it spiraling through the sky, before impaling his eye. He knew it was the coveted golden arrow.

"Nay, nay, dear brother," Godwinson said, and with an evil glint, he smote his brother with his sword.

Watching the life ease from his eyes as he held him close, Tostig jabbed deeper and deeper. Any kinship he had ever felt to Har, his own flesh and blood, was washed away, consumed by his raging power and greed.

The ground heaved and groaned with a clap of thunder across the sky. Hardrada lay on the ground as life seeped from his loins. Godwinson stood over him with his war sword, and in one swoop, Har was beheaded.

Godwinson charged that his brother's head be taken instantly from his sight. "Get these eyes away from me."

"And the gold on the arrow?"

"Bury it with the head. Don't tell me where you have laid it. But be warned that the arrow is cursed. Let him be buried without riches, so that he will be denied from Valhalla."

Har's head was carefully wrapped in a royal cloak and placed inside a wooden sepulcher, carved with the emblem of his Dragon boat. A fiery, crimson ruby was placed in the etching of the Dragon's eye with hopes of Har having a chance to still see the world.

Two supporters, Mali and Gurd, carried the box to the moors of northeastern Yorkshire, to the grand underground chambers, site of past pagan rituals. Others captured a wild boar to sacrifice in a ceremonial burnt offering.

Chanting and wailing vibrated through the next night, a mournful grieving worthy of the King of Norway. A collection of meaningful items from the men and a cache of jewels salvaged from the longboat were buried with enough silver and gold to ensure Har's spirit would be well provided for, in spite of Tostig's demand.

With the last sentinel of his soldiers lingering, his son Olev mounted the limestone stairs to the burial chamber, marking a final message in sheep's blood on the walls.

Cut from the cliffs, a giant slab of titan limestone was wedged securely, taking the might and muscle of many men to embed it into the land. A black stone, measuring eight feet, was pounded into the soil at arm's height, as an escape lever should Har's spirit decide to leave the burial chamber.

Olev made a final etching and pressed a ruby into the carving, then graced the entry with crossed torches, oiled and soaked in animal fat and wrapped with hair.

"If I should ever come this way, dear Father, you will see me," he declared.

Brush and rocks were piled on the limestone slab to protect it from animals and hide it from curious generations.

For centuries, it remained untouched. The surrounding land eroded into dales and gullies, and the titan was consumed with heather and moss. The mist of the moors gave birth to crustaceans and plant life, devouring signs of the chamber at the end of the Roxby Beck in North Yorkshire. Although Har's body was buried in the grave at Pevensey by his son, Olav, his head was missing when that site was later exhumed.

After the battle, the Viking soldiers scattered into the woodlands, and many died of famine or exposure. For days Tostig celebrated jubilantly, feasting and drinking into a stupor with his army.

William, Duke of Normandy, was furious at Hardrada's death and ordered that the lands be salted to prevent foliage and crops in the Yorkshire Moors, as an act of vengeance.

Rumors prevailed for centuries that the ghost of Hardrada remained in the moors, his presence signaled by claps of thunder and deathly moans from the underground tunnels.

On rare summer nights, guttural roars were said to rise from Whitby Abbey, Helmsley Castle, and Roxby Beck, claiming by every generation to result from wizardry and mythical gods seeking revenge.

Erosion over hundreds of years of abandonment produced fields of heather, dales and glens, burying the dry river beds that had carried the Norsemen from the briny sea. Hulls of longboats and skeletons of pirates of yore remained untouched until the latter part of the 19th century.

As mines were dug to bring out iron, occasional hoards surfaced with coins and Viking remnants, and by the early twentieth century, treasure hunting was becoming English sport. Museums were bursting with medieval antiquities, and pockets of farmers and hunters challenged by the prospect of rich rewards.

British Museum Thirst for Archaeology

THE APPETITE FOR new artifacts of old civilizations could hardly be met fast enough in the information-mad twentieth century. Excavations in Egypt were enthralling academics with the 1922 discovery of King Tut's tomb, the boy pharaoh from 1322 B.C. By the 1970's, the exhibit became a hit in Europe and a tour of a thousand artifacts bringing in North America.

It was Patricia Farrow's tenth year employed at the Natural History Museum in California, and she relished the new assignment as a clerk to schedule classroom tours for King Tut's exhibit at San Diego's Balboa Park in 2014.

Patricia was divorced, living with her son Gabe in nearby Sherman Heights, within walking distance to her work on sunny mornings.

Gabe was excelling in University, with his passion for archaeology paralleling his mother's. With regular museum exposure, his knowledge and familiarity led to part-time work as a tour guide for the Tut exhibit, with authorized access to its vast inventory of archives.

Long past closing times, Gabe stayed and studied ancient history, noting and scrutinizing artifacts. Lloyd Swanson took note of Gabe's passionate interest and sought to recruit him into an internship program. Swanson's endorsement, as Gabe's advocate, opened the doors for the young academic to gain entry status and opportunity at the Museum of Natural History in New York.

A few days before leaving San Diego, Gabe stopped in the hall, overhearing an intense boardroom discussion amongst curators about English hoards and the complications of the Treasury. The door was ajar, and Gabe leaned to the wall to listen.

What piqued his interest most were the medieval artifacts buried in the countryside of England. When the meeting broke, Swanson was the first out the door, and was startled by Gabe's presence.

"Ha, the desire to overcome history is in your veins, Gabe. After a few months under your belt in New York, look into their exchange program to England. You'd be smack dab in the middle of a medieval world," Swanson said.

"You've been very kind to me, Mr. Swanson. I plan to make you proud . . . and yes, I will pursue that road too."

Gabe's mother was saddened by his plan to leave, even across the continent to New York.

"I always wanted to give you a better life, Gabe. A family, with brothers or sisters. When your father and I married, I had Cinderella plans, but one night after work, our lives all changed.

"He was devastated he'd lost our entire savings to a UK gold scammer. A Florida schemer had enticed him to buy gold, with the certificates held by a London securities firm. Your Dad learned that day that police had raided the Florida office and closed it down. Obviously, there never was any gold.

"I said it didn't matter, we could start over, but his pride was damaged with a deep shame he couldn't overcome. That's why he left. He swore he'd get even and come back with our savings. I never saw him again, Gabe, although for the next five or six years, modest funds were deposited to an account for you every year on your birthday.

"If you ever do get to England, be wary of precious metal scams. You never get the genuine goods."

Gabe had said little as he listened intently, and she changed course. "Perhaps at Christmas, you'll come home?"

Packing his future into a small duffle, Gabe retrieved a packet from his drawer. Years before, he had discovered it in one his mother's photo boxes. He had scant memories of his father and had been taken back with photos to the anguish and realization that his father had abandoned his family. He always knew he would never see him again. The family photos had the face of his father clipped out. Over years, that hurt turned to anger.

At the bottom of the box was a newspaper clipping taken from The London News. Gabe held it close to examine the faded print, of several men at a reception in London, England, receiving some sort of honors for service in protecting history.

Perhaps if I can get to London, I can track down these men. My heart tells me that one of them is my father. I'd like to meet the man and see how his life has prospered with his new family.

Gabe placed the folded paper in the back flap of his pocket book.

In New York, Gabe applied in a flash for placement in Medieval History of the United Kingdom. His reference letters earned attention and priority, and within days he was assigned to the studies of Viking archaeology. He studied the museum's exchange policy for internships, first requiring a minimum of twelve months in dedicated studies.

Walking home from the West Central Park museum on his first day, he formulated his plans to get to London.

I'm onboard for that. In my spare time I'll attend community college and acquire trades skills. One starts next week on glass blowing with another in gas-fitting to complement the certificate program. Could be fun.

New York was vibrant, a world apart from California's freeways. Gabe kept to himself, preferring to be a loner and faceless. Taking a room in Hamilton Heights, he was a short walk to the train and twenty minute commute from Central Park.

Passing 5th Avenue at 79th, the aroma of grilled sausage with sauerkraut lured him in the first week and became a daily routine.

The faces of the same newsboys, shoeshine kids, the gyro carts, fake Rolex kiosks and handbag sellers kept the same spots as he passed daily, whether morning or evening. They were nameless, but were the extent of his friends, other than workers at the museum.

The streets bustled at supper hour and weekends, with entertainment by mimes, magicians and gymnastics. An accordion played lively music near his flat, with an audience mix of homeless and Armani's. Gabe never felt alone.

Nightly, he pored over online subscriptions to British newspapers. Enthralled with a new hoard discovery near Whitby in the North Yorkshire Moors, he researched the topography and history of the coastal villages, and matched them to Norsemen routes in the medieval artifacts rooms.

On paper, he knew the land so well by now that he bantered to himself that he could walk the terrain blind-folded.

But equal to his passion for the discovery of hoards, was his curiosity about the men in the news clipping. The paper was unfolded and tacked to the wall.

Who are they?

A letter waited in his box. He knew it was his mother's handwriting, but seldom heard from her. A premonition and sense of misgiving needled him even before he ripped open the envelope.

Dearest Gabe,

My news is sad today and I'd prefer to say this in person. Uncle Hermes unfortunately fell on hard times. A man in the city sold him tainted gold with a guaranteed return, but the fellow then absconded with the fortunes of many folks who wanted to put a little away for retirement.

Hermes is a proud man and didn't boast of his misfortune. He couldn't bear to tell Aunt Viola that they had been wiped out and regretfully he took matters into his own hand, with the hopes that his life insurance would provide for her. Everything is a horrible mess.

The funeral will be on Tuesday in San Diego. We all understand if you can't make it.

Lovingly,

Mother

Gabe read it twice.

Today's Tuesday. I've already missed the funeral.

He phoned his Mom, knowing she was alone with that grief, and they both acknowledged comfort from the contact.

Over pizza, he opened his laptop and pored over pages of web links to gold scams. There weren't any reports of the one that targeted Hermes, but Gabe opened pages of many others, with theories and methods of enticement and some on smuggling.

This is so much bigger than the San Diego scoundrel. Someday, Uncle Hermes, I'll get revenge for you and Aunt Viola.

The letter found its way to the back of Gabe's wallet, folded with the newspaper clipping.

Spring in New York was dazzling, with blossoming cherry trees, music festivals and art exhibits. Central Park was lush with greenery and bicycles.

Gabe had a skip in his step on his way to the museum; it was time to plan his travel adventures, and map out the next year of his life.

Today, he'd attend a symposium held by an entourage from the British Museum, with the curator accompanied by a medieval historian and two interns.

On their arrival the day before, one of the young women had caught his eye, but she hadn't been close enough for more than introductions. They called her 'Clay', and he was taken with her appearance, a single blonde braid and a brush of freckles across her nose. Even across the room, he thought her blue eyes could be the color of the sea.

As guests collected coffee and donuts in anticipation of the PowerPoint, Gabe spotted her again at the back.

"Hello, Clay," he said, hoping to break any ice. "While in New York, will you gather information from our museum, or is the trip mainly to share your knowledge of medieval times?"

She seemed impressed with his professionalism, and the conversation continued with Gabe complimenting her accent, then pointless prattle about travel. It seemed to him to be going well, and they advanced to half-hearted laughs.

"Please take your seats," the Director announced. "We have fascinating content to share this morning." Gabe followed her to the board table and claimed two seats, reserving his own with his coffee and portfolio. The New York museum was represented by one of the curators, two Directors, and three apprentices.

He felt elevated to have been picked. Captivated by Norsemen legends and lore, his imagination traveled through time at the images of artifacts. Forty-five short minutes later, the lights went up.

"Daunting, isn't it, Mr. Farrow?" Clay whispered. She could see he was overwhelmed, and he breathed once deeply before turning to her.

"Oh yes. I'd love to work on projects like that on the North Sea."

His nonchalant comment was what she wanted to hear, and his wildest dream was about to start.

Clay tilted her head to watch his reaction. "Actually, one of the objectives of our group is to recruit an intern as an undercover agent to place in a seaside village up in the North Moors. Someone that wouldn't be recognized or draw suspicion and without attachments back home. It's an excellent medium for information-sharing across the borders."

By gosh, how could the door of opportunity swing open any wider?

"How do I apply?"

"First of all, make an impact on our Director. You need at least two recommendations by our committee. You'll have my vote but you need his too." She glanced across the boardroom and pointed discreetly.

"Excuse me, Clay. Save my seat."

At the intermission bar, Gabe found Director Shipton in light discussion with another intern. Time was valuable and he couldn't lose this chance.

"Director Shipton . . . Gabe Farrow. The presentation was captivating. I feel archeology and historic retribution in my bones."

Intrigued, Shipton looked over the top of his glasses.

"Well, Mr. Farrow, clarify for me what you mean as historic retribution."

"Since a teen, I've spent every available moment in ancient history. I see these historic revelations of Viking hoards off the North Sea as important to the British people and their rich heritage, even who they are."

The Director listened in silence and the other intern shied away. Gabe continued.

"Perhaps retribution is a bit too harsh, but I believe the law and the rights of any land be protected and preserved.

"Unfortunately, today I am a bit fired up for a personal reason; you see, my uncle was victim of a gold smuggling scam. I can relate my own story somewhat to swindlers who deny history its right to its people."

He watched for approval and decided to wrap up.

"The hoards of England must be preserved and accounted for by the governing board."

Mr. Shipton's voice was deep, and his manner was gracious to ease Gabe's nerves. "Well, Mr. Farrow, you've said a mouthful. But I am impressed with your passion; perhaps we could have dinner together tonight. I'd like to hear more of your perspective."

Second foot in the door.

2

Stranger comes to Staithes, North Yorkshire Moors

RIDING THE BUS to the seaside village of Staithes, Gabe Farrow struck up a conversation with a British passenger who boarded at Harrogate. He'd spent the previous day shuttling on Northern Rail trains, and was here at last.

The abrupt exit from New York was long past, and he regretted the harsh words with his mother about the photo of his father. But his lifetime anger from abandonment was too much not to linger. In his wallet were the UK clipping and the letter about Uncle Hermes.

Shipton had installed a laborious initiation in New York, then Gabe was assigned three months working in security for an international organization in London. His craft abilities as an artisan would be the ideal foil for his mission and life in the coastal hamlet of Staithes.

Farrow and the stranger opted for the bus to the Dalehouse stop at Staithes Lane, rather than hang around for the scenic steam train between coastal villages.

From the window seat, the intoxicating scenery mesmerized Gabe, with miles of brooding moors, green dales and valleys. On the lush fields, hundreds of sheep grazed between strips of broken ancient stone walls and sinking ruins. It was hypnotic, until Gabe realized his travel partner was observing him in the glass reflection of the window.

"Ah, it looks rather lovely," Gabe said. "I didn't mean to be a rude companion with my silence. I haven't been this way before."

"Ye, 'tis rather grand. I'm sorry to say I have to wrap up my digs at Mrs. Capps' Boarding House in town. I've been called away to attend to family business and won't be coming to Staithes. There'll be no time for seashores, I'm afraid," the mate said.

"I've never seen the moors before. I took a leap of faith and replied to an advert in the Harrogate Adviser for a glass blower at the Mill—it's outside Hinderwell at Staithes. It's not often I see a need for my artisan craft, you know. Fortunately, they hired me from a phone call," Gabe said.

"M' name's Bradley Turner." The man extended his hand.

Gabe sized Bradley as a self-assured bloke with leadership qualities, who liked to be heard. With buzzed ginger hair and a wispy moustache, he was straggly and travel worn.

"Sorry, Mate; call me Gabe. Gabe Farrow from Bristol."

"I could tell from your accent you weren't from the north. We have our own dialect, some say it's almost Scottish. Do you have a flat ready for ya, Gabe?"

"No, the fellow at the factory said there would be adverts at the bus station for billets."

He laughed. "There ain't no bus station—it's Stand No. 11. But how would you like to take over my place? I'm paid up at the Blue Cove 'til the end of the month. It's the only place you can let rooms with board. That'll give you three weeks to sort yourself out. Pay me whatever you like," Bradley offered.

"Do you think Mrs. Capp will have me?"

"Of course she will, but one thing I know is she won't give me a refund." He pressed his finger to the window. "It's this way, just a sprint up from High Street."

As the coach approached the hillside hamlet, Bradley gathered his pack and rang the bell for the next stop at Lane's End.

Gabe watched through the same glass reflection, as Bradley moved a shiny object from his pocket to the backpack, then saw the tattoo on his left hand.

A three-headed serpent, what an odd tattoo.

"Hope you don't mind, Gabe, I'll collect my mail at the Post Office. It's not far, over thar on Church Street. We'll pass a few craft and china shops on the way, and that'll get your bearings."

"I'm not expecting mail, but makes sense to set it up for the rest of the month."

"That'll be good. If any of mine comes to ya, send it on to me in Harrogate."

"Sure will."

From the bus depot, Captain James Cook's Memorial Museum and Whitby Abbey's spires were visible over the hill. Gabe knew the distinguishing landmarks from the travel brochures and folders of Yorkshire he'd read.

The Post Office hardly lived up to its name, as a tiny kiosk next to the news and smoke shop. The few patrons in the store fell silent as he entered, but turned to see a newcomer in town. Gabe momentarily sensed he was one against the crowd.

Bradley nudged Gabe's elbow. "You'll get used to it. It'll stop before long."

"I know small towns are territorial about folks," Gabe said.

"True, they'll get curious and maybe even some gossip too, but if you need help, they'll give you the shirts off their backs. Do they say that in Bristol too?"

After transactions with the Postmaster and with suitable information dredged from Gabe, the pair head to the tavern for a pint. "You'll be at home at the Endeavor, Bradley said at the door. I'll introduce you to Mary Jane. She'll give you good service. Prefers M.J."

Mary Jane had a distinct brogues dialect, veneer smile and a pencil behind her ear. "Ah, Bradley, you've brought me a new customer! First one's on the house! Two pints of Black Sheep Ale coming—it's from neighboring Masham."

Gabe saluted from the bench seat. "Gabe Farrow . . . nice to meet you, M.J."

The waitress was a slight, plain-looking woman of early thirties, with worry lining her brow and a captivating smile.

"I'll be heading back to Harrogate. Gabe's taking over my room for now. He's a glassblower." Gabe nodded as Bradley blurted the quick resume of his new friend.

Without realizing it, Gabe was officially introduced to the community. Mrs. Capp would hear the news of her new boarder even before his arrival.

The storybook hamlet in the North Yorkshire Moors had been an ancient port in the days of the Vikings, with myths and legends surviving and thriving. Every resident of Staithes would have a story to tell, more thrilling than when last heard.

Outside the tavern, the two men walked the cobblestone main street, passing a tourist's treasure of fossil and ammonite shops, and colorful Bed & Breakfasts.

The afternoon fishing boats were beginning to return to the cove, a natural harbor, with ropes, buoys and lobster traps.

The salt water breeze carried the scent of the basins of fresh herring.

"Ah, so that's sea air," Gabe joked.

Gabe jogged the first incline to keep up with Bradley.

From the Blue Cove hill, the panoramic view of rocky cliffs and sandy beaches stretched to Roxby Beck. Above the fishing town was a flat, rocky peninsula of stacked houses wedged between one another. Other streets followed the course of the creek, becoming a mud flat at low tide, and consumed by the ocean at high.

Climbing to the upper terrace, Gabe and Bradley came to the boldly painted, blue stacked house. Gabe had visualized a stern Tugboat Annie character ruling the boarders, and grinned at first sight of the house—he wasn't far wrong. A middle-aged woman, with broad hips and carpenter's apron waited on the porch with her arms crossed. When Mrs. Capp saw them approach, she pretended to be busy sweeping, with her red kerchief tied tightly about her head.

"Well's about time you landed, Bradley. I've got your things packed and your room cleaned out fer ya," Mrs. Capp said. She relished her efficiency on the spin of a dime after M.J.'s call.

Bradley gave the ample matron a hug. "Dear Maude, you needn't have troubled yourself. You look as young and lovely as I've ever seen you."

"Pshaw, you young men, trying out your flattery. But it does seem to work." The matron broke into her chortle and Bradley reveled in his Eddie Haskell spoof.

"Well, come on Mister Gabe Farrow. Bradley can show you around the place."

Maude's hands were on her hips as the captain in charge. Her eyes were fixed on Gabe to see his next move—the moment his fate was sealed in Staithes.

"I've heard wonderful things about you and your boarding house. Thanks for permitting me to take over Bradley's digs."

"You're welcome, Gabe." The adoption was complete.

"However, Gabe, I should explain that while the Blue Cove is called a boarding house, we don't serve any meals. You have a hot plate and sink in your room."

On the main landing by the center hall spiral stairs, a call box with a row of buzzers rang to the tenants' suites.

Bradley stopped at the wall mantle by the buzzers. "Mail goes here . . . both in and out." He proceeded to thumb through a stack of envelopes. Gabe supposed he was looking for something specific, by the flash of anger cross his face.

The flat was a large room with two windows—one in the galley kitchen and the other by a metal coil spring bed. The sparse kitchen had a single-burner hotplate, an antique icebox and basic utensils and worn linens.

"Sorry, Gabe, it's on the third floor, but check the view of the North Sea; you can even see the spire of St. Mary's Church and the old Abbey."

"Perfect, Bradley. I'm a man that's easy to please."

"I took out my phone but the hardware's there if you want to hook it up again. One more thing, you'll need to shower early to get hot water. After 8 am, it turns cold."

"That's all cool. I'm an early riser so that suits me fine."

"If you need your shirts washed, hang them out the door on Thursday morning before 6. Mrs. Capp prides herself on fresh sunshine laundry. It's the only time she comes further than the first floor, with her swollen ankles. I heard her say it was 'gout' or 'goat'. All it'll cost you is a chocolate éclair from the bakery. The best baker is up at Saltburn-by-the Sea, a short walk on the seashore cliffs."

"That sounds like more than a fair trade."

Gabe leaned out the window for the full view.

With the coast clear, it was the chance Bradley needed to retrieve an item he'd hidden; he knew he couldn't return to Harrogate without it.

Gabe heard the sound of the floorboards creaking as Bradley popped one up. It was awkward now, but too late. Gabe looked out again and waited to change the subject.

"Is the boarding house full of tenants?" he asked. "Did you get a chance to meet the others?"

"Mostly traveling workers that you don't see until the weekends. I kept to myself, but for anything you want to know, Mrs. Capp has an inside loop."

"I've always been a bit of a loner myself," Gabe said.

"Well, pal, I'll be off. I've got some visitin' before the bus returns from Whitby. I can't be late back in Harrogate to catch the evening train."

Gabe sighed with relief as the door closed.

Finally, introductions are done!

Bounding downstairs, he took long strides to High Street and halted in front of Pickersgill's, inspecting the window, then the overhead sign.

Pickersgill General Store. I'll get by with some tea, sugar, lemon, and a half loaf of bread. That'll do me fine to start.

The grocery clerk added a tin of meat, a potato, mushy peas and brown beans into the brown bag, then referred Gabe to Church Street where he found a dairy.

"Yes, I'm that Gabe," he clarified, sampling the Stilton. "I'll just need a quarter stick of butter and cream."

With the weight of the cans and a bottle of milk, his paper bags were tearing as he walked back. He passed an old bicycle with a 'for sale' sign, propped in front of the Endeavor Ale House. The metal basket seemed secure and it took only little pondering to convince him.

"Hello, barkeeper. I'm new to town and I'd be interested in the bike out front."

"It'll need a new chain soon, but you can take it for £8. There'll be a police fee for the new tags—their office is across from the old bus depot that's now a library. Tell them it was registered to Jimmy Reagan; they'll know about Jimmy."

"Thank you. I'll take care of it." Gabe handed over a £5 note and three £1s.

With his groceries stored behind in the rusty basket, he rode and walked to the seashore and parked the bike against a boulder that protruded near the wharf.

He stopped under a bright yellow police dingy on a hoist above the pier. Next to it was the place he'd been told about—a ticket cubicle and equipment hut. The sign boasted they had anything a tourist would want to rent.

"Hello, Sir. Do you rent fishing poles and sell bait?"

The man sized him up. "Sure do lad. The best way here is to fly fish." He pulled out a pole.

"Here's a good starter. If you catch two, one for me and one for you, and there'll be no charge."

"I'll do my best!"

"If you find you like fishing, there's a shop called 'Sand and Surf' up the road. They have nicer ones for sale," the clerk added.

Gabe glanced to the pier. The thrill of the first hook as a tyke with his grandfather flashed to his memory.

He sorted the tack on a bench and picked the silver lure and hook. With his lungs filled with sea air, he spun the reel and released it high into the sky. It splashed, then with a yank it boomeranged back. A second time, then a third.

Gabe rolled his jeans up to below his knees and waded into the surf, sinking his feet into the gritty mud.

"One more cast."

A long and high throw hooked a suitable brown river trout escaping with the tide from the mud flats of Roxby Beck. After icing a young sturgeon to join it in his pail, Gabe observed the air bubbles in the sand. With a broken sea shell, he dug out a few clams and mussels, and with a salt water rinse, he had his dinner haul.

Dusk was settling on the shimmering sea, and he wondered about the calling of the ancient deep, its mystique and its power in the past. He watched the dark green water splashing to Roxby Beck from the North Sea, a reminder that it held such mighty secrets.

The clouds momentarily cast a shadow, and Gabe stood with his hands locked behind his neck to stretch his shoulders. A cold shiver overcame him as he imagined the dragon head of a Viking ship crashing the rocks.

Is this place haunted or sacred? It's exactly like the legendary stories in those books.

His vision receded quickly, but the haunting remained.

No one else was on the beach to hear the muffled sounds of a boat motor. The shadow, in a nautical shape, passed Seaton Garth where the water widened at the harbor. Shielding his eyes, Gabe squinted to make out the form of a trawler, now moving beyond into the next bay.

From what I saw from my window, that bay is too rocky for a light craft. I can't worry; if someone's in danger, the Light House will see him.

Riding up High Street, Gabe's nagging psyche made him stop and look again. From the rocky outcrop stubble at the river's mouth, he saw three figures—from a distance, the lead outline was stocky and muscular, the other two taller and perhaps younger, he thought.

It's incredible how deciphering controls the mind. My grandmother said curiosity killed the cat, and it's had me in trouble before. This time no one knows what I'm here about, but I'll always listen to my subconscious.

Again, he witnessed the intense flash of the dragon head thrashing in the North Sea.

Blimey, what the heck? The sea . . . now the beck!

Shaking his head to reality, he scanned again for the men, but they'd gone.

Have they retreated? Maybe they spotted me watching. Or more likely, it's my vivid imagination.

Soon he heard the motor of an ATV revving up in the former direction. The boarding house was around the bend and he was relieved to see Mrs. Capp waiting on the porch.

He waved the pail. "Good evening, Mrs. Capp. I've caught my dinner on the beach. The mussels and clams were begging to be brought home, but you can see it's much more than I can eat. Can I fill a pot for the house?"

"Kirby from the wharf called to let me start boiling the water," Maude said.

"Kirby?"

"Yes, the fellow that rented you the fishing pole. There ain't no secrets in a town this size. Don't take offence. When the day comes and you're in trouble, be assured the authorities will come to your aid sooner than you can bat an eye. We look out for one another."

Maude leaned over the catch, poking and checking the color of the clams.

"I'll be taking the clams then if you don't mind, Gabe."

"Happy to give them to you."

Maude brought an old coffee can and a pair of kitchen tongs to the porch and went about picking out her dinner.

"Hank told me about the bicycle. I found an old lock in the tool shed for you. Nobody from Staithes would take it, but I can't guarantee the tourists wouldn't. Lock it onto the porch."

Third floor, I'll be getting my exercise now.

Gabe looked up the spiral staircase to the floor. A glimpse of a black jacket passed his door, and a second later a door slammed.

So I do have neighbors up there.

Gabe laid the filleted brown trout in a fry pan with butter, salt and pepper, and lemon, then placed chunks of potato and onion. Leaving it to sauté, he rinsed the sandy mussels in cold water, then plopped them into a pot with a bottle of beer and butter to simmer.

Two TV trays were attached to bent metal frames.

Reminds me of Grandma; she loved these things.

Savoring his fisherman's delicacies, Gabe found local news on the television with intermittent, snowy static. At the back of the set, he adapted wires until two other channels came through, both in reruns of Coronation Street. With tinfoil and more wiggling, he got a clearer channel.

The first news item was a railway accident at Harrogate.

Bradley! Can't have anything to do with Bradley!

Static overruled the rest of the news, leaving Gabe pondering his new friend's fate.

The room was stifling, with both windows already open. Gabe threw off the top bedding and stared at the ceiling until well past midnight. In the strange environment, every sound was unique—even the still air and walls vibrating. Twice, a door slammed nearby, followed by irate voices. He sat up to listen closer as a broom banged from somewhere below, and got out of bed at the buzzing.

He traced the noise to a conduit box, attached to an outlet on the wall under his bed.

That's more than hypnotic. It'll drive me crazy.

He plugged in his alarm radio, hoping the news would drown it out, and in seconds a voice echoed from the second floor.

"Be quiet up there!"

Turning down the volume, Gabe drifted back to sleep. The vibrating turned to mumbling and at five in the morning he was awakened by the ringing of a telephone.

What the heck! I don't even have a land line.

Tracking the sound to the conduit, he knelt by the bed to listen. Someone picked up a phone nearby and Gabe strained to hear the muffled conversation. The voice was gruff.

"Did Bradley see you? Does he know the route? I've received confirmation that the package arrived in Staithes."

Glassy-eyed, Gabe rubbed his aching temples.

It's like one of those dreams, waking up in the night and it won't go away. First day of work and I'm far from rested. And what package?

Getting an early hot shower, he whistled a tune that might bring him relaxation. With his travel stubble shaved, he groomed his golden brown curls in the mirror and stuffed them under a grey wool toque. He rolled his sleeves to his elbows, and checked that the crease was still in his pants. At the door, he brushed off his shoes.

At 6:30 a.m., Gabe crept past Mrs. Capp's porch, walked the squeaky bike to the road, and coasted downhill in search of a coffee shop.

"At least somebody else is up," he commiserated, seeing the cawing seagulls swarming the beach.

Riding past the Brewery onto Beckstone Flats, he stopped at Fisherman's Square to pick up a coffee. Continuing the downhill grade of High Street, he passed the Endeavour and spied an original red telephone booth.

Time to check-in.

Inserting a prepaid phone card, he asked the operator for a connection to a number in London. A female voice picked up.

"What is your code, Mr. Farrow?"

"Hardrada, with three A's."

The clerk set the phone on her desk. Instead of on-hold elevator music, Gabe heard her heels shuffle across the floor and a door open, then her distant voice.

"Sir, it's the call you've been waiting for."

Click, click.

"Hello Gabe, you settled now?" Gabe recognized the voice as his contact at the London museum. They hadn't spoken since he left New York.

"Yes, Mr. Davis. I'm already onto a suspicious trio of blokes that don't fit into this quaint hamlet. I've established several points of contacts to verify information. Everything is going like clockwork. The Bradley lad even sat beside me on the bus from Harrogate."

"Splendid. Our research indicates that the Cobb fellow at the mill can be trusted."

"Thank you, Sir. Will the parcel be sent directly?"

"Marjorie is preparing it as we speak."

Into a padded envelope, the secretary at WC1B inserted a flash drive and a rectangular instrument with parts for a transmitter.

She sealed it with a magnetic strip, and Davis handed her a slip with the address of the Blue Cove in Staithes.

3

THE OUTDOOR SIGN said 'Open 8 a.m. to 8 p.m.', but Gabe got to the Cleveland Corner Café an hour earlier. Theo Arbuckle was sweeping the threshold and setting out bistro tables.

"Good morning, Mr. Arbuckle. That's a fine smell of fresh baking. Makes a man mighty hungry."

Theo stopped, relishing the newcomer's chat.

"You must be the Farrow fellow. If you bring out the rest of my tables and chairs, I'll give you fresh coffee and my wife's warm blueberry scones. They're the best in town," Arbuckle boasted with a laugh.

Gabe's broad smile was answer enough. He laid his bike on the resting rack and lifted the tables, then chairs two at a time.

"One at a time, so you don't knock the paint, Farrow. There's no hurry to be had at this hour. Where ya from?"

Gabe started his practiced patter. "Bristol . . . well, I'm not exactly from there. That's just where I landed in England. I came on a freighter. My career training is to be a gas-fitter and electrical engineer but I get more satisfaction creating glassworks. I'm on my own and enjoy traveling about the countryside. You have quite a gem here by the ocean."

"We do indeed. I've lived here twenty years and pride myself on meeting most folks that pass through. I have an indelible memory for faces. We're an artsy town and have festivals several times a year, so you can't help but meet a lot of new ones. I was trying to figure the accent. Have you been here long? M.J. says she met you yesterday."

"I've been told my accent reflects both my American and English background. I'll work on improving that. And, yes, I came yesterday. I'm taking over Bradley Turner's flat at Mrs. Capp's place."

Gabe knew he hadn't satisfied the baker's curiosity and continued without prompting. It seemed that the skill of real gossip was to add another tidbit to the original story with each new person.

"I start work today at the artisan factory at the old mill between here and Hinderwell Road."

"I know the place—Cobb's is it? What's your particular skill?

Gabe wondered why the man with the indelible memory had already forgotten that he mentioned glassworks.

Is this a test?

"If I may say, I'm rather good at my craft but not many towns still appreciate a good glass blower. Apparently Mr. Cobb has a demand for colorful glass buoys."

"If ye'd been here last summer, we were flooded with tourists when the Tour de France came through. Every room in town was booked. The place was like a boiler ready to blow, with money spent everywhere. Folks couldn't get enough local crafts and souvenirs."

"I'm afraid I was on the Black Sea then, but maybe next time if they ever come back, Mr. Arbuckle."

Mrs. Arbuckle, a jolly, middle-aged women, carried herself carefully with a tray, walking toward Theo and Gabe. Proudly, she laid the tray on the table nearest the door.

Her voice was high and shrill. "Here are fresh scones with Devonshire cream and my homemade triple berry jam. A steaming English Breakfast is steeping in the pot."

"Very kind of you, Mr. and Mrs. Arbuckle. You'll be seeing me a lot in the next few weeks. Do you ever make chocolate éclairs?"

The Arbuckles broke into laughter.

"You're at the Capps' Place, ain't you?"

The low fog remained heavy over the moors as Gabe crossed the bridge from lower to upper town. There, in the underbrush high on the riverbank, was the back end of a red ATV. Gabe glanced behind for intruders as he inspected the ground for clues.

Could be the motor from last night. It hasn't been here long, it's relatively clean. Footprints lead to car tracks on the shoulder over here.

Gabe imagined he saw a path wide enough for two tracks, wide enough to belong to the suspect ATV.

Not enough time to take comparative measurements.

The piercing steam whistle turned his head toward the trestle, as the North Yorkshire Railway locomotive chugged over the river from Dalehouse Station on its way to Herriot Country. A steam tour guide at the front prepared the conductor for a face-to-face with some annoyed sheep as it slowed. A crowd of delighted tourists lined the windows, snapping fields and heather moors, and each other.

The steam whistle is something I could get used to.

The growing clatter of the train drowned out the ATV motor, closing in.

Leaning on his bike, Gabe watched the train pass. But suddenly, two lads not more than ten years of age barreled along the walking path, feet flying to outrun the old steam tank.

Gabe screamed to them as he could see it all.

"Hold on, boys! A vehicle is cutting you off . . ." But it was too late, as the boys flew into the air, landing in a swampy bog.

The red ATV with three accomplices tore across the trestle with no regard for pedestrians. Instead, they cursed and shouted at the boys, with their tires spitting mud.

"Are you alright, lads?"

Dragging sore limbs, the boys climbed up to the path but the mangled bikes had already drifted and sunk into the river. Too late to salvage the bikes, Gabe raised his hands in the air.

"Sorry, I can't give you a lift. I'm on my way to work, but I can get help for you."

"Naw, Mister. We don't have far to go, but Mum worked hard for that bike," the freckled one said.

"Where do you live?"

"We rent a loft over the Endeavor. My Mum's a waitress in the pub."

"She's a nice lady. If I see a used bike for sale, I'll be lettin' her know."

The boys renewed their spirits as they started skipping stones, sauntering toward the beach.

Gabe scanned the other direction for the ATV. The muddy tracks went toward the upper Cow Bar Bank. His eyes followed to the natural wharf from the beach, then up the north side.

Cow Bar Lane ran along with the creek from Wesley Square to the rows of quaint fishermen cottages and guest houses.

But he saw no sign of the ATV.

Seems out of sorts to me, but best to mind my own for now.

Niles Cobb was setting out his wares on a narrow table in front of the stone mill when Gabe arrived. Built of sandstone and beams, the old matriarch was several hundred years old, once the glory of a wealthy Earl or Lord. Colorful hand-painted glass buoy balls, tethered to trapping lines, were the main feature, filling several baskets. Pieces of driftwood were artfully molded into garden furniture, including tables and rockers.

Cobb had greying hair sticking out from under an English tam. His face lit up as the bike rolled into the front car park. Wearing a cable knit seaman's turtle neck and dungarees, he wiped his hands on a leather apron.

"Ahoy! You must be Gabe Farrow. Glad to see you made it all the way to the North Sea. I heard you've taken over Bradley Turner's flat."

"News travels fast in a small town."

Gabe parked the bike at the side of the factory and walked toward Cobb with his hand outstretched.

"Pleased to make your acquaintance, Mr. Cobb."

"Other than Mrs. Capp, no one calls anyone Mr. and Mrs. in Staithes—we're like a big family. C'mon, I'll show you around as the kiln's getting warmed up. Mandy Arbuckle said you were on your way."

Gabe concealed his amusement at the speedy grape vine.

"I'm looking forward to refining my craft here."

"As you see, we get a lot of call for the glass buoys. The more colorful and unique, the better they sell. I guess the lobsters like 'em."

Cobb laughed at himself, and Gabe knew he'd hear that one again, so let the man's sense of humor have its way.

"We have an order from Saltburn to fill today."

At Gabe's work table, he was given goggles, a blast shield, tweezers, glass cutters, gloves, an insulated apron and his choice of milk stool. A variety of Chinese, German and Indian Glass filled the shelves in various colors and clear weights. Anticipating no further chitchat, he settled into his station.

Life couldn't be more perfect if I were an artisan.

But Niles was the sort that needed to talk, and also eager to learn. He came by repeatedly to scrutinize Gabe's techniques, even looking for tips to add to his own skills. By the time the order was completed, Gabe had acquired a wealth of knowledge of the community and residents.

He started home on his bike, then got off to walk as it would serve him better. Along the way, curious townsfolk came out to stop him for a talk, and after an hour of socializing, his voice cracked from the pat explanation, and smile lines stuck like glue to his face.

At the Cod & Lobster Pub at the end of High Street and Seaton Garth, he lucked out to get a seat with a view of the fishing boats and lobster traps. In his mind, he dwelt on his growing concern about the town's curiosity.

I feel a creeping ownership of my presence here, by everyone in town. Their phone lines are on overdrive.

Framed, monochrome photos adorned the walls in shades of gray, evidence of the pub's fortitude through past storms and gales. Whenever the foundations had been threatened, the breakwater seawall was re-enforced.

Among the pictures was a movie poster of Harry Potter, who claimed High Street as Diagon Alley in the Rowling movies.

Gabe stood to examine it, all the more fascinated by the town's secrets. Someone touched his shoulder from behind.

"Hello, Gabe . . . I didn't mean to startle you. We have a whole lobster special, and Theakston's on tap. My name's Crystal, like in crystal ball."

"That'll be easy to remember. The lobster special and a pint of the house ale then, Crystal. If the lobster's not too much to handle." Gabe's stomach growled in agreement.

"Chips too?"

"Sure, add those. Is that Potter thing really true?"

She held a finger, "Wait, I'll give the cook your order first."

Crystal needed little urging and was back to him.

"I had a bit part in one of the Potter movies. The costumes were like a fantasy, and I spent hours in makeup. But it paid well. They made Staithes into a wizardry, fictional High Street in old London. It was like being in a storybook, and I threw myself into the part.

"Our cobbled streets became movie sets and this pub was converted on the outside to the 'Leaky Cauldron'. The street was taken over for months. I played one of the Snatchers. Do you want to see autographs I collected? I got Ian McKellan, Daniel Radcliffe and Alan Rickman; so sad he since passed away.

"Staithes was flooded with crew, trailers and construction. Truckloads came from I don't know where, with enormous equipment, fancy camera tracks, and director's chairs. Cameras and lights hung over the streets and I experienced sights and sounds I could never imagine."

"It's all glamorous and fascinating to me. I'm afraid I didn't catch the movies, but everyone knows of Harry Potter and Diagon Alley."

Crystal returned with a glossy of the fictional street; three signatures were scratched in the corner: 'To Crystal, may we meet again in your crystal ball'.

"You are the town's celebrity, I'm sure," Gabe smiled at her blush.

"Well, as it happens my last name is Ball, and I've heard every joke about that all my life."

"Order up," the kitchen called.

Crystal tied a plastic bib around Gabe's neck, and centered a steaming plate of lobster, melted butter and lemon slices beside a shell bucket. Fiddling with the utensils, he picked at the lobster. With nobody watching, he gave up on manners and his fingers tore the succulent flesh from the mangled shell.

At the Blue Cove, the foyer was empty when Gabe checked the mantle for mail. There was nothing for him by name, but an envelope 'To the Occupant of 3B'. It was a form letter from the phone company, inviting him to reconnect the service. Tucking it in his shirt pocket, he looked up the staircase; the third floor seemed a long way up after a work day.

Turning his key, he heard a ruckus from below. He looked down at the spiral landing. It was the three men from the ATV, and the arguing became violent. He tucked into his doorway out of sight, and listened as Mrs. Capp came from the landlord's apartment.

"Quiet down, you boys. If you want to brawl, go to a pub."

The shorter, older fellow stood firm and came closer to Maude.

"I'm not afraid of you, Hennie," she said. "Your type lives in the gutters of London."

Too late to take back, she realized her insult would cut deep. One of the taller men gripped his hand on Hennie's shoulder to calm him. By this time, other patrons of the boarding house had their heads out the door, listening but afraid to be seen.

The taller man, referred to as Fergus, had a shaved head and spoke with a low, deep voice. "Our apologies, Mrs. Capp. We got carried away with our disagreement. We'll be quieter in future."

Fergus was the type of character that seethed in his soul and had his own agenda, but Hennie didn't seem to mind the intervention.

"Yes, Mrs. Capp. My apologies too," Hennie shrugged.

Easing his door closed, Gabe listened for the footsteps to pass. Two did, but the third man stopped at Gabe's door and whispered. "I know you're in there. Stay scarce or you'll wish you'd never seen this place."

Gabe's heart raced, but he didn't move until the footsteps retreated and the door of 3C closed.

He had trouble sleeping, from the glow of light into the room. He stood at the window, watching the beam of the Lifeboat Station at the Seaton Garth Harbor. The town appeared at peace under the half moon.

Bradley Turner. What did you do to stir the wrath of these scoundrels? What's your connection to these ill-behaved tenants next door?

Exhausted, he fell into a deep sleep. Again, at 5 a.m., the telephone rang as it had the previous day, with buzz, static, and garbled voices from the phone outlet. He opened his eyes, imagining Bill Murray in Groundhog Day.

There has to be a stop to this. The buzzing and static are too much.

"Did Turner tell you where they were?" a distance voice asked.

"Bradley skipped town, but a new fellow's in his unit. We need to get in there and make sure Bradley didn't leave the map hidden somewhere."

Gabe was sure it was Hennie's voice.

The reply from the caller faded in the static, then Hennie ended the call with "Hydra. Wednesday."

With his ear against the joining wall of 3C, Gabe tried to make out the mumbled argument. He found a flathead screwdriver from the kitchen and loosened the conduit box. An exposed wire gave him a bit of a shock, and at the back of the box he found a tiny microphone, the source of the static.

It's a one-way, intended to intercept conversation from my unit 3B. But someone reversed the wires to send the one-way from 3C to 3B. Must've been Bradley.

Gabe's first instinct was to toss the bug.

Darned if I do and darned if I don't. But I don't talk to myself, so what's the use of anyone listening to my room?

His mental calculation ruled out Davis or anyone connected with the British Museum.

Bradley stepped on toes and drew attention from London . . . but no, I think it's the local trio with the ATV. Whatever, I can't blow my cover the first day in town.

Gabe unlatched the window, hoping the breeze would help him relax and catch another hour's sleep. With his eyes closed, he fancied floating on a raft in a gentle sea, but didn't sleep.

Peddling was faster in the morning, with no locals along the way. At 7:45 a.m., Cleveland's Corner Cafe was filling with fishermen, packing in a hearty meal before the morning catch. Gabe gravitated to a corner window, folding the local newspaper from the cashier. He checked the chalkboard and read the early bird special to himself.

£4 for black pudding, poached egg, back bacon, browned beans, stewed tomato, fried potatoes, toast with jam or marmalade, tea or coffee.

A waitress arrived with a coffee pot the moment he sat down. He glanced at her hair net under a short nurse-style cap. Her voice boomed, but he liked her down-to-business flair.

"You must be Gabe Farrow, the fella at the Cove. What'll ya have?"

She tucked her chewing gum in her cheek and tilted her head to a chalk board behind the serving counter. He nodded, understanding it was the only menu. "By the way, Stilton cream sauce is extra," she said.

"Yes, the special. That's what I want. And black coffee."

Jotting what the cook would understand, she flipped her notepad closed and returned to the Bunn.

Out the window, high tide was now changing the harbor's nature, dragging shore boats with her will. He looked over the colorful rigs the locals called cobbles, anchored to cement blocks along the shore with iron hooks. At the distant Cow Bar Wharf, Gabe could see lobster traps being prepared and he focused on the glass buoys.

I wonder if any of those came from Cobbs.

His substantial order arrived, filling a large plate, and he took a second refill.

The bell over the door jingled with new customers, and Gabe cringed at the sight of the two taller men from 3C. They surveyed the room from the front, and he sat back with his paper. It worsened when they took the table behind Gabe.

"Mornin' gents," the chewing gum waitress said.

"Two specials, Linda."

"You got it, Axle. You boys going out to the hills this morning?"

"Thanks, Linda, but it's none of your business."

"I knew," she said.

Gabe unfolded the Saltburn & Staithes newspaper again to avoid eye contact, but an uneasy feeling spoiled his appetite. Collecting his hat, he rose from his chair.

"Don't do that. Stay put. I haven't had a talk with ya yet," Axle said without looking. "I said stay!"

The second request left no doubt. He was speaking to Gabe.

"Me! You talking to me?" Gabe said, his eyes wide with confusion.

"Yeah. Don't make this so obvious, fella."

Gabe lowered back into his chair. "What do you want with me?"

"We need to talk with Bradley."

"I don't know Bradley. I only sat beside him on the bus and he offered me his room. That's all I know."

"Where is he?"

"Ask the Postmaster." Gabe's impatience was thinning.

"No, I'm asking you. You're part of this now."

"Sorry gentlemen, but I must be off or I'll be late for work."

"Alright, go; but I'll find you later. Bradley left something in his room that belongs to us," Axle warned. "We'll be watching you." He forced a growl. "And by that I don't suggest anything neighborly, if you get my drift."

Gabe left on foot for the glass mill, his face bearing the dread from these minutes; he'd get the bike later.

Rifling his jacket, he found Bradley's paper and forwarding address, but no phone number. He'd almost tossed it a few days before, and was relieved it was there.

Crossing Roxby Beck, Gabe saw the ATV hidden in the brush, the same as before. Muddy tire tracks led away toward Upper Cow Bar.

They couldn't have been here long.

He kept his eyes to the ground, searching for anything. At a good distance past Roxby, he heard the ATV engine. Picking up his pace, he jogged to Niles Cobb's place, panting on arrival.

Cobb came out to greet him. "Ahoy, there Gabe! You look like you've seen a ghost."

"No . . . just troubled."

"I can loan you an ear. Folks say I'm a good listener."

Gabe struggled, whether to ask about Bradley Turner, weighing the consequences in a close-knit town.

There's no point bringing Niles into something like this. Maybe one question, or two.

"Did you know Bradly Turner, Niles?"

"I can't say I did, but I was aware of him stirring up a commotion a time or two at the boarding house. Mrs. Capp is the best person to tell you about that."

"Thanks, I'll do that. Some nasty blokes are on my back looking for him."

"I know who you're talkin' about. They don't talk much to the locals, but it's obvious they're up to no good."

Niles was a kind gentlemen, beyond retirement age but young at heart. When Gabe saw him lifting a load of supplies, he tried to take over, but Niles took offence.

"C'mon laddie, we've got a large order from Robin Hood's Bay. They requested the shipment be delivered Friday afternoon as there's a weekend bus tour coming in."

"I'll make a variety of sizes then. Does Robin want their name etched on the glass as a souvenir?"

"You got that kinda skill, Gabe?"

"Sure do." Gabe was amused by his foil. Signatures were the first thing he learned at occupational college in New York, to identify his own pieces.

"I'll be, land sakes alive!"

Donning the blaster shield, Gabe tuned out Niles, driven by the pressure to fill the new order.

In the background, Niles continued to talk, but his words were drowned out to Gabe by the noise.

"Hmm . . . Bradley Turner. The boy brought kin from Leeds one day. It was an odd place on the Mineral Railway . . . Hunslet Carr. Yes, that's what it was. Those bad seeds he hung with warned me off with a rifle when I was walking my dogs up in the pastures. They had a soddy by the old alum mines and didn't want folks around."

Cobb went about his chores, striking up a jolly whistle to the tune of 'Whistling Gypsy Rover'. Bradley Turner vanished from Gabe's thoughts, but he ruminated over today's encounter with the ATV and the collision with the local boys.

Whatever they want must be long gone with Bradley, so it's obviously Axle's game to intimidate me. Good they don't know that I'm beyond being curious, I'm obstinate and crafty. I always balance the odds.

Cleaning his bench at 3 p.m., Gabe left for Saltburn in Cobb's delivery truck. On the way, his mind chewed over the interferences since arriving in North Yorkshire.

With luck, the afternoon delivery went past Liverton's Bakery. Today was Thursday and Gabe needed éclairs for the landlady. He'd get an extra one for information about Bradley, plus one more for the way home.

The buzzing, the phone and telepathic messages must stop. Once I figure their schedule, I'll use Mrs. Capp's master key and put my own transmitter in 3C.

At the boarding house, Gabe found Maude on the porch, her ankles crossed and nylons rolled to above the ankle. The Oxfords, with brown laces, hadn't been polished in a while but completed her ensemble.

"Hello, Mrs. Capp. I have some éclairs from Saltburn for you."

She smiled broadly and reached out her hands. "Thank you dear boy. You needn't go all that way for éclairs. Next time ask at the Seadrift on Seaton Garth. They take special orders."

Gabe nodded once and she sensed disappointment.

"But the ones from Saltburn are the best."

He left her peering into the baker's box, dipping a finger into the soft cream. In the foyer, he scanned the mail. This time an envelope was addressed to Bradley Turner, and a yellow card for 3B, of a parcel left with the landlady.

The three musketeers either didn't notice, or left it here deliberately to see if I know Turner's address.

He tucked the brown envelope in his jacket and turned back to the porch.

"Mrs. Capp, did you accept a parcel for me from the Post?"

"Oh yes, Gabe, Mr. Marlowe let me sign for it. We had a bit of a discussion about whether or not I had authority to take it. He's a stickler for rules. Anyways, I put it in your room with the clean clothes."

"Thanks, Mrs. Capp. Should I tip you or Marlowe?"

Maude grinned. "Townsfolk take care of one another."

At the top of the spiral stairs, Gabe's door was slightly ajar. He ran his finger down the gap.

I'm sure it clicked tight when I left . . . or did I forget? Or has someone other than Maude been in my room?

Easing it open, his three laundered and ironed shirts hung on a kitchen chair and his denims were neatly folded on the table.

"Ah, must've been Mrs. Capp," he said aloud.

Beside the jeans was a padded envelope the size of a pocket book. It had no return address, but a typed label that he recognized from the British Museum in London. His close inspection lent suspicion that someone had tried to bypass the magnetic tape and seal, but failed.

Now . . . was this Axle or Maude?

At the table, he opened the parcel, first removing a burner phone, preloaded with a dossier and contact numbers. Deeper inside were enough small parts to build a transmitter, receiver, or a GSP tracker; then a mini cam for his cell.

"Bless you, Marjorie, you've even included a micro set of instruments."

Gabe unfolded a parchment letter written in code that he deciphered from memory.

This feels like Mission Impossible; is something going to self-destruct in five minutes?

He found humor in his imagination.

In his cell phone, he accessed a preloaded geology report from an area northwest of Roxby Beck. Another protected file had archaeological details of a suspected find of a piece of drift wood with indentions similar to a Dragon Head.

"A thousand years old," he read out loud.

Finally, he opened a detective's report on Bradley Turner's background, photos of the men Gabe had come to know as Hennie, Fergus and Axle, and a coded text message.

In a freshly pressed shirt, Gabe headed out for the Cleveland. He stopped this time to read the biography on the door, named for its location leading to the cliffs by Cleveland Way. It said the Arbuckles were from Chicago, and as coffee bean roasters, were famous beyond the seaside hamlet.

"Hello, Gabe, right over here."

Arbuckle led him to a window table. "I recommend my specialty—a thick, halibut steak and my own crispy chips or Mandy's Crab Pasta. Leave room for dessert, we have fresh lime tart and dark chocolate cake. We guarantee you'll leave with a full stomach without emptying your wallet."

Gabe felt at home with seemingly genuine folk. "Theo, do I really need to order? Just send me the chef's special."

At 6 p.m., the high tide was ready to peak. Fishing boats wedged onto the sand for the night, and lobster traps were stacked safely by the rocky barrier near Cow Bar Wharf. The buzz of comradery filled the restaurant.

Searching the faces, Gabe had already met many of the locals on his rounds, but only remembered a few names. He knew he'd need to improve on that, as they'd each hope to be addressed by name.

Crystal Ball walked past to begin her night shift, and stopped at the sight of him.

"Hello there, Gabe. I'll be taking over your table. I see your order will be up in a jiff."

"I thought you worked at the Cod & Lobster?"

"I do, but that was Monday night and Arbuckle's are closed on Mondays so I work across the street."

Crystal didn't seem anxious to leave his side. Tucking the order pad in her apron, she stood with her hands on her hips, waiting for information. It was an expected courtesy, and he found some small talk in a hurry.

"I filled a large order of glass buoys over at Cobb's. We'll be shipping the lot to Robin Hood's Bay tomorrow," Gabe complied. "I do admit they are a fine looking batch. I put my own initials on each one discreetly."

She displayed some interest. "As you can see Gabe, we have a nautical theme, with souvenir mugs and tee shirts. But would you mind bringing a few to put on our shelves on consignment? Every tourist wants a unique souvenir of Staithes. There'll be busloads in a few weeks when the season is in full swing."

The cook's bell rang.

"Must be yours."

Crystal returned with a steaming plate, and Gabe wanted to glean some information this time.

"When I was here this mornin', a pair of fellows sat near me, tall, both with black leather jackets.

"You mean Axle and his pal."

"Yes. Are they locals?"

"They don't say much, but ask Niles about the time they warned him off with a rifle while he walked his dogs. I'm glad to see customers come, but I'm gladder when those leave. Enjoy your Fish and Chips."

Gabe left a generous tip, a prepayment for future gossip.

4

THE ODDS & SODS shop was still open when Gabe left the restaurant, and he went there directly. An overhead doorbell clanged as he stepped inside, and in seconds, he winced at the musty air from boxes of dusty nostalgia.

The storekeeper paused from rifling through vintage postcards on a counter that Gabe thought must have aged at least two hundred years.

The man had a full head of black groomed hair, with precision trim like Gabe's mother used to do with a cereal bowl. His mechanic's shirt was buttoned to the neck, partially covered with a shoe repair apron.

Fumbling into cartons of transmitting equipment and adapters, Gabe settled on a good condition AC/DC, then an old battery operated transmitter radio. He held it up to the light wondering if it worked. He asked the clerk for a bag, and added a pair of earphones, a broken telephone with a jack line attached and a soldering iron. In a wooden crate, he recovered a small pencil drill. At the till, the clerk threw in a roll of electrical tape.

"Come back anytime, Gabe, I've got everything you could possibly want." He was no longer surprised hearing his name.

"Thanks, I'll be back."

Room 3B was buzzing when Gabe got upstairs, and he noted the time and issue. From his new treasures, he found a miniature Philips screwdriver and a dull cheese knife.

Gabe went about splitting, stripping and twisting copper wires he'd yanked from the radio. Cracking open the adaptor, he connected the green and red wires to opposite ends of the power terminal. The soldering pump needed a bit of priming but did its job. Unscrewing the phone conduit box, he fitted the adaptor and ear phone.

Ah ha, the tables have turned, gentlemen. I bet I'll get to the bottom of this. What does Bradley have of theirs? And what the heck is Hydra?

Listening against the wall, he deduced that the next unit was vacant. Drilling a tiny hole, he inserted a mini spy cam and directed it under an end table.

While waiting for footsteps to 3C, Gabe pored over the detective's gatherings about Bradley. It seemed that his ginger friend had built a large debt through gambling, and that his parents had cut off funding. At his wit's end, he made a bar acquaintance at the Bluebird one night while in Harrogate.

With a zoom of a photo of Bradley meeting his uncouth partners, Gabe noted that two of the men were Hennie and Axle. The file then revealed a plot to recover a hoard from under the nose of a shepherd owning a Yorkshire Moors pasture.

A piece determined to be part of a Viking ship had been recovered but it had no treasure trove value in silver or gold and went unnoticed, although illegal. It was thought that the finder misrepresented the discovery, and an investor from Harrogate hired Hennie and Axle to delve further into the find.

The illicit activity went on for several months, and the museum feared that Harrogate thieves would access a new hoard outside of Britain's Treasure Act. In the Act of 1996, if a landowner discovered any artifact or antiquity more than three hundred years old, it must be offered for sale to a British Museum, with the price determined by an independent board, and the value shared between the museum and the landowner.

So Bradley caught wind of the scheme and tried to outsmart the pair, but tripped himself up here in Staithes. It's a map and documentation about the find that Hennie wants back.

The geology report zeroed in on a location, based on assumptions that a thousand years ago, Roxby Beck was a full river, bringing Norsemen inland. The ancient site of a Viking village had already been unearthed, giving credence to the lifestyle of the pirate breed. But a second site at the old Ironstone Mine at Port Mulgrave remained unresolved, with only bits of pottery surfacing.

His wait for them was worthwhile. After eleven, the neighboring door slammed, vibrating Gabe's kitchen wall. Resting on his elbows on the floor, he watched the scene with his cellphone and ear plug.

Feet walked near the cam under the table, as Hennie started up.

"Axle, have you tracked Turner yet?"

"I have a lead about a sighting and I've set a trap at the alum mine. He's not dumb enough to think we won't be coming after him. He traded his grief to the glass blower. I got into his room yesterday, but couldn't find anything Bradley Turner left behind."

"I've heard excuses before, Axle."

"Are they sending a surveillance man for the weekend?" the third man asked. "We need eyes on the train station for Turner."

The heavier fellow that Gabe recognized as Hennie sat on the couch. Axle paced in the kitchen and the other tall one lit a cigarette and slumped into an armchair, yanking the footrest into position.

So there's a point man in Harrogate.

Hennie waved a finger at Axle. "Old lady Capp is too curious about us—don't trust her. Axle, keep an eye on the nosey busybody. If she comes to our place again, there'll be a price to pay."

Axle acted tough for Hennie. "She steams open the tenants' mail, I know that. I caught her red-handed looking through the mail of 1C. You know the gal with the kid?"

"Stay clear of her for now. I've got more important things on my mind," Hennie said.

Gabe's internal clock opened his eyes at 5 a.m., and he waited in the dark for the phone to ring. There it was. Click! Buzz!

"Yes, boss!" It was Hennie's sarcastic voice.

"Darby on the train this afternoon . . . yes, of course. Axle will be there to meet him, I assure you."

As brief as it was, Gabe knew something else was said that upset Hennie.

Friday morning had heavy fog and drizzle, and the heather moors looked like a sea of rising mist. Mrs. Capp heard him on the stairs, and intercepted him at the door.

"Morning to you, Mrs. Capp. Off to the mill, but with the rain, I won't be biking." He stepped to the porch, hesitating as rain poured over the eaves trough.

"Wait up, young man." She was back in a shake to offer her husband's rain cape.

"Bill ain't come back for it, so you might as well put it to use. You'll get soaked to the bone the way you are."

"That's very kind of you, Mrs. Capp."

"It's time you call me Maude."

"All the same, Maude, I appreciate your thoughtfulness."

It wasn't a downpour, but was accompanied by a damp mist that chilled Gabe into shivers.

I don't want to be predictable, so today I'll avoid the Cleveland. Maude mentioned the Seadrift. It smells good from Seaton Garth whenever I pass.

The Seadrift Café was famous for Grumpy Mule Coffee, and he knew from Martha to have the Staithes Coble cake, with apple, walnut and cinnamon, and Devonshire cream. At the door, he breathed in the warm baking. A breakfast bagel sandwich with lox and cream cheese was written on the specials board beside the Coble. Gabe was surprised to see Mary Jane at the till.

"Good morning, M.J. I thought you worked at the Endeavor."

"Oh hello, Gabe. I work at the pub but they don't open until eleven, so I take an early shift here. Helps pay the bills with a growing kid."

"I'm as hungry as an ox, so give me one of each of the specials on the board. And, of course, a Grumpy's coffee, double."

"How's your boy?" he asked. "I saw the accident by the bridge a few days ago. Too bad about his bike."

"It was his own fault. Shouldn't have been riding over there at that hour of the morning. Was supposed to be on his way to school."

"Have you tried the used shop for another bike for the boy? The Odds and Sods, I think?"

She laughed. "Oh, Horace, you mean. He's got a few in his back shed that need repairs but never gets around to it. He's a procrastinator."

Gabe said, "Why don't you pick one out and I'll make the repairs. I can do that."

"I'll owe you big time if you do."

"I confess, M.J., I have an ulterior motive."

Mary Jane looked disheartened. "What's the catch? I thought you were just being a nice guy."

"No, no. Listen to me first before you judge me."

His strides started out long in the rain along the pathway beside the creek, but crossing the bridge, he was slowed by deep puddles and mud. His mind wasn't on the weather, but contemplating a discussion he would have today with Niles.

It's what Crystal said last night, that Niles was warned off with a rifle by one of the ATV blokes. I need to know more.

It was slow trudging the muddy tracks from the creek to the mill, and he stepped to the side with the sound of a pickup from behind. Uncertain, he looked away from the road as he walked.

"Get in. I'll give you a ride to the mill." His face brightened, as it was Arbuckle.

"Oh, much appreciated, Theo." Gabe shook and wiped off the rainwater, not to drench the seat.

"Don't worry about that, kid. They're vinyl and will wipe."

What makes him assume I'm a kid? I'm twenty-five and spent three years in university. I've travelled the oceans and I've been shaving since fifteen.

Arbuckle continued. "It'll clear up before noon, but it'll be soggier for the weekend."

"As long as business is good, we'll roll with the punches," Gabe said.

Pulling to the mill, Gabe gushed his gratitude and promised to come by the Cleveland soon.

The mill was cozy and he rubbed his hands, inside the door. "Good morning, Niles!"

"You look like a drowned rat, Gabe."

Shaking Bill Capp's raincoat out the door, he hung it on a hat rack over a mat. At the base was a vintage umbrella holder.

"It was teeming, but Theo rescued me part way, or it could be worse."

He sat at his table, then tilted his stool toward Niles. "Oh, by the way, Crystal at the Cleveland says we can put some glass buoys on her shelves for the tourist rush."

"Good prospecting, Gabe. If we get to it Monday, they can have them for the Victoria Day weekend. You can promise it to Crystal.

"In England, we call it Corpus Christi holiday; it runs over to the bank's Monday holiday, and no one works when the banks are closed."

"I wanted to ask something else, Niles."

Niles looked up, ready to listen.

"It's about the three outsiders from the boarding house. Crystal says you had an encounter with one of them, when out with your dogs."

"Yes, I mentioned that to you."

"The way I heard it, the one called Axle pointed a loaded rifle at you to keep away. What was he protecting?"

"The soddy up beyond the sheep pastures. I take my setters along the stone fence in the upper lea. About a mile from Boulby Cliff."

"Exactly where was that?"

"Come here, Gabe." On a piece of parchment, Niles drew a map from the mill to the pastures, then a line to the soddy.

Gabe studied the sketch. "Looks like the road you drew to the top of Cleveland Way ends at the cliff ridge. From that height, could someone look down to see remnants of the old alum mines?" He already knew, before Niles could respond.

"And who owns the land?"

"You're mighty inquisitive; what's this really about?"

"These guys are my unfriendly neighbors. I'd like to know about my opposition."

"Let it go, Gabe. Nothing good can come from tracking those blokes."

Gabe said, "I suppose you're right." He knew it was what Niles wanted to hear.

"So . . . on with business. The shipment to Robin's Bay is about ready. Could you take the truck and deliver it there? It's along the coast, about five miles south of Whitby."

"Not at all. I'll get the crates. Robin Hood's Bay is a curious name for a fisherman's village in the North Moors. What's the story on it, Niles?"

"Legends and lore . . . makes it hard to know the truth. They say Robin Hood fought off an assault of French pirates that pillaged fishing boats off the coast. Since then, it was a smuggler's haven for gin, rum, silk, and tobacco in the 1800's, even tea. It's good enough to bring intrigue to our seaside villages, and to draw the movie companies. Robin Hood's Bay is the setting for the Bramblewick novels and a few years back for a movie, Wild Child. Never saw it myself."

"Hmm. The cobbled streets of quaint villages leaning over the sea; that does indeed inspire fantasy and mystique. I'll do some reading to catch the spirit if I can."

"Try the used book store on High Street."

"That I will," Gabe noted.

Robin Hood's Bay was nestled between a fissure and two cliffs. Rows of picturesque houses with red tile roofs snuggled tightly, around New Road and King's Beck.

Gabe maneuvered the delivery truck past the crowds on Lea Street, then followed to the Victoria Hotel. Ahead, a tour bus was idling, then moved on to park with a hissing sigh, blocking access to the loading bay. In twos, an archaeological group exited the coach, many in tour-issued, rubber wading pants, and a few with straw hats from the gift shop.

The hotel terrace overlooked the North Sea. Below, tourist lineups received fossil-hunting instructions on the beach, with maps of precious finds distributed.

The commissaries waved Gabe's truck from the entrance.

"It's a delivery for the Gift Shop. Where can I unload?"

"Follow around the road until you come to sea level. You'll see a sign at the back with an arrow for deliveries."

Gabe wound down to the turnoff near the Coastguard Station, and parked as close as possible to the Victoria Gift Shop. He loaded three crates on a dolly, and wheeled to the door. The sign over the window blind said 'Closed for Tea'.

It's Friday . . . and the mill closes at noon today.

He checked the time, and dialed from the sidewalk.

"Niles? I'm outside the shop and they're closed to noon. If I wait, I won't make it back before you close. Shall I wait?"

"That'll be fine. When you're back, park the truck in the lot and toss the keys through the door slot."

"Will do, Niles. See you Monday!"

At half past noon, Gabe was on the road again. Driving inland to connect with the cliff road, he likened the panorama to a storybook, like a snow globe. He pulled over to scan the distant boulders of the North Sea, where they met with Seaton Garth and the guest houses on Upper Cow Bank. On the horizon, the moors and green pastures were dotted with Swaledale horned sheep, bloated with ripe, straggly wool.

He argued with his conscience and a temptation to explore.

Do I take Cleveland Way and head back to the mill over Roxby Beck, or do I look now for the alum mine from Boulby Cliff?

In Nile's glove compartment, he found a pair of binoculars. He opened the door and stood on the running board. The sun was out but the mud hadn't dried.

Through the glasses, he followed the red ATV as it sped beside the stone wall toward open pasture.

The landscape dipped and peaked with a grass covered conal shape not far from the stone wall.

I know where he's going.

Gabe took Niles' sketched map from his pocket, and in that moment the decision was made.

He took off, with tires sliding in the mud and stayed in the sight of the moving red dot. It disappeared, and he waited for twenty seconds, hoping it would reappear at one of the rugged detours. At Boulby Cliff, he waited another fifteen minutes.

Tomorrow, I'll go up to the ridge on my bike.

Back at the mill, Gabe took buckets and brushes to the muddy pickup, leaving it spotless in the lot.

He remembered his promise to Mary Jane, and walked directly to the Odds and Sods shop. Horace was working at the counter.

"Did Mary Jane come by about a bike for her boy?"

"It's you, Farrow. I was expecting you earlier." Horace sized up Gabe's condition. "Been through the wringer today, eh?"

Looking down, Gabe saw that his shoes were still caked in dried mud and his jeans splattered to his hips. "I'll leave my boots outside."

"No, don't take your boots off. Go around back to my workshop. I'll meet you at the door."

The back area smelled of both motor oil and musty leather. Wooden shelves floor to ceiling held unmarked crates that bulged with parts, and tools hung over them from the rafters. At one side, half a dozen bikes in degrees of attachment hung from the ceiling, over a stack of tires and tangled chains.

One corner had semblances of abandoned movie equipment, with a wind machine and broken projectors. A large box of Foley sound equipment appeared untouched.

"Looks like you have enough here to build an airplane," Gabe laughed.

"My wife says I'm a hoarder. I do get attached," Horace sighed. "Can I leave you to your repairs? Take whatever you need to put together a reliable bike for M.J.'s boy. Just last week, one of those Orange Pro 5 bikes was stolen from a lane on Dalehouse. Its tourist season, and you'll need to make sure the kid keeps it locked up."

The doorbell chimed in the front and Horace left for it.

"Holler if you need help."

Gabe stood on a carton, up on his toes.

It's like a candy store. There's too much to pick from.

He didn't choose the most intact skeleton from the ceiling, but lowered a rugged ten-speed mountain bike.

Mud traction and getaway speed.

It took little more than a better tire, greased chains and gears to make it roadworthy. He scrubbed with rust remover until shards fell off, revealing clean chrome underneath.

It has to dry, so I'll paint it tomorrow.

A windshield caught his eye from another bike.

Perfect. I'll attach it after the paint. My young point man deserves nothing but the best.

"Horace!"

The storekeeper was impressed at Gabe's progress and assured him he'd be open at nine for the painting.

"Keep this under your hat, Horace. I want it to be a surprise for M.J. and her boy."

"That's a tall order in this town, but you have my word."

"Horace, do you mind me asking if Bradley Turner ever came into your shop?"

"Turner . . . Bradley. Oh yes, the fellow from the city. He barged in one day and asked if I had any mine goggles. What a weird question to ask these days. Nobody's mined around here in decades."

"Did you have any?"

"I said I didn't because I was too lazy to look through these bins. Do you want one too?" Horace looked confused.

"Not today, but maybe soon," Gabe laughed.

He was just about to leave the Odds & Sods, when he turned back.

"Just one more question. Horace, what about the threesome staying at Mrs. Capp's house. They keep to themselves, but I was wondering if they asked for anything unusual as well."

"Well, I remember the one with the name of a grease monkey. Rod . . . no, Axle. He wanted a spool of wire and as much cable twine as I could find. I sent him to the Fish & Net at the Harbor. I don't know where they get the line for their traps."

Horace bit his lip. Gabe waited for him to go on.

"I didn't say anything at the time, but a heavy duty spool of line went missing from the Lifeboat Station a few days later. My instincts warned me not to mess with those blokes, so I didn't say anything to the shore authorities.

"The marine squad was upset about the theft. That kind of thing doesn't happen around here. We're the type of village where we look out for one another. We know everyone in the Fishermen's Choir, the Chamber of Commerce and Tourist Board, the Gallery Group, and the congregation at St. Stephen's. We even know who doesn't show up for Sunday morning service."

"Thanks, Horace. You've been helpful."

There's no mystery here. Someone knows something, I just have to find that person. Tomorrow, I'll wander by the guest houses on the cliff. See if anyone's seen anything peculiar.

Gabe stayed in for the evening and warmed a Scottish meat pie from Pickersgill and a portion of slaw and potato salad. With a rare glass of cheap, red wine from the grocer's cooler, he allowed himself to relax.

The envelope to Bradley Turner was still on the coffee table.

It's an offence to open someone else's mail. But if I mark Bradley's forwarding address for the postman, Hennie will see it.

Gabe put his feet up on the coffee table and continued with his second glass of wine, staring at the envelope.

I don't want to be responsible for harm to him. What did you do, Bradley, to have Hennie turn the tables on you?

The image of Bradley looking under the bed on the first day returned to Gabe's memory. Getting to his knees, he removed the foot mat and ran his fingers around the corner of each floorboard.

Between the two slats closest to the wall, he suspected a gap. A cheese knife pried one of the boards free, and he stuck his fingers into the flat slot, searching for anything.

There—something cold and hard. A tin. Sharp on the corners.

Inside the long, flat tray, Gabe found an over-sized, pencil lead box. The supplier's name was printed and its location indicated 'Harrogate'.

"I wonder how long this has been here," he whispered as he wiped away the grime. "This is an antique."

The lid's edges stuck together and he took it to the table to open. An article from the Harrogate Advertiser from 2007 was folded inside.

The headline identified a new hoard discovery at the time at the Vale of York, describing the discovery in a farmer's field, of 617 Viking coins from the 9th century in gilt and silver. Two farmers made the find with metal detectors.

The item referred to finds at the Cornwall Toldish tunnel, closed in 1874, and Prospect Crimple at Harrogate, closed in 1848. Other hoards in England were mentioned, suggesting more exist in the North Yorkshire Moors where the Vikings came ashore from the North Sea.

The newspaper quoted The Treasure Act, with statements by the museum curator reminding the public of England's rights. After evaluation, a portion of the 2007 hoard was returned to the two farmers.

Why would this under the floorboards?

Treating the fragile paper with care, he caught a tiny heading from an article on the back of the page.

Lone Gold Coin Found

The item was just one column and an inch at most, mixed in near the social columns, but he jotted the details. The Museum Curator had identified the found coin to be from the era of Hardrada and Tostig Godwinson, who fought for English supremacy in the Battle of Stamford Bridge in 1066.

Feeling inside the tin, his hand caught on something razor-sharp, leaving a gash on his hand. He clenched his fist, but protruding from the wound was a sharp fossil, long and narrow. Gabe applied antiseptic from the cabinet and a bandage to stop the bleeding, and returned to the table to examine the fossil.

In disbelief, his eyes widened—the boney imprint was threaded with pure gold.

It's time for me to take an interest in those fossil shops and the local museums. They claim to have fossils from a thousand years.

With precision, Gabe returned everything to the floor and covered the board with the mat. He lifted his head as footsteps approached the third floor, and readied to listen at the receiver. The door to 3C slammed shut.

"Hennie, I'm going into the alum mine in the morning to search for more of that Dragon hoard. Darby is on the morning train and is posted to watch for Turner—or generally any men in suits. On a hot weekend, tweeds and suits are warning signals that the British investigation is getting close," Axle theorized.

Gabe returned to the laptop to study the dossier. Searching online archives and links, he stalled at a photo at a museum ribbon-cutting at a Norsemen exhibit. He couldn't identify the museum, but it was clearly Bradley Turner standing in the corner.

I'll need more equipment from the Odds and Sods.

He set his alarm to be out the door first thing.

5

SATURDAY MORNING seagulls were in full voice over the harbor. The town had been buzzing in preparation for Victoria Day, anticipating the miraculous annual influx of tourists. Nobody was disappointed with the crowds again this year.

Along the boardwalk peninsula, tourists jockeyed for the choicest seats for the Lifeboat Regatta. Brindley, from the Gallery, assembled a class of art students with easels to show off watercolor instruction to passersby. His scattering of supports and easels obstructed part of the boardwalk, but he was oblivious and others thought it added to the charm.

The morning sun projected across the congestion, and Gabe stood to observe the motion on the walkway. A crowd of old-fashioned bonnets passed him with baskets, and he followed them toward the Farmer's Market in the Square, where hawkers imported for the weekend were peddling high-priced wares in competition with local merchants.

The Ladies Horticulture group was festooned in bustles and hoops of a bygone era. In white braided and powdered wigs, they resembled Queen Victoria in all sizes and shapes, in remembrance of the celebration. Mrs. Arbuckle was among them.

High tide would be in less than ninety minutes, when the muddy trough of Roxby Beck would flow with salt water, with whitecaps again dancing.

Outside the Odds & Sods, Gabe waited for Horace to open shop. He held a cup of takeout coffee in each hand.

Horace arrived red-faced, riding Gabe's patched bicycle.

"You gave me your word, Horace!"

"I haven't said a word to M.J. or her boy." Horace thought that would do as an explanation.

Gabe made a faint attempt to disguise his irritation. "How much do I owe for parts and equipment? I'd like to rectify my obligation. I'll paint it later on my own."

"It's a good solid bike, easily worth £20."

Gabe stuffed the pound notes into Horace's hand and rode off, afraid if he lingered, he'd say something in the heat of annoyance. Understanding the value of keeping good terms with Horace and his need for future parts, he held his tongue. Wheeling the bike around the back alley, Gabe went uphill on High Street to a concrete landing between two old buildings.

Just enough space to sneak across and save time.

On the rise to the cliffs where the two roads converged, Gabe discovered an option, an abandoned petrol station. He looked inside through a broken window, and stepped through tall grass on the side of the building, to an unlocked washroom door.

No traffic around here—it must be a back road to Runswick. I'll stash the bike in here and get it in a few hours to do the painting myself.

Back on High Street, the shops and tea rooms had lineups already, with lively conversations, tea, scones and berry jams.

With throngs of tourists on the streets, Gabe felt like a town native. He strode past the newly painted, red doors of the Butcher Shop, then the blue doors of the Endeavor, and stopped at the bay windows of the Staithes Gallery. Several paintings were creating chatter as they were set on easels outside on the walk.

"Hello, Mr. Milner," he called in an exaggerated whisper, just loud enough to be heard over the crowd.

Milner nodded and made a gesture that he wanted to talk, but needed to finish his negotiations with an elderly couple from Grimes Guest House. They were holding a Martinsdale original bold with reds, yellow and blues, depicting the ocean and spring eruption of the countryside, and Milner was well into ensuring they wouldn't escape without a purchase.

The Gallery doors were propped open and Gabe stepped inside. Interpretations of tiled houses were displayed on an easel near the door, but his eye was on an older oil painting further on the wall. Unlike the vivid, gay colors of the ones in the window, it had natural hues, and buried in the mystique of the painting was a glimpse of yellow light coming from a tunnel.

Drawn by the perception and intensity of the tunnel's depth, Gabe was transfixed on a glow in the color that he thought leered at him like a pair of eyes. The painting's card said 'Staithes Viaduct–Beach Street', and he thought about the setting and its familiarity.

Is it on the way to the mill? Or in the bush upwards from the creek where the ATV gets stashed? Staithes Viaduct . . . would it be from the old days of the Whitby-Loftus line? Like a ghost from that old railway.

He observed that for the occasion, Milner was featuring a vintage railway theme in this cubicle of the gallery. Nearby was a plaque and faded photo of a derelict train station, 'Staithes Train Depot – closed 1958', and beside it, a framed newspaper clipping of a vintage steam locomotive running between Staithes and Runswick Bay. At the counter, a set of four poster reproductions were available in tubes as reasonable souvenirs of local memorabilia.

A small wall ad described the North York Moors Railway's steam section from Whitby to Pickering in high season commencing this Saturday morning, with 1940s apparel and exuberant décor from the period. In the photo, the Engineer in the cab was waving to the crowd, like Santa Claus.

Gabe heard the lengthy toot of a steam whistle outside, and picked up a copy of the full Victoria Day agenda.

VICTORIA DAY CELEBRATIONS

9 A.M. TO 6 P.M.
(FIREWORKS AT 10 P.M.)

Old Jack's Boat – storytelling segments from the writing of Bernard Cribbins
Story-Telling & Tour of Diagon Alley (Harry Potter)
Pop-Up Galleries on High Street
Street Parade on Beach Street
Reel & Rod Casting Competitions – Seaton Garth peninsula
Hot Air Ballooning – Boulby Cliff
Capt. James Cook Museum – Special Tours
Vintage Railroad rides at Saltburn Station to Runswick Bay
Hiking Tours – Check at Lifeboat Station
Fossil Hunt – Register at Cod & Lobster
Harbor Regatta – Register at Lifeboat Station
Fly casting off Rocky Isle Peninsula – Register weights at Seadrift Café
Marching Bands in Market area – 10 a.m. 1 p.m. 5 p.m.

At the door, Milner winked as Gabe left. He was showing the same customer a matching acrylic to go with the first.

A brass band was cued on the street, and across he saw M.J. setting out bistro tables at the tavern with wild flowers Troy had picked from the upper bank.

She caught a glimpse of Gabe watching her and waved back. He had no choice but to go to greet her.

I'm not ready with the bike, and for sure she's going to ask about our last conversation.

"It's a fine morning and too bad you have to work, M.J. What does Troy do on a Saturday?"

"Why are you asking?"

"You've been in Staithes for some time; I'm interested in knowing the lay of the land. Boys will be boys and thrive on adventuring . . . I'll have the bike ready this afternoon. Maybe Troy could be my tour guide?"

M.J. studied Gabe's face as he continued.

"I saw a newspaper item at the gallery about old tunnels, train routes and aqueducts. Would you mind if I borrowed Troy to show me? Of course, I'll compensate him."

"Those areas can be dangerous. A kid went missing a few summers back and they found him in a collapsed mine shaft. Folks started locking their doors—something a village like Staithes takes as an offence."

"Let me try to convince you then. I have a first aid kit, was a Boy Scout leader and I'm cautious." She listened as he ramped it up. "I'll give you my mother's address and my military service credentials. If it makes you more at ease, I'll sign over one of my kidneys." Gabe pulled a pouch from his pack. "See!"

Mary Jane burst in laughter at his charade.

"Alright, alright! He's doing chores. You'll find him looking for seashells at Seaton Garth. It's a safe way to pass the time, but the beach is so sandy, it takes all day to find a decent pair to sell to the Boat & Anchor."

"I'll find and feed him and he'll be home before supper."

She called out as he left, "Be careful on the trestle; it's got weak spots."

Troy and Gabe recovered the bike at the petrol depot, chained to the sink's plumbing with a cable and generic lock.

"Wow! This is a super bike. How much does my Mums have to pay for it?"

"Not a dime. I'm handy with that sort of thing and just put together a bucket of parts. It'll be fast. Ten gears!"

Gabe made a final check of the spokes, and dug in his pack for a can of spray. "Blue metallic," he said. "Do you want to do the honors, or shall I?"

"May I?" Troy had a Christmas morning look.

Sitting cross-legged in the grass, Gabe quizzed Troy about secret tunnels and sights that only a boy would know. With a finger, he gently touched the drying paint.

"Still a bit tacky," he said. "Troy, other than the day the ATV ran you down, have you seen those fellows around?"

"Don't tell my Mums. I'm not supposed to go near the cages that block the old train tunnels. I did see two of them with metal detectors over in the mounds though. They're pretty thick with brush, but the legends of Norsemen leaving treasure have always brought greedy prospectors. You're not one of those, are ya?"

"I'll admit my curiosity is peaked." Gabe looked into the boy's wild eyes. "How old are you?"

"I'm eleven next month. My Da's a mariner and every now and then we see him, but he loves the sea more than me."

"You and your Mum are a fine pair. Chin up!"

"Naw, I don't cry or nothing; I just feel a hole in my heart. But don't worry about me, I do fine as the man of the house."

Gabe took a swipe at the cross bar of the bike. "Feels dry enough to me. Give it a test there on the road."

Troy's smile, minus two front teeth, struck a chord of remembrance inside Gabe.

"You're the leader, kid. Let's go."

Near Boulby Cliff, they detoured into a rocky terrain where Roxby Beck dwindled into thick gully of brush. The stone cliffs showed years of crumbling with old Jurassic shale and whinstone.

"They say the Viking paths are somewhere here, but must be buried in heavy thicket," Troy said.

Laying the bikes in the bushes, they trudged toward the viaduct, now partially visible.

"Do you know where this goes?"

"Naw, but I brought a metal detector here once and it went wild."

Troy led the way, maneuvering through a thorny hawthorn. "Over there, I'll show you where." The soil and rocks were loose under their feet, and they raised their arms for balance.

Under a pile of dead tinder, Troy exposed a wire gate with a recent padlock. To the left, an immeasurable slab of titan limestone was imbedded in the bank, upright on an angle. Gabe examined the exterior rim of each side. The years had taken back its own. He leaned his weight on it but the massive stone wasn't budging.

Seems out of place for heather fields. I'll check the topography maps. Maybe something connects.

Gabe fingered a carved indention.

This black rock has an etching. An animal head—a dragon maybe.

Some loose rocks rolled and crumbled under their feet and Troy slid on his backside down about ten feet.

"Troy! You okay?"

"I'm fine. You can come this way."

Gabe tendered his footing and reached for a protruding iron bar near the grate.

"Careful, touching the metal. It's corroded with rust. I got a nasty scratch that was infected for weeks."

A noise above them took their focus.

Whoosh! Whoosh! Blast!

Whoosh! Followed by sublime quiet.

Overhead, a hot air balloon coasted in silence. Gabe had forgotten the event on the day's itinerary, with pilots from across the UK competing over the Yorkshire Moors. A second was now in sight, and others rising from Cowbar Bank.

The baskets barely cleared the tops of trees, and the voices were clear as a bell.

"Look down there. What are they doing?" a passenger asked.

"Probably a misguided tourist," the pilot said. "Along the coast are ancient hoards. Most treasure hunters have stars in their eyes, but no idea what they're doing."

Gabe and Troy stayed under cover as the convoy of balloons swept overhead.

Hmm. Aerial maps over the moors must be available.

Before they could proceed, a distant noise alarmed Gabe.

"Troy—over here. Stay low and scamper up the ridge to the bikes. I'll follow you."

"What is it?"

"Can't you hear that? The sound that ran you down on your bike. Those guys are up to no good . . . they're dangerous, I say."

At a high vantage on the ridge, they waited for the ATV to pass. Hennie was driving, and slowing on the old tracks below. He looked up and stopped.

The pause was agonizing for Gabe and Troy, and in silence they watched the sun's glint on the vehicle's glass, waiting for it to move on. At last it continued, following an old mine road barely visible to Gabe that took them up to the top of the cliffs.

He finally spoke out loud to Troy, lying in the shrubs. "You can sit up now; I didn't mean to scare you. Are you alright?"

The boy was on his feet in a jiffy. "I ain't scared. Why, are you?"

They lifted the bikes high over some thistles and back to a rideable path. Nearing High Street, they were both in good spirits from the adventure.

"Do you like fishing, Troy?"

"Sure do. We can fly fish off the end of the rocky pier. Even now, if you want?"

"Come with me. I'll be less than a minute getting my gear at Mrs. Capp's."

The veranda rocking chair was empty, and Gabe assumed Maude was on Main Street, socializing with the Queen Victorias.

The house is empty, with Hennie and Axle at the moors. Otherwise, I don't dare leave the boy alone while I go up.

"I'll wait on the porch," Troy said.

Against better judgement, Gabe bounded upstairs.

The house was quiet, and grabbing his rod and reel and a pair of sodas from the fridge, he beetled back down.

Hennie had Troy by the arm. "Where were you, boy?"

Troy's eyes were wide with fear, but he clenched his teeth with the bravery of a soldier.

"It ain't no business of yours. Who are you?"

"Hennie, get away from the boy. If you have something to say, let it be man to man. Only a wimp would intimidate a boy."

Gabe stepped forward, the muscles on his neck taut and his fists buckled. The fishing rod fell to the ground.

Taking the lad from Hennie and Axle, Gabe stormed down the hill, with Troy keeping pace at his heels.

"Don't give them the satisfaction of looking back, Troy."

His hand wormed into Gabe's fist. "Thanks for rescuing me, but we both know I could've handled it on my own, right?"

The two men laughed.

With a heavy pail of cold brown cod from the rocky pylons for the Endeavor, Troy was content with the events of the day with Gabe.

"Better not to alarm your Mum about our run-in though."

"No way. She wouldn't let me go with you again, but I'm available to be your guide next time if that's okay?" His bare hand stretched out for the promised tip.

"Is a fiver good enough? I don't want my confidence man to be on the financial outs."

"Mighty pleased. And thanks for the bike . . . I'll chain it around back so it don't go wandering away."

M.J. was at the door with no questions, but enjoying some glee on her son's face that she hadn't seen for a while.

Troy raised his hook of cod. "Can Gabe stay for dinner?"

"Thanks Troy, but I have things to attend to," Gabe said without even a fluster, sparing M.J. the embarrassment.

Gabe peddled directly to Captain Cook's Museum and Heritage Centre, hopeful to find any relic maps, drawings or pictures of the tunnels in the bowels of the moors, where the legends of ghosts swarmed.

The Firths, Reg and Anne, were in convincing period costume at the door, about to recreate James Cook's grocery store, where he had apprenticed before falling prey to the romance of the sea.

"Welcome to Captain Cook's Museum," Reg announced, greeting each person one at a time that passed the threshold.

"Delighted to meet you, Mr. Firth. My name's Gabe Farrow."

"Yes, the fellow from Mrs. Capp's. Nice to finally meet you. You've almost passed the stage of a newcomer."

"I see you're busy today, but I'm interested in the lore of the moors. I'm intrigued by the tales of the tunnels. Can you point me to any information?"

"On the upper floor, that's where. You'll need time to thumb through the books, some two hundred years and more. And manuscripts, letters, old paintings—even a semblance of recovered Viking coins and pottery. Yes, that's the place to start."

Gabe thanked him and was about to head upstairs when it donned that he'd forgotten his English manners. He turned back to see Reg Firth still watching him.

"Reg, perhaps we'll have tea later in the week. I'd like to hear your story."

"I'll look forward to it." Reg smiled slipping his fingers into his suspenders with satisfaction.

The museum was meticulous in its dossier and archives of the British sailor. On the second floor, a hostess guarded the antiques and locked cases of delicate manuscripts.

"Good afternoon, Sir. These manuscripts are personal diaries of Captain Cook. Besides old archived books, there's a wealth of references about North Yorkshire."

"I'm interested in the old tunnels of Staithes. Is there anything that would reference the moors?"

The archivist thought about a few books at the counter: Atkinson's Legends of the North York Moors; Spirits of the North Yorkshire Moors Railway; Hidden Places of North East Yorkshire. Oh, and Fodor's book, Secrets of Moors & Dales.

"There must be a dozen more too, at least. We charge full price here, but I know for a fact that a few end up at the Odds & Sods."

Time passed without notice and at five o'clock, Reg came up to find him. "How did you do, young man?"

He looked at his watch with chagrin. "Oh my goodness, time did get away from me."

"Not at all. It pleases me to see this. If you'd like to purchase any books, my wife's at the till. She'll give you a discount, just so you'll come back."

Settling on two, Gabe headed toward the Cleveland Café with his parcel under his arm. A long queue waited outside for tables to empty.

A portly lady in the line behaved like she was in charge, wielding an imagined influence over the naïve.

She boomed to Gabe, "Give yer name up front. Then get at the back of the line. That's what they said."

"Thanks, Ma'am."

At the front, Theo Arbuckle was adding names to the list.

"Hi Theo. You look busy."

"A bit more than we can handle," Arbuckle admitted, his face red and showing stress.

"Tell you what, Theo. Get me a spot or chair at the counter and I'll hang around after and wash dishes."

Arbuckle pointed to the wall. "This way, my friend."

A narrow table with one chair satisfied Gabe. When Crystal came with the water jug, he said, "Don't fuss with me today, just the special. After I've eaten, I'll lend a hand in the kitchen."

"You're a doll, Gabe."

Waiting for his serving, Gabe dug into his bag of books. In a chapter linking Robin Hood's Bay and the abandoned railroad of Deptford Junction, he was stalled in a section on the ore mines. He pored over the lore of mysterious hoards and mythical ghosts.

"Here you are, Gabe."

Crystal straightened a plate of haddock and chips in front of him, with a side of homemade tartar sauce and a nappy of slaw.

"Theo says when you're done, check with Mandy. There won't be a bill coming; they really appreciate you pitching in."

When Gabe approached Mandy at cash, the bossy woman from the queue had just arrived at the front of the line to be seated. She glared at Gabe. "And who do you think you are butting in out of order? I saw you."

Mandy gave Gabe an apron and he headed to the kitchen. On a top shelf, he deposited his books beside a stack of folded linens.

At six p.m., he started washing dishes, alternating to tossing salad, and finished at nine. As a teenager, he'd spent weekends cleaning dishes at the local old folks' home, and Arbuckle's dated equipment was familiar.

"Land sakes, Gabe, you really saved us tonight," Mandy said.

"That's just being neighborly, right?"

"So you've already got the Staithes blood in ya."

"If you're done with me, I'll be off to find a seat for the fireworks at the beach."

Theo looked up from the till from counting receipts. "Hey, Gabe, can't say enough. Anytime you want a seat and there's a line, remember you rate preferred seating. I should give you a badge or something."

Gabe laughed to avoid the awkwardness. "No gratitude needed—I'll be happy waiting my turn."

With a skip in his step, he felt like a million bucks. Crystal came running after him. "Gabe, you forgot your books."

"Thanks, I would have remembered before long."

"Do you mind if I join you for the fireworks?" Crystal had a beach blanket rolled under her arm.

"Sure." He took the blanket. "I think the Lifeboat Station's best. Looks like they're keeping folks back from the rocky pier."

"I see a spot."

She nudged Gabe at a grassy knoll, and he hailed a drink hawker. "Two cokes and a pack of your sparklers. What else is your fancy, Crystal?"

Crystal set them on the ground with a giggle. "I'll take one of those neon bracelets and a pink candy floss too.

"Thanks, Gabe. I never miss Victoria Day. My favorite is the cascading fountain, the highest ones. Then the booming missiles."

"Or Roman candles and burning stars?" he added.

After an hour of oohs and aahs, Gabe walked Crystal to her flat over a guest house in the upper Cowbar Bank.

His room at Capp's was quiet, with no buzzing, talking or shuffling, but his kitchen table had a form and a clipped note. 'Gabe, if you want to stay on during tourist season, I'll have to up your rate. Let me know as early as possible.'

Heck, where would I go? You've got me in a tight situation, Maude. I'm known in town as the fellow from Mrs. Capp's.

He sat to mull the dilemma and how long his mission could take.

It'll be yes for July to September. But so far, I've found no traces of the board or what Bradley discovered. And now new expenses for London. I might need the weekend job at the Cleveland to pay rent.

Exhausted, he fell into the sagging bed and his mind went to the alum mines and Axle.

The five o'clock telephone rang right on cue.

I'll have to fix that.

Down on the cold floor, he inspected the conduit box, now convinced the call was an automated system controlled outside the house.

The lines for 3B and 3C are connected to a single line.

Finding a Customer Service number in the phone directory, he called on his cell. An automated voice said he'd wait twenty minutes for a representative, and he was determined enough to wait, to find the source of the calls. In thirty minutes, a real person answered.

"This is Sanjeep. What's your number and how can I help you?"

"I'll give you my address—you should be able to find the number from that."

"What's the residential number of your account?"

"That's part of my problem. I don't have a telephone number but my phone rings me every morning at 5 a.m. I need to find who and where these calls come from."

"If you're not a customer of the telephone service, I can't assist you, sir."

Facing a brick wall, Gabe shook his head, but had already invested forty-five minutes.

"May I speak with your Supervisor?"

"I'm sorry, sir. As I told you, if you are not a customer, we can't help you."

"Let me tell you again, Sanjeep. You have a live line into my flat."

With Sanjeep's pause, Gabe sensed a crack of progress and in the man's perseverance.

"The number is registered to Bradley Turner. Have him make the inquiry directly."

"I assume this call is being recorded and you will be rated on how you remedy the situation."

"Yes, sir, it is recorded."

Gabe's voice raised. "Who calls me at 5 a.m. every day?

"It's from Harrogate, from Dodds & Turner Gold Exchange. The direct line of Mr. Ian Dodds."

"I appreciate this—thank you. Can you give me that number, I don't have a call display."

"There is an unlisted request on that line." Sanjeep wasn't going to budge again.

"Thank you, Sanjeep. Have a nice day."

Gabe recalled the name 'Dodds & Turner' from the museum's dossier, and he google searched for anything more. Twenty years earlier, a client of the firm recorded the discovery of a hoard between York and Harrogate, in a closed vein of an abandoned mine. Most of the evaluation fees went into the account of Jarvis Turner and Ian Dodds, with only a pittance returned to the British Museum, with fudged excavation reports.

An archived news article had a photo that mesmerized Gabe enough to pull the news clipping from his wallet.

Bradley set me up as his patsy when he first saw me. He couldn't do the job, so he put an innocent tourist on the hot seat. Guessing he was in cahoots with the gang but double-crossed them.

3C's door slammed and he counted what he thought to be three sets of feet.

Today, I'll tail them.

He pulled on jeans, a tee, and a khaki fatigues hoodie. Scampering downstairs in his socks, his shoes waited outside at the front. In the distance, he watched the three men head for the foot bridge, and on the other side, they dragged the ATV from the bush by the creek.

Hennie revved the engine and they headed uphill traveling on the Cow Bar. Jogging far behind now, Gabe kept pace with his eyes, but out of sight. At Roxby Beck he detoured for about twenty minutes.

At the top of Cleveland Way, the ATV veered toward the moors along the crumbling stone wall. They skidded to a stop. Hennie cut the engine and Axle jumped out reluctantly.

"Pick you up in one hour," Hennie said. "Exactly, from now."

"You sure about this, boss? We've never sent a man alone for the run through the mine. Do you want me to take an inventory?"

"Ha, don't you trust me?" The two glared at each other, both in suspicion.

Hennie eased the ATV out of sight down into a knoll, and roared along the cliff toward Staithes. Fergus hadn't spoken since leaving the house.

Gabe lay on his stomach in the shadow of the stone wall, hidden by the rugged mounds. Ten minutes had passed and Hennie hadn't returned, and Gabe was gauging it was safe to move now.

He focused on the mouth of the old mine, for any sights, sounds or activity at the point he last saw Axle. It appeared to him to be a soddy of sorts, with the entrance covered by a military camouflage blanket.

Alum was mined in the 16th century for medicine and vegetable dyes, with miners hacking through the shale into bands of ironstone and alum. But as fifty tons of shale only produced an inch of alum, the mining was redundant by 1860, and the mines closed and sealed.

Looking back at Boulby Cliff, Gabe considered it safe to venture under the backdrop of the entrance, and crawled close enough to hear water dripping from somewhere in the depths of the open cavern.

Must be a deep mine.

Adjusting his eyes, his hands felt the way, as he eased along the wall on the decayed remnants of an ancient scaffold. Broken shafts of light filtered through the netting of the camouflage blanket used at the mine opening.

He froze at a splash near him.

A rock falling. Water sounds deep. Was that me . . . or Axle?

"Who's there?" Axle yelled. "Hennie, is that you?"

Gabe's feet slid a few inches downward, toward the ruins of a rotted shaft. In a crouch, he watched the moving beam on the walls of Axle's flashlight.

It looks like an old silo buried in the ground.

Feeling around the frame, Gabe gripped onto heavy hemp rope used for shinnying into the bowels of the mine, the kind used at the Lighthouse Station.

Common sense took hold of Gabe, knowing he was chasing a dangerous man into a dark hole without a weapon or any reasonable rescue tactic.

I could be trapped in here with Hennie coming up behind, or just left here in my grave.

Near the exit, he caught the whiff of rotten eggs and sped up. Barely outside, he heard the ATV, and holed up behind some rocks to wait it out.

At Odds and Sods, Horace wanted only a paltry sum for two used metal detectors, a crow bar and fifty feet of heavy, yellow camp twine. He even threw in a pair of mine goggles at no cost.

"Horace, do you have one of those oxygen tanks that old people sometimes carry around? I know it's an unusual request, but I have a good use for it. I'm going spelunking near Whitby on Monday, and I'd like it for safety precaution. Sometimes old gases get trapped in forgotten crevices."

"You are an interesting man, Farrow. And yes, I happen to have one. One of the old ladies from the nursing home passed on and a family member brought it to me like I was a pawn shop."

Next stop was the Cleveland. Theo was outside sweeping.

"Ahoy there, Gabe." Arbuckle put his broom aside to speak. "I was wondering . . . since the town is overflowing with tourists this weekend, could I hire you tonight between five and nine? I'll gladly pay you the same as the rest of the staff, plus a percentage of tips at the end of the night."

"Thanks, Theo. As it happens, Mrs. Capp has raised my rent and I'm a bit short. So it'll help both of us."

A handshake sealed the deal and Gabe continued on downhill to the beach, whistling.

From an honor pay box, he picked up a newspaper and proceeded to the Seadrift for a black tea and lemon. Spreading the classifieds, he zeroed in on a single column of used cars.

Used Cars . . . cheap used cars. Here's a ten year old Vauxhall hatchback. Not a bad price and sure would make life easier.

He rang a number in Harrogate. A Scottish man answered.

"Yes, we're open for the long weekend, but only between eleven and five on Sunday."

"I'll come tomorrow by train. I'm interested in the silver Vauxhall."

Gabe rifled in the news section for anything about hoards, thefts and archaeological items. Nothing was there, but the Society column caught his attention, with an announcement of tickets to a reception honoring Mr. Ian Dodds' appointment to the UK Treasury Board—the garden reception to be Saturday afternoon on King's Road, Harrogate.

Gabe pulled up the bus and train schedule to Harrogate. From Staithes, he'd connect to another train at Darlington, then an hour and a half to Harrogate.

I'll need to be back at the Cleveland before five for the job.

At the boarding house, as he showered and shaved. His face in the mirror surprised him, with so much sunburn, and the sun bleaching his brown curls. His nose was long and he clenched his jaw as he shaved, now reddish from so much time outside.

Gosh, I'm starting to look like my grandfather.

With kitchen shears, he trimmed his locks, taking away the brunt of his boyish looks.

Sitting on the side of his bed, Gabe reached down to touch the tracks of mud on the floor.

"Someone's checking out either the phone line or the floorboards."

Voices were rising next door. "Darby has been at the train station since yesterday. He recognized Turner and tracked him to the mine."

"Blasted! Did you say anything to him—I mean Darby? There's no point in him knowing anything more than the essentials. I don't trust outsiders," Hennie barked.

"No, but there was a commotion near the mine entrance today. Someone or something knocked some rocks down the chute."

"Probably a rat. I was up there and didn't see anyone."

"Will Darby keep his mouth shut?"

"Dodds vouched for him," Axle said.

"What makes *him* think he's calling the shots?" Hennie was getting angrier by the minute.

"He's the one that turns the stuff into bouillon. Apparently, the Cash for Gold scam is under scrutiny and Dodds wants to distance himself from our operation. Unfortunately, we need him to filter the gold to the market."

"Enough talk! Just get the bounty from the mine ready for pickup," Hennie demanded.

"All of it?"

Hennie didn't answer, but the scowl to Axle was enough.

"And take the train to Harrogate. I'll call Dodds and have a word."

"Fergus, you need to be available for lookout. It isn't enough to follow us around like a puppy. We need a driver for the ATV tomorrow."

Gabe had yet to hear anything from Fergus, the taller one, and wondered if the man could even speak.

Hennie dialed Harrogate on his land line, and Gabe picked up the earphone.

Ring . . . ring . . . ring.

"Hello."

"Dodds, is that you?"

"You know it is, Hennie. What do you want?"

"I'm sending Axle to Harrogate tomorrow with some gold coins we found in a cache at the alum mine. Not a motherlode there, just a random find. First, I'll send Axle into the alum mine to finalize it, then we'll move to the Runswick site."

"Now hold off a bit. I told you I've been appointed to the Treasury. I can't afford any questionable meetings or contacts right now."

Hennie said, "Darby tailed a bloke from the train yesterday that checked out the mine."

"You know what to do about that." Dodd's line went dead.

To the background of the men arguing, Gabe returned to his maps and file.

I've got to get to the mine, but I need a lookout, like Troy. I'll take the oxygen tank. That whiff of rotten eggs suggests methane. The setting is ripe with decayed agriculture and dripping water.

The gauge on the tank was three-quarters full, enough he thought. With a balloon aerial map of the mine terrain and the museum cartography, he made precise measurements.

Not far from the alum mine was a dark spot on the map, under the surface of the moors.

"Possibly the main find is here. Fortunately, Hennie hasn't gone this direction, at least as far as I know.

The topography is rugged. After a thousand years, erosion should have evened out unless there is a deep cavern, so something's not right. Hennie's men identified Dodds' role to convert items to gold bullion, but the farm operation needs investigation.

Gabe emptied his backpack and reloaded his hiking and survival tools.

Tomorrow he'd get the train to Harrogate and return with the Vauxhall.

I'll be back in time, then I could take M.J. and Troy to brunch—I'll beg for him to be my lookout guy. I can't fit in Dodds' reception. Funny about kids—they are observers and mimickers, but they can keep a secret from a parent. I have to earn M.J.'s trust.

She answered at her loft above the Endeavor.

"M.J.—it's Gabe. Captain Cook's Inn serves a nice Sunday brunch, and if you and Troy would like to join me, I'd be happy to have your company. Do you mind walking to Staithes Lane and meeting me there at 1 p.m.? I'll make a reservation."

Her voice sounded either surprised or reluctant, he wasn't sure which. "Sounds fine, Gabe, it is kind of you to invite us."

Mary Jane was a nice girl, seven or eight years older, and he didn't think of her in a romantic way. She was the forgotten wife of a mariner, doing her best to raise her son with her waitressing earnings.

I'll kill two birds with one stone. It's a friendship I can trust, with people that are becoming my substitute family. I feel like I'm establishing roots.

Gabe was waiting at the auto dealership at 10:30 a.m. Through the fence, he examined the silver Vauxhall by the Service door, until one of the salesmen unlocked the gates for him.

"Take a seat in the salesroom, Mr. Farrow. Baldwin will be with you straight away."

After five minutes, Baldwin appeared with keys and a dealer plate. "Shall we take a spin, Mr. Farrow?"

Sliding into the driver's seat, Gabe felt a familiarity. Rubbing his hands over the leather covered steering wheel, he decided the car was his.

"Can we arrange for insurance? I *might* take it today."

"We can issue a temporary transfer permit, but you'll have to get a permanent plate within ten days from a government office."

"Is £1800 your best price?" They were barely out of the parking lot when Gabe began his negotiations. He gunned it onto the street and the pickup speed from the ramp to the thoroughfare was impressive.

"The car is in excellent shape," Baldwin said.

"But the miles on it are high for its age," Gabe challenged, too late to appear disinterested. £1500! That's the bottom."

"Deal, Mr. Baldwin."

6

MARY JANE AND TROY waited inside. She was in a floral, pastel sundress, and a straw summer hat with fresh wildflowers in the band. Troy wore shorts with suspenders, a pressed white shirt and argyle knee socks.

"Hello, Gabe. Doesn't Mums look nice?"

Gabe and M.J. laughed at his spirit.

"She does indeed. How's the new bike?"

"Super great."

"You must let us pay you something for your work and the parts," she said. "Horace says you're a magician in the workshop."

"No further discussion about that. But I might borrow Troy again for more adventuring with me. I'm teaching him about being a Boy Scout." Gabe winked at the freckle-faced boy.

"We'll talk about that later in the week." M.J. looked directly at Troy, but Gabe knew her stern point was also for him. "You still have a few more weeks before school is out and I don't want your studies to falter."

Gabe's face sobered and he leaned forward.

"M.J., do you know much about the history of Staithes and the area?"

Gabe waited as she took another bite to think.

"Well, I know the Lambton-Hetton-Staithes tunnels ran under Beach Street until it was shut down in the late 1800s. It was a couple hundred feet of line, I'd say, and was connected to the Deptford Junction."

Gabe was impressed already, and she put her fork down with another thought.

"The old railway station became a private residence, and when under construction, they found tunnels beneath it. Also, the family at Boulby Grange estate have stories of old smuggling routes in the mines. Then there are centuries of tales from the days of the Norsemen. I don't pay no mind to them, but I hear things."

Troy wiggled to the seat's edge. "Can I go with Gabe and look for tunnels?"

M.J. found both pair of eyes staring and waiting.

"The two of you are in cahoots—I can see that."

Gabe said, "I'll get some metal detectors and a GPS transmitter. You'll *always* know exactly where we are."

"But it's not safe," she said.

"And you can call my cell anytime. If at any time I feel Troy's safety is in jeopardy, we'll come straight back."

"Troy, you know your Da would say no," M.J. cautioned.

Mary Jane stared into Gabe's eyes. "Mr. Farrow, what is it that you're really looking for? Are you one of those crazed treasure seekers?"

"I agree I owe you the truth, but this can't venture through the grapevine of Staithes. Sometimes secrets must remain protected for the safety of others. You understand?"

"Alright, I vow it won't become gossip through these lips. I promise."

He scanned the tables. Nobody was in earshot, but he whispered regardless.

"The fellow Bradley that gave me his flat is mixed up in something shady. Whatever it was, Hennie and his men believe I know more than I do . . ."

He wanted to say more, but he had taken an oath with Sean Davis in London.

"Don't say more," M.J. said, and covered her eyes for a second. "Once, I overheard Hennie and Axle at the pub, talking of Boulby Cliff and Runswick Bay. It's known that pirates stole from the rich and gave to the poor, like the tales of Robin Hood. Gossip spreads in town from time to time of pirate treasures found in the passageways and tunnels. Who knows for sure if they're even true?"

"Wow! Awesome Mums! I'll like be joining Robin Hood's band of Merry Men in real life when I go with Gabe. Maybe I could be Friar Tuck." Troy's pupils darted back and forth in imagination of the days of yore.

Gabe said, "Every child deserves to have a fantasy and imagination. I know Troy's a man I can trust. He's wiser than he gets credit for."

"We'll try it as an experiment. GPS and phone *must* be turned on though." M.J. again covered her eyes and forehead.

"Awesome!" Troy wriggled.

Gabe whistled back to the Blue Cove, and M.J. heard it from the next block until it faded. She smiled about Gabe's determination, and watched Troy's face as he kicked stones and skipped.

Jotting measurements into a private log on his cell, Gabe calculated a scheme of his own—one that even Davis didn't know. With a quick shower, he jaunted to the Cleveland Kitchen, welcoming the relaxed atmosphere as weekend tourists were already heading back to Harrogate, Manchester or London. By nine, there were no stragglers, and Arbuckle locked the front door.

Sitting at a circular table in the dining room, the tip jar was opened. Each of the staff took a pile to count, then Theo divvied the pot between two cooks, two servers, two kitchen helpers and two bussers. The English were known to be generous when on holiday and Gabe was more than happy with a nice hundred quid.

"That should keep old Maude happy," Theo laughed.

"I keep her sweet on Thursdays."

With the last coffee cup wiped, the staff rambled to the door in a group. From the steps, Gabe saw Troy coming from half a block away, bounding and bobbing in the direction of the beach fireworks.

In a flash, his visual perception made him glance across the street to the eyes of an unfamiliar man. On being seen, the bloke shifted his face—at first feigning confusion, but then his eyes burrowed downward to hide the deception.

Guilty of something, that's for sure.

Gabe examined the man's wiry physique, and his straggly brown and ginger beard. His rugby cap promoted a team from Harrogate. As a flock of tourists passed toward the beach, he vanished.

Maybe my imagination.

"Hey, Gabe! Ain't you coming to the beach?" Troy called.

"First, young man, you mean '*aren't we*'. Ain't is not a word men use . . . also, where's your Mum?"

"She's got a headache but said I'd be safe with you."

A warm feeling overcame Gabe. He wasn't accustomed to anyone needing him on a personal level. Life had been all business.

Troy knelt on the picnic blanket on the knoll, his face tilted high toward the rockets and flares launched to the sky. He covered his ears before noticing that others were braving the noise.

"There's something I should tell you, Gabe. I never told my Mum, but those men you talked about . . . I've studied in mythology and I'm certain they're wizards."

"Why do you say that?"

"I watched them take the Dragon's head from the seashore. I learned at school about the Viking longboats that came from Norway into the North Sea. The sea is a monster and rises up in a fury. In the olden days, probably before your time, the Roxby Beck was wider and deeper and flowed inland some distance.

"I used my Granddad's old binoculars. I keep them in my room as Mums says he left them for me when he died.

"From my spot, I saw them ride beside the ancient river bed along Creek Lane. They stopped every few feet to use poles with beepers on the end. Then they pulled it from the water—a piece of driftwood, but not like anything I'd seen."

Troy stood and stretched both arms.

"At that moment, the sky turned dark and rumbled with thunder. The wind was strong and I know I heard the Vikings roar. I knew then that the men were wizards. This sounds made up, but I heard words. I can't forget as I've repeated them over and over. 'En taks noa gawm, ban'. The words were in a roar over the river."

"Later they spread a rumor it was the Dragon's head of a king named Harold and claimed to have found it at Runswick. But I saw it different—I know what happened.

"This is important, Troy. Have you told anyone else?"

"Nah. But if I told my teacher, she might give me a pass in Geography."

Gabe was rattled that Troy had experienced this horror, but hid any sign of alarm.

"I'll guard your secret. In the past, I studied legends of the infighting of Kings from Norway and England. What you heard is indeed an Old Norse dialect . . . so I believe you, but can't explain it. Maybe someone was playing cruel tricks.

"I have a secret to tell you too, Troy. You've no doubt heard in your History studies at school about The British Museum of Antiquities in London."

"Yes, they collect the old artifacts people find."

"Much more than that. They protect national treasures and the rights of property owners. I work for them and came here on assignment. Nobody here knows my true purpose for being so interested in Viking treasure. Give me your word this stays just between us."

"Like a pledge of honor. Do we need to spit on it?"

"No, I see that you're a man of your word." A handshake sealed the new incorporation.

From the street, Gabe saw the lights on in 3C. Sneaking up the stairs, he turned the key slowly. The room was black and he knelt to listen to the transmitter.

"Dodds is getting paranoid. He's preoccupied with his new celebrity and power since he joined the Treasury Board. He obsesses about the security at the farmhouse in spite of the new high tech cams."

"I don't care how he views himself as long as he keeps taking care of the gold," Hennie said.

"What about the neighbor?" Axle asked.

"Farrow? He's a red herring, I saw him at Arbuckle's last night," Fergus added.

"Tomorrow, we'll do more digging at the mine. Axle, it's your turn. Fergus, you ride shotgun to Runswick and I'll meet you at the access point."

Gabe tiptoed down the staircase and planted a GPS bug in the lining of Hennie's boots at the front door and another in Axle's shoes. He started up the Vauxhall and idled gently so they wouldn't hear it, then drove to the abandoned petrol station and returned soon after for the night.

The next morning, Gabe rode his bike to Cobbs.

"Good morning, Niles!"

"Mornin'. I saw you at the Cleveland Saturday night. Are you moonlighting?" Niles teased.

"Ah, 'twas a busy weekend." Gabe didn't offer a further explanation, leaving Niles wanting more.

"Theo gave the okay for you to make up an order for the Cleveland on consignment. We can set our own price. Use your creative talents and make something unique for them using brighter colors."

"Glad to—would the smaller German glass be best?"

Niles didn't reply.

"You don't mind me helping out weekends for Theo, do you? Maude raised my rent and I was strapped. No other place I can go now in tourist season."

"No, no, I was teasing. You're a young fellow with lots of energy; glad you found something that suits you."

"On Sunday, I went to Harrogate and bought myself a used Vauxhall. I find the North Yorkshire Moors and the villages fascinating, and I'll be able to get around and explore. Besides making the éclair run easier."

"I've had a few Vauxhall's in my time. Did you bring it today?"

"No, I came by bike."

"Next time at the Saltburn Bakery, ask Priscilla to make one for me. She uses real Devonshire cream. My mouth's watering to think about it."

"Perhaps I should place a regular order and set up a route," Gabe joked.

Niles' voice sobered. "I walked my dogs on the weekend at Boulby Grange. I saw that pair go into a mine entrance, and my curiosity got me too close. I'm sure they didn't see me or hear the dogs."

"Careful, Niles. Let's keep that between you and me for now." Gabe stared intently without being offensive. "Those fellows are up to no good. I hear things from my room, so don't say anything to put me in jeopardy. Gossip moves fast in town."

"Sure, Gabe. I don't want to cause trouble."

"My instincts say they found some old hoard or Viking ruins. They are pilfering outside the law and I'm convinced they're dangerous."

Niles' cheek was twitching and Gabe saw his hands shake. "What is it, Niles? Should I know something?"

"I don't know about the mine, but there were rumors last year about some artifact found in Roxby."

"It was you, Niles, wasn't it? It was you that found the artifact . . ."

"I don't want trouble with the Treasury Department. I was just using a metal detector. Everyone in Staithes, at one time or another, goes afield with one."

"What did you find?"

Niles opened a hutch with drawers where he stored nuts and bolts. He removed a drawer at desk height and reached deep to a concealed compartment.

Unfolding a cloth, he revealed a tarnished red ruby with gold backing. "My guess is that it's about a thousand years old."

The awe of its medieval survival hung over both of them.

"Your secret is safe with me, Niles. Return it to the hiding place. We'll get this sorted out, but for now, I've got souvenir buoys to make."

"I feel a fire in the ruby when I hold it . . . a strange presence. I'm sure it came from the eye of the Dragon head. It's like it has a spirit of its own."

The ruby was returned to the sanctuary of the hutch, and the men's thoughts became absorbed and drowned by the sounds of the oven firing and the pumping of billows.

At the end of the day, the buoys were crated, and Niles suggested Gabe take the truck to High Street.

"Will do, Niles. Sometime, would you show me where you found the stone?"

"I'll draw you another map. I paced it out so I'd find the exact location again. But I don't want to go back, it felt haunted."

Niles returned from the hardware drawers with a scratchy map, and distances marked out in feet. The size of Niles' feet, specifically. Gabe dropped his pen and bent to assess Cobb's shoes.

At the turnoff from Mill Road to lower town Staithes, a blaring sound approached, then red flashing lights in the direction of Boulby Cliff.

"Niles won't mind a delivery detour."

Parking clear of converging emergency vehicles, he moved in on foot.

It's the alum mine.

A fireman staggered out to the grass near the yellow barricade. "What's happened?" Gabe asked.

"Some idiot was treasure hunting. There was a mudslide, but what got him was the methane gas. He didn't have the common sense to wear a mask."

"Did everyone get out?"

"Can't say for sure. Right now, a crew's down there on their bellies trying to dig a man out."

"Is he alive?"

"Don't know. Look fellow, I got to go and take my place in the drag." The fireman pulled an oxygen mask up over his face.

"Thanks, buddy. Good luck."

Awe struck, Gabe recalled Hennie's words overheard last night. "Axle it's your turn."

Poor Axle.

A backhoe arrived and the silo was gingerly opened up to expose a gaping hole. A muddy stretcher hoisting a black rubber body bag was brought to the surface.

Wasn't worth a life.

Behind him, he heard the roar of the ATV. He turned as Hennie got off, his face angry that Axle had caused such attention. Then his face whitened at the sight of the reality.

There was time only for an instant moral decision, and Gabe took it, approaching Hennie.

"Sorry about Axle. It seems either a mudslide or methane gas got him. My condolences, Hennie." It was the first time the two men made eye contact.

Before Hennie's guard shot up, Gabe wondered if he saw a glimmer of humanity.

"Was his own fault then," Hennie snapped back.

"Can I ask what he was doing down in the mine?"

"No, and mind your own business."

Hennie stomped away, with no interest in identification.

Even the unwrapped delivery crates clustered with hemp rope captivated the Arbuckles, who stood at the door as Gabe carried them in. The crates were stuffed to the top with curls of wood shavings to protect the glass, each wrapped in vinyl crepe. Gabe laid the manifest on the counter, detailing each buoy by number and its brilliant color.

Holding the first to the light, Theo admired the gold etching of 'Cleveland Corner Café' on the bottom. "How be, I clean off the post card shelf and set up a display by the door? Folks can't miss them waiting for a table—they'll sell themselves."

Gabe went about staging the shelves, as staff dug in to hand up their favorites. He grinned, hearing some oohs as the reds, yellows and blues came out, and stopped to watch their faces as they got to the bold purples, oranges, and greens.

"Very nautical," Theo said.

"Glad it suits."

With the crates stashed in the delivery bay, Gabe walked uphill to his flat, hoping he might cross paths with Hennie.

He'll take the loss of Axle like a left punch and go on without as much as a goodbye.

Maude was on the porch, and he heard her soft sobbing as he mounted the steps. News had filtered in to the Blue Cove and across town moments after the accident.

Gabe gathered her hands into his and leaned to look into her pooling eyes. "C'mon Maude, I'm taking my best girl for some ice cream." She dabbed her handkerchief, covering the red streaks.

"Looks like we're both softies."

Maude stood in a flash, first rolling her pressure stockings up to her calf, then tucking a wisp of grey into a braid twisted under her hairnet. She slipped her arm into Gabe's waiting elbow.

"How about the Ice Cream & Donut shop? It's a wee walk."

She said, "I don't understand how Hennie doesn't show an ounce of compassion. They've shared that room for close to two years. Axle wasn't kind or nice to me but he was a human being—I presume he has a family somewhere."

"Two years! A long time. I guess you got to know them well."

"No. Just comings and goings. I had a few run-ins with them about the noise and bringing their mud into the house."

Gabe glanced at the place by the front door for shoes. Hennie's and Axle's boots were gone.

"Did anyone come to visit?" He hesitated, then braved another one. "Someone perhaps from Harrogate?"

"Not for Hennie or Axle, but for Bradley. A snobbish man in a suit—said he was from Hunslet Carr. They argued and it got boisterous, then Bradley told him to get out. I heard him sayin' he didn't need him anymore, he could do it on his own."

"Did you ever hear talk of the alum mine or tunnels?"

"Everyone knows about the tunnels under Runswick and hobs holes along the shore. Some under Robin's Hood Bay too—you have to practically stand in line to see them. I'd say there's more myth than legend with the moors. You'll get drawn into it soon enough too," Maude said.

The ice cream was only a block and a half from Blue Cove. Gabe opened the door for Maude and she blushed.

"Aren't you the gentleman? My Bill used to be good with his manners when we were first married, then he stopped being nice."

"I'm sorry for your loss, Maude."

"Oh no, needn't be. I'm glad he's gone. He ain't dead, Gabe, just don't come home anymore. Since you're interested in the old tunnels, I'll let you have a gander at Bill's boxes in the basement. He liked local history too. Last I heard someone saw him drunk in Leeds with a hag half his age."

"I'll hold you to lettin' me poke through the boxes."

Maude polished the cherry custard sundae and strawberry sauce and Gabe escorted her back to the Blue Cove, his mind set on digging in the boxes.

If Gabe had looked up at the Blue Cove on approach he would have seen the man in the rugby cap watching with binoculars. Within seconds of Gabe's arrival, he was gone.

It took him three trips to haul the dusty boxes to the third floor.

Rifling in the first, Gabe pulled out maps of the Grinkle Mine tunnels from Runswick Bay to Port Mulgrave. The Grinkle, an ironstone mine from 1875, had deteriorated into a maze of relics, then the Ridge Lane tramway ran the tunnel circuit until the Easington Beck culvert collapsed, cutting off access to Mulgrave in the early 1900s. With subsequent slides and groaning, the county barricaded entrances to prevent snoopers causing more cave-ins, but the most determined folks always found their own way in.

Documents showed a visual trace of a series of hob holes at the edge of Runswick Bay, and Gabe noted the aerial map's long indention near Lingrow Beck.

One of Davis's reports identified a magnetic field in the same area.

He unfolded another map, with indentions between Roxby Beck and Cleveland Way running across a field to the top bank, showing similar readings.

Tomorrow after work, I'll go. Three to investigate—Runswick, Port Mulgrave and the residual of Roxby Beck. And I still haven't followed up on the dark markings at Staithes.

In a long gaze at the bay from his window, he couldn't make out the detail in the darkness. The half-moon twinkled on the waves with enough light to accent the boat silhouette, the one he'd seen the first night at Seaton Garth.

Hennie and Fergus expected to be incognito. Returning from Runswick Bay, they pulled into a shallow cove on the other side of the Garth. By the time Gabe returned from the kitchen with binoculars, all signs of their boat had gone.

Fifteen minutes later, 3C's door closed with a slam.

Gabe gave a last look at the books on the table. In a double-take, he saw the image of a glow and eyes in the train tunnel. He held it up closely to study it.

Déjà vu.

7

WEDNESDAY, FROM THE MILL, Gabe pedaled full tilt to the Endeavour. His small friend waited outside in britches and rubber boots, and M.J. cleaned tables inside with an eye on the window. She relaxed her shoulders in relief that he had arrived.

Gabe put the bike on the kickstand. "Ahoy there, matey."

"Sorry about the man in the tunnel," Troy said with more maturity than his years. "Was he a friend of yours?"

"Mighty fine of you to say so, but no. He wasn't a friend of mine, but you might remember him from Mrs. Capp's house. I can count my best friends in Staithes on one hand and you're the first one on my list."

Gabe tousled the boy's hair. "Glad to see you're wearing your gun boots. Get your metal detector and we're ready to go."

M.J. signaled Gabe with a hand at her ear to remind him of his promise to phone. He nodded with thumbs up, and she watched their bikes as far as Creek Lane and over the toe bridge.

At the end of the creek bog, they covered the bikes under some branches, to walk with the metal detectors. The path had become a mixture of leftover gravel and shrubs, and the weeds and ground cover would leave no signs they'd been there, and provided no trace of predecessors.

"Troy, do you know exactly where we're going?"

His lips were already moving silently. "Oh yes. I'm counting my steps. Red scout boulder to my right, step of grey flatstone, and walk to the gumtree root . . ." Troy's chant reached a rhythmic hop scotch patter, until he halted it with a raised hand.

"See! Under the roots, there's the cave entrance. I've been inside once, but it felt weird . . . like I was in someone's place."

"Was it like the wizards?"

Troy pondered. "Yes, that's what it was like."

"Maybe it's an old pirate's lair."

Standing on a tree root, Gabe surveyed a plateau of purple heather to the right and deep vales just beyond. Troy jumped to a rock for height and pointed to a rocky mound several yards ahead.

"There!" Their metal detectors began screaming.

"This is a lot more than a ping, Troy."

Past more tree roots, the ground underneath felt soft like sponge. Gabe reached for some hanging boughs for balance, exposing some rusted bars from an ancient aqueduct. He inched forward, then yanked on the iron grill with his work gloves.

"Stay safely behind, Troy, till we know the ground is solid enough for us."

The grill was connected to more iron bars, and Gabe followed each section to the joints.

"It's a gate of sorts," he said. With his next yank, the rusted hinges fell away, clanking to the ground.

"Yikes!" Troy exclaimed.

"Well, it doesn't look like anyone has been this way in a long time. I'd guess that the grate was put here in the 40's or 50s."

Gabe edged himself into the gap behind the corroded shackles, sliding his shoes for a safe footing.

Beep, Beep!

Troy answered, seeing M.J, on call display. He listened, and covered it with his hand.

"It's Mums. She wants to know where we are." Troy and Gabe exchanged nods, knowing not to alarm her. The two remained frozen during the call to prevent noise or any unexpected surprise.

"Hi Mums . . . I'm in the lea still looking for metal. Yes, safe and sound." Privately, Troy was glad she worried, but was too proud for her to know.

Caution helped Gabe slide his left foot. He eased it down. "Troy, watch my feet and step exactly where I've stepped."

Gabe knotted a camping twine to a tree that angled over the mound. With a cable securing his belt, he stepped between the menageries of the ancient roots to cut away the shrubs to make a path.

"It's damp in here," Troy shivered. "A kid from school believes in these hobs and goblins. He was with his Dad when they ventured into a cave—just a big hole, not a railway tunnel."

"What did he say, Troy?"

"He could have exaggerated, but said he heard voices in there, then some giggling. Shadows on the wall. I don't pay much mind to those stories, but he was convinced they were hobs from the dale."

"I've heard the winds myself, and they groan as if they're warnings," Gabe said. "It's not farfetched that folks could believe the fantasies the winds create. And books and movies stoke the imagination, like the fabled Bramblewick books or the Potter movies."

Troy said, "When I was small, I heard talk about an exorcism near Paddy's Bridge, about horrid goblins that quickly vanished."

"My metal detector is going wild!" Gabe interrupted.

"Mine too!"

Stumbling over driftwood, they moved along the whetstone wall and switched their military-issue headlights to high beam.

"Here. Along the floor," Gabe said.

On his knees, he dug at the dirt, shaking each handful like a sieve to filter even the tiniest remnant they might find. First, they came across a broken piece of a broach, then shards of driftwood.

"Troy, we're on the brink of finding a treasure, I feel it in my bones."

"Will I be able to buy Mums a new dress?"

"Any gold we find has to go back to the British Museum. However, I told your Mum I'd pay you for your guide services. If you save that, we can go to Whitby and do some shopping."

Gabe found fault in these words, knowing that the Treasury department had loop holes and gold-diggers were out for personal fortune.

Ten feet further into the tunnel, the cable tightened. As Gabe reached for a piece of metal protruding from the wall, pieces of decrepit wood and shards of metal rust crumbled in his hands.

This has to be a plant by someone . . . it's much too convenient.

"Gabe, I hear a vehicle."

"Cover yourself with bush and stay still . . . Troy . . ." he whispered.

He waited for a reply.

"Troy!" he said louder, and turned abruptly. The cable was slack.

"Farrow, I suggest you come out here."

"Coming out, leave the boy alone."

Gabe retreated over unsteady rock and out into the blinding sunlight. The silhouette of the man had Troy by the arm and his hand over his mouth.

"What the . . . what the heck! You're scaring the boy, he's done nothing to you. Let him go!"

Gabe was in no mood for negotiation. Bradley shoved Troy into a bank of soft shrubs.

"Troy—go and wait in the car!" Gabe tossed his keys and they dropped to the ground. He repeated it. "Get in the car!"

His pupils had adjusted to the light, and the first clue of the man was the serpent tattoo, then the ginger brown.

"Bradley!"

"Bet you didn't expect to see me again. What are the pair of you doing up here?"

"I was going to ask you the same thing, Turner."

"Relax. Let's sit down and have a chat." Bradley sat on the angled bank.

"How long have you been following me?" Gabe said.

"You're not the only one with trackers. I saw you park the Vauxhall at the petrol station and I took the opportunity. It's under your back bumper." Turner smirked, reveling at his stealth.

"It's time you come clean, Bradley. I checked into your family business and see you're on the outs with your Dad. And

I know of Dodds' appointment to the Treasury Board. Together, these set a stage ripe for clandestine activity."

"Indeed. Or so appearances would indicate."

"Care to explain?"

"My father became suspicious after a hoard was discovered near Harrogate two years ago. His partner, Ian Dodds, fared much better. It took my Dad off guard as they had a long, trusting relationship. We needed inside data to expose Ian.

"In a public audience, my father set the pretense that he'd cut me off from my leisurely life. Dodds bought it all. I love my father and would do anything for him. We have a discreet regular contact while I penetrate Dodds' pilfering scheme."

Bradley never looked Gabe in the eye, raising Gabe's suspicion.

"I followed Dodds one day to a meeting in Harrogate. It was with Hennie—his gang is always looking for a quick buck regardless of who gets hurt in the fray. Now I hear about poor Axle, that his pals didn't even put in for a funeral. The village welfare system is paying to have him buried."

As Gabe listened, his thoughts compared the story with the accounts in Davis's dossier.

"Go on, Bradley. It interests me, but I haven't decided if I can believe you."

"I followed Hennie and his partners to a tavern where I threw back of couple of ales. To get close, I feigned a drunken episode and moseyed into their conversation, convincing them I was furious with my father for cutting me off. They seemed to know that already, no doubt from Dodds. So they fell for my act.

"I let them convince me of their fool-proof plan to get back at my father, Jarvis Turner. If I wanted to make a few bucks, they'd cut me in, and I agreed to collude with them. Hennie runs the hoard hunting while Dodds controls a get-rich gold scam."

"Stop for a minute—then why did you part company and leave Staithes?" Gabe asked.

"On the bus, my instincts said you were a smart bloke, so I picked you. Better still, being in my old room would get your curiosity going. You can see I'm good with disguises; I've more or less bumped into you a few times. You can almost see my new digs from here. On Cleveland Way, climb the steps to the top. From there you look down on Robin Hood's Bay, an easy jog to Staithes. My room's near King's Beck—the hostel with the red tiled roof."

Gabe needed more. "Either you or Hennie has uncovered a Viking treasure, I presume."

"The alum mine was a decoy. I'll admit it was me that first found the Dragon head driftwood near Roxby Beck, then I planted various pieces around in bogus locations. The gem that Cobbs has is fake, as is the one you have there in your pocket. The real find is in Runswick, where there's a land depression near Lingrow Beck.

"Now it's time for you to come clean with me. What are you doing here? I see you and the boy are prepared for pirate searching with your metal detectors and equipment."

"It seems our missions are coincidental," Gabe said. "How do I know I can trust you? Are you on the side of the law or the criminals?" Gabe was leery about this new information directing their search in Runswick.

"Absurd! I just explained what I'm doing here."

"If I tell you what I am doing, how do I know I can trust you? You could be a ruse sent by Hennie and his Harrogate collaborators as a smokescreen. And what gave you an impression I have anything to do with a search for the Runswick hoard?" Gabe asked.

"No one knows for certain if there even is a treasure," Bradley said. "The entire coastal area beyond the moors is seething with troves, as for centuries pieces of Viking ships were washed to the surface from watery graves. If you know the history, many seaside villages collapsed into the North Sea from erosion, and since that time breakwaters and sea walls were built to reinforce the land."

"You seem knowledgeable enough," Gabe said.

"What can I say to convince you that I'm on the side of Justice? Hennie and his gang are not the first unethical searchers for buried gold. They are, however, the ones connected to Dodds. My blood is my loyalty. Do you wish to call my father to verify what I have said?"

"What's his direct number?

Bradley handed his phone. "Here."

Gabe phoned a different number.

"Hello Davis, I need you to check out a story surfacing in Harrogate. Can you call Jarvis Turner at this number and get confirmation that his son, Bradley, is working undercover to expose Dodds in theft of antiquities in the moors. I'll hold. It's important, I have his son right here. May I have permission to reveal myself in return for his cooperation?"

"Sure, Farrow." The line went silent as Bradley and Gabe remained on tenterhooks.

It was a long five minutes before Davis returned.

"Farrow, you've got a go. The story checks out and you have clearance to show your identification. We will back you up."

"Thank you, Sir. I'll be in touch shortly."

Gabe pulled out his wallet and his photo ID badge as an investigative agent of the British Museum Department of Medieval Antiquities.

"I'm curious about what put you onto me, but I've been given authority to work with you with the understanding that the British Treasury Act supersedes the destiny for any find."

Bradley appeared stunned.

"Medieval Antiquities?"

"Do you have a problem with me now?"

"No, Sir; you take the lead. But take my advice, it's too dangerous for the kid. Next time *I'll* go as lookout. Agreed?"

"Agreed. Now I do have to talk to Troy. He's a tough kid and I won't rule out him as he is smart as a whip and knows the lay of the land better than any of us."

"He's M.J.'s boy, isn't he?"

"Yes, and you might apologize for scaring the wits out of him."

At the Vauxhall, Gabe was alarmed. Troy wasn't in the car. Frantic, he turned to Bradley. "He's gone!"

"Gabe, I'm up here." Troy warily emerged from a grassy hill, his eyes showing fear and rejection. "I heard everything. I want assurances that I'm still the point man."

"Troy, accept my apologies for yanking you the way I did. As it turns out, now we are a gang of three sworn to secrecy. Are you in?" Bradley put his hand out.

"My Mum always told me that when you trust someone, you should expect they give you trust in return. Is that right?"

"We have a pact!" Gabe said.

Reaching under the bumper, Gabe pulled out Bradley's tracker. "Here, use this for something better."

"Let's take the car to Runswick for a bite, then I'll show you where I think we should dig. Stop at the fish and chip cart at the beach. It's the best cod and fries you'll ever eat. Of course, if that's okay with you, Farrow," Turner said. Troy jumped in the back.

Before reaching the beach, Gabe said, "You know that Hennie is focused on the Grinkle? He's carrying one of my GPS trackers that says he's on the move now in the old tunnels."

"Yes, they go regularly to the bay with a skiff. I've seen the boat sitting on rocks. They shuttle any find from bay to bay, then Axle takes the train to Harrogate. Dodds smelts the precious metals without log notations, and they feed them to the black market, higher than fair trade value. They nary say anything to my Dad about it."

"Is this justice, Bradley, or revenge?"

"I gave you my word—it is family honor for me. My father's reputation is of first importance, to separate him from Dodds' dishonesty."

Gabe missed a cell call and clicked for voice mail. It was from M.J. about when Troy might be home. Gabe texted right away.

'We're having a great time and I'll return him before 7 if ok. Going now to Runswick for a bite of supper, assuming you have an evening shift at the tavern.'

"Troy, you'll have to come up with some truths about scouting from today. Remember the difference between a lie and withholding information. If you get backed into a corner, omit details on this one."

"Perhaps you should teach me something."

"What do you think, Bradley? Maybe fishermen knots, identifying poison ivy and fossils, building a pyramid campfire?" Gabe asked.

"After lunch, we'll check out the lobster catch on the beach and learn some cable knotting. Then we'll go to the Grinkle," Bradley said.

"Deal, now how about the fish and chips you offered," Troy bantered licking his lips.

Three orders were wrapped in newspapers, with tartar sides and cokes. At an umbrella table on the sand, they dug in, allowing Gabe to ramble this time without interruption.

"The mine is dangerous," Gabe started. "It's from cave-ins and flooding."

Troy spoke up with food tucked in his cheek. "In one unstable area, you can hear the roar of falling rock. People say they've heard a crashing noise preceded by a wailing call, with visions of a Boggart-like creature and a deciphered Viking dialect uttering the words, 'Nay Mell On En Higg'. I memorized that too."

Gabe said, "I've studied that. Supposedly a warning not to meddle or more rocks will be thrown."

"Sounds like the wizard I met near Roxby Beck," Troy said. "Legends say King Har, beheaded a thousand years ago, has come back for his brother."

"It's more than a myth, Troy. There was a real Hardrada—a Viking," Gabe said. "Books say he and his brother Tostig fought over England's throne. Tostig shot him in the eye with a poisoned golden arrow. The body was found, but his head isn't buried with it. Legend says his men buried the skull near one of the Becks, along with the golden arrow."

Troy's eyes were transfixed. He'd heard the tales before, but at this moment he knew they were more real than ever.

Gabe went on. "For centuries, Scandinavian countries fought with Britain and Normandy over birthrights to the England's throne. In the thousand years, most of Europe challenged the English throne, cousin against cousin, brother and brother, and even father and son. Legend says Tostig hand crafted the gold arrow, building feathers of fish bones and bird quills. A gold monger's value is a hefty fortune."

"Nay, nay!" Troy laughed in his best Viking imitation.

"These days are long with sunshine," Bradley said. "We can still get in a few hours at the mine."

"Let's get going then. We have supplies in the trunk. Helmets too."

They hid the Vauxhall under a trio of giant oaks, and sorted armfuls of supplies—breathing masks, harnesses and rope cables, whistles, a canteen, and camouflaged helmets with flashlights—all from Odds & Sods.

Bradley snatched the lead, suiting Gabe, and the three stepped in single file around a pot of soft soil. They stopped to assess a visible land depression extending a hundred feet, then continued warily.

"Hold right there," Bradley gestured. "Remnants of an old stone wall . . . actually a tunnel entrance that few know about. Gabe, can you find Hennie's location?"

"Troy, stay here in the brush outside and control the tension and length of the cable. Two tugs means we've been spotted. Three means to relax the rope and give more latitude. If we don't reply with a single tug, blow your whistle and tug again."

"What if you don't come out?"

"Here's my cell. Call your mother and ask her to send Mr. Cobb or Jimmy at the Lifeboat Station, but only if you absolutely need to. He'll know what to do."

"Okeydokey." Troy's freckled face tightened with his responsibility.

"Good man! Now Bradley, let's get going. Hennie's a good distance away."

"I was with them one day when they stumbled across a few pieces of pottery and a pair of gold coins—my guess from the eleventh century."

"What happened to the coins and pottery?"

"The coins went to Dodds and the pottery to the alum mine stash."

Past the thick huckleberry bushes, Gabe and Bradley entered the decrepit mine.

"Did you examine the coins? Did they have Har's symbol of a triquetra?"

"I don't know what that is." Bradley's voice echoed and he hushed in mid-sentence.

"It's not important right now. Did you notice signs of methane in here?"

"No, not until I got in pretty deep. Then I smelled rotten cabbage. The gas is light in weight and rises to the surface of the ceiling, so you're safer crouching close to the ground."

At twenty feet in, Bradley veered off to an earthen tunnel that had not been part of a railway route since before the 18th century. The ceiling and walls were propped with ancient boards, likely reinforced a century ago.

"This is where I found the driftwood," Bradley said. "This is a medieval Norseman's cave. Keep your eyes on the metal detector or signs of previous tourists."

Gabe picked up a low reading on his meter, and slowed his pace as it strengthened.

"Over here, Bradley! Along this wall. Look—these stones are put together. Possibly an ancient vault."

"My meter activity is fierce," Turner replied. "We're onto something."

Gabe hacked at the bricks with his hatchet until the first wiggled loose. "Yes! I can squeeze my arm through and there's open space behind. Can we open the wall in less than an hour?"

"I'm wiry and lithe. If we take out a few more I can squeeze through," Bradley said.

Twenty minutes later, Bradley entered the cavern.

8

TROY WAS BACK at the Endeavour by seven. M.J. looked cool and collected, but relieved.

Within minutes, she confessed her worry to Gabe. "I'm not used to my son being out with strangers for so long. You must understand."

Troy waited for her long hug and glanced at the other men.

Gabe ventured some honesty to satisfy M.J. "We did peek into the old tunnels. Troy was a master as a lookout and cable controller. Couldn't have done it without him."

Troy jumped in. ". . . And we helped a lobster fisherman in Runswick to cable his catch ropes. Do you want me to show you?"

M.J. spied an arm-waving customer. "Maybe another time, sweetie. I have to attend to this now."

She pirouetted. "Wait here, Gabe."

In minutes she sprinted back to the front. "I'm not off until nine. Gabe, would you mind taking him to the loft? I can tell he enjoys spending time with you."

"I'm the lucky one. He's a great kid. Can he help again after school on Friday?"

Her answer was quick this time. "Yes, that's fine. I'll be working the evening shift."

With Troy delivered, Gabe drove up Staithes Lane to Dalehouse Bank. He'd heard of the Fox & Hound, perched on a hidden dale beside a row of antiquated stone cottages. At the door, he looked to the back to see only strangers, then spotted a dimly lit table near the fireplace, a place to relax with a pint and sort his thoughts. He was sure no one here would recognize him.

"Hello, my name is Vera, can I take your order?"

"I've heard in Staithes that you feature Adnams Southwold Bitter. Is that good?"

"The best, and right now it's the only beer on tap. Folks drive from villages all around to try it, then become regular customers.

"Well then, bring me a pint."

His fingers combed through his hair, then he rubbed his temples to ease the tension.

I'll stay on guard about Bradley. Finding clues to a hoard in minutes was too easy. He's gullible if he thinks he has me by his little finger.

"Here's your ale, Sir. It's after the dinner crowd and we still have our Saltburn special. Would you like to try it for a good deal?"

"Sure—and what's the special?"

"Homemade steak and kidney. You'll want chips and slaw with it."

Bradley assumes I'm green about the geology here, but with Davis's training, there's little I don't know about it. I get it that the terrain is full of windypots, hobs holes and ancient fossils ideal setting for buried treasure.

Delving into the pie, Gabe forgot about his issues. Downing his bitter, he took a sigh of satisfaction in front of Vera, who was still watching for his reaction.

"Thanks, Vera. Yes, that hit the spot. This is the perfect place for a tourist vacation?"

He left cash on the table, and at the door, he thanked her again.

"I'll definitely be back."

Mrs. Capp's boarding house was suffocating. Hennie, on the other wall, was convenient for spying, but the surveillance twenty-four seven was fraying Gabe's nerves.

How could Bradley subsist under the microscope? Who's the man Maude brought up that visited? And what's the farmhouse situation?

On the laptop, he opened Davis's dossier, and matched the area where Bradley had taken him. Noting his conclusions, he sent a secure report to Davis.

What kind of man plants Viking pieces around the neighborhood?

Hennie and his gang showed on Gabe's cell tracker to still be in the Grinkle mines.

"It's no longer moving. They must've found the tracer in the boot."

Gabe arrived in the morning at Cobb's mill half an hour before opening. Firing up the equipment, he checked the order file and began.

When Niles arrived, he was perplexed that Gabe had already punched out several orders.

"Couldn't sleep, Gabe?"

"Things on my mind, that's all. It's good to take out frustration by working with your hands."

"Do you need a friendly ear? I'll put on the coffee."

Niles slowly went about with the same routine Gabe had seen every morning since he arrived. He returned with two mugs of steaming coffee, and pulled up a milk stool beside Gabe's.

"What is it, son?"

"Sometimes I fool myself, thinking I'm getting a clearer viewpoint of things as a stranger. Then as I get involved in people's lives, it changes and becomes complicated."

"I don't know what you mean. I've never been a stranger."

"As you've gotten to know me, we've shared a few secrets. I know about your past and you think that you know mine. I'm trapped in a situation where I need to trust those around me, but I'm bound to the spy hideout for the summer."

"Has something happened?"

"Could I examine the Viking gem?"

"Sure."

He was back right away with the pouch.

"Gabe, did you know that off the galley kitchen back there, we have another door? It's a bedroom that hasn't been used in years. On rare occasions I've stayed overnight. It's always unlocked, so feel free to use it to get away from the boarding house. There are blankets in the closet."

Laying the gem pouch on the corner of Gabe's table, he took his seat.

"Have you ever had this examined or evaluated?"

"No, you're the only one that knows I've got it."

"Would you trust me to send it to London? I have a friend there that can find its history and value. He specializes in medieval antiquities . . . I recently heard that someone with access to the Staithes tunnels has planted fake paste gems."

Gabe removed the broken broach from his pocket to make comparisons.

"Is it Hennie?" Cobbs said.

"I'm sorry, I'm not at liberty to say."

Niles pursed his lips in dejection. "You don't trust me!"

Gabe wrestled with showing Niles his true credentials.

That would make three—Troy, Bradley and Niles.

"I trust you, Niles, but I don't want to put a burden on you to keep another secret. If you insist, you can be an accomplice in my extracurricular activities. Is that what you want?"

"For heaven's sake, Gabe, I'm getting on in years and if you can tell me something to add excitement to my life, you'd be doing me a favor."

Gabe reached for his wallet. Without a word, he displayed his British Museum seal of authority.

"By golly, this is big, Gabe. So you want to send the stone to these people in London?"

"Yes, it will go to the Department of Medieval Antiquities."

"Of course, of course."

Niles picked up the pouch and extended it to Gabe.

"I'll leave it with you until the end of the day, Niles."

"I'm happy to cooperate if it's with the government."

Just before 3 p.m., as Gabe prepared to leave at the end of his workday, his cell vibrated. The phone display said Bradley Turner, and Gabe didn't want to miss it.

"Hey, Bradley, what do you want?"

"Can we meet?"

"What's the reason?"

"I'm going to the Viking cavern at Runswick. What else do you think I want?"

"In a few minutes, I'm leaving work and I'll meet you there."

"Okay. On my way too now."

I don't know for sure where he lives or how he gets around. And he's always up to date about Hennie, when he's so invisible.

Gabe wouldn't get Troy's help until Friday, so he went directly to the mine alone, and parked the car in the same place, waiting for Bradley.

From a footpath near the mouth of the mine, Turner appeared. "Hello, Gabe!"

"Hello yourself. Where'd you come from? You've got to tell me how you stay under the radar?"

"Those are a lot of questions."

"Then there will be a lot of answers. Go ahead."

"I see distrust on your face, Gabe, and it disappoints me. What happened since yesterday?"

"You answer my questions first."

"Take it easy. I'm staying at the Runswick Hostel like I said. They don't ask questions there. I'm registered as 'John Mann'. I didn't turn in my front door key to Maude when I left. What I gave her were some old keys, but she won't notice for a long time. I wasn't able to put a bug on Hennie, but I put one in Dodds' phone in Harrogate. I get enough information to keep me ahead of Hennie."

"The GPS tracker is frozen in the ironstone mines, so obviously it was discovered," Gabe added. "It'll put Hennie on guard."

"Yes, Hennie called Dodds this morning and told him about the bug. They were both upset. So watch your back."

"When you gave me your room, what did you expect would happen?"

"The buzzing and phone ringing would make anyone curious. And I made enough noise when you pretended to look out the window, as I dug up the floor board. I was back one day and saw the newspapers folded differently."

"Yes, I remember. You left mud on the floor."

"I apologize for putting a tracer on your backpack. I couldn't hear anything but I generally knew where you were."

"Why me?"

"My instincts proved right, didn't they? Dodds said he overheard my father talking to me, apparently about Staithes. He's understandably paranoid as there's a lot on the line for him."

"I'm hearing a lot of double-talk, Bradley."

Bradley brushed off the insult. "I gave you my word."

"Alright, alright. For now, let's take a look at the cavern that you found so handily."

"No, Gabe, it was *you* that found the stones."

"Without Troy, we'll hook the harness to the cable and hope no one sees us."

Inside, Gabe removed the stones one by one, enough that both could wiggle through into the cave.

"It's eerie, like we're being watched," Bradley said.

"Its history. History has eyes and ears."

"Are you trying to scare me?"

"Stand still and listen." Gabe's neck shivered as the tunnel echoed a deep groan.

He deepened his voice and lowered his chin, surprising Bradley with a Viking dialect he'd learned.

"Beini vinatta en saemd," he boomed. "We come in friendship and honor, Sir Godwinson."

"What the heck is that about?" Bradley asked.

"Shhh.

A gust of wind swept through and the groan closed in.

Did you hear it?" Gabe whispered.

The whirring and rumbling persisted.

"Perhaps the noise is outside."

Uncertain what to do, Gabe continued, projecting his voice at full volume, echoing into the tunnel.

"Sir Hardrada Godwinson, rightful King of England! The golden arrow that pierced your eye can be used to shame Tostig. We have come to take you and the arrow to a better place of rest and honor."

Bradley shook his head. "You're losing it, Gabe. There's no one there! Who do you think you're talking to?"

"You know the story, Bradley, that Hardrada was murdered and thrown headless into his grave. His men retrieved the head and buried it in the moors."

Bradley cracked up. "That's a fantastic tale, Gabe."

Suddenly, the ground heaved, and a slab of stone dislodged ten feet ahead of them, producing clouds of dust. When it settled, they stepped toward a new, gaping hole in the side of the tunnel. Gabe peered in, knowing the somber reverence of a presence inside.

"Stay right here, Bradley. I'm going in first this time."

It was dark, but he found his way to the center of the room to a crude wooden table. He leaned close to examine an ornate carved box on top, with the symbol of a Dragon's Head and fiery rubies and emeralds inserted in the eyes. He reached to feel it, but had second thoughts.

"Don't touch anything Bradley. I'll notify London."

They stepped outside for cell reception.

"Davis, Sir, I believe we may have discovered the vault or tomb of Godwinson's head. I don't want to breach protocol or destroy any validation of a Viking treasure. I'm sending you a picture of the artifact. The first rumors that get out will bring curiosity seekers in droves. How can I secure the area on behalf of the Museum?"

"Is the Turner fellow still with you?"

"He is."

"We'll get your GPS coordinates and dispatch a recovery team. You'll have to remain with the vault personally until relief arrives."

"When will they be here?"

"We'll have them on a private plane within half an hour and they'll be there before seven."

"The sooner the better. Now Bradley Turner is a co-partner involved in this finding. Anticipate a future claim from him if it should be the golden arrow."

Static intercepted on the line and it died.

Bradley was inching backwards toward the vault, and Gabe saw his intent. He raised both hands. "Turner, we have an agreement. Don't do anything you'll regret."

Turner stepped inside, his eyes darting between Gabe and the trunk. "I've invested a great deal of time in this discovery and now you've arranged for government agents to scoop it out of my hands."

Bradley's fingers were already gripping the box when a loud groan shuddered through the walls.

"It's going to cave!" Gabe shouted and backed toward the access hole.

Bradley lunged to grasp the wooden compartment, as the tumbling of rocks began, crumbling on the walls around him.

"Leave it Bradley! Come now!"

"I'm not leaving without it! I want to make my father proud."

His eyes flashed with envy, seeming oblivious to the impending crash. Gabe headed for the entrance, and looking back saw nothing but falling rock and dust.

"Turner! Turner!"

At the first chamber, Gabe tugged at the cable line. It was heavy and immovable, and his only choice was to release the harness attachment.

He continued shouting to Bradley, and finally heard a faint muffle. He dialed Davis.

"The tunnel collapsed. Send EMS fast with a recovery team—a copter, men and equipment. Bradley's buried inside."

With the pick axe, he chopped and dug with vigor.

"Bradley, I'll get you out. Stay calm!"

Picking and hacking, he broke a tiny hole through, enough to feed an air tube from his supplies.

Twenty minutes passed before he heard the thrashing of helicopter blades outside. He ran out, waving his arms as it set down in the field of heather.

"Farrow? I'm Commander Nichols. Here to assist."

A rush of six military uniforms was heading his way, thrashing through the debris.

"Hold it, Nichols. The tunnel is unstable. Hold your men back until you've reinforced a passage. Send in a medic, my partner is trapped in a collapsed section. I pushed an air hose through but I've had no response since."

Nichols and a lone EMS member approached Gabe. "I need the coordinates of your partner and relative directions to the box."

"The trove is the last thing on my mind. My partner is Bradley Turner. He's behind this mound, about eight or ten feet. The cavern is not properly reinforced and appears to be ancient. The area has been isolated for centuries with no plant exposure and sign of animals other than some minute scratches on the box.

The beams are rotting, and support a fragile roof of crumbling limestone. It's still vulnerable."

"Okay, Marks and Sandler will take over the recovery. If you don't mind standing back, Mr. Farrow, my men will bring in some equipment."

An extension ceiling jack was installed in minutes to support the work area, then a series of pipes were hammered into the wall. When he was certain the pipe was through, Nichols called through the mouthpiece.

"Mr. Turner, we're coming in. Use the plastic tubing for fresh air. Tap once if you understand."

In deafening silence, the men worked, calm but sober. Finally, a barely audible tap eased the tension.

"Received, Mr. Turner. There is a wider metal pipe near the tubing, we will now insert tubes of water. Drink if you can to stay hydrated."

A second tap got new enthusiasm outside, and Gabe wiped the sweat from his forehead. Twenty minutes later, a private squeezed through an opening to grasp Bradley's hand. "Got him!"

"It's under control now, Mr. Farrow, if you want to wait outside."

"Absolutely not! Your first command from Mr. Davis would be to secure a newly discovered artifact of significant value. It is still my responsibility to oversee that."

"Yes, Sir. I only meant that you might like a bit of fresh air and a coffee. We have security now for it."

Bradley was carried out on a stretcher and attached to intravenous and oxygen. Gabe was by his side. "Turner, what happened to the trunk?"

His answer was feeble through the mask. "Don't touch it. Don't go back in there, Gabe—it's haunted, like trespassing on a tombstone."

"It's guarded from this point on. You did fine, pal."

Gabe followed to the copter. "We'll take him to the Whitby Hospital in Springhill. You'll find him there," Nichols said. "Or come now."

"Thank you, Sir. I'll remain. Where's the carved box? It was in the cavern on a table. Tell your people it can't be opened in a space not properly humidified, or deterioration can degrade the artifact. The carvings might be fragile, encrusted with rubies and emeralds."

"A specialist will preserve it in transit, with proper casing and humidity meter. Will you accompany the box back to London? Security and skilled archaeologists will manage the site, with others to begin excavation and preservation. I assure you, precautions will be taken so the area is not contaminated."

"Yes then, I will come with you. But first, I need to take photos to document the discovery site."

Gabe snapped pictures every angle of walls and ceilings, and a panoramic video with supporting narrative. A close-up of a corner of the ceiling revealed a few orphaned roots of grass.

Hmm—plant life. Perhaps the tomb has not been as isolated as someone wants us to believe.

Nichols had left Gabe to complete his examination and waited in the helicopter.

On his knees and elbows, Gabe inspected the floor, using the powerful flashlight beam. He zoomed his camera at a faint impression of a shoe print, barely discernable.

Nike. Bradley wasn't wearing that.

The anticipation to open the box was invigorating, and Gabe wanted to be in London when it happened.

In the air, his face was against the window, scanning the site that was now surrounded with headlights and a swarm of official vehicles. Rising high above the cavern space, he saw a lane with tire tracks in proximity to the collapsed chamber.

He opened his camera to scroll the digital photos from the rescue site. The interior images showed a consistent dark blob in the interior images, closely behind Bradley's location.

Has to be an energy source. But I heard those groans.

He zoomed his lens for a better image of the tire tracks.

9

MOST OF THE TOWN saw or heard the helicopter hovering, or were told about it on the grapevine. In no time, a crowd of onlookers had circled the yellow tape to watch stages of the rescue in progress, hoping to see something gruesome.

Among the curious were Hennie and Fergus arriving on foot. They cared little about the victim taken out, but the officials representing the museum infuriated Hennie who considered the moors his personal digs.

"It's Farrow. I knew he was bad news," Hennie moaned.

Fergus said, "I heard a man say that after Turner is at the hospital, the chopper will go to the Whitby airport, for their private plane back to London."

Hennie watched every move. "One, two, three, four—four men setting up a restricted perimeter around the cave-in and an excavation tent, just over there. A few have jackets that say BMMA. What's that mean?"

"I'll try to find out, Hennie," Fergus said.

He was back in an instant. "You won't like this, boss. It's the British Museum of Medieval Antiquities. They've secured a wide area now, and no one without official status is allowed beyond the tape."

Hennie's face was steaming. "They have no right in taking a hoard from under our feet. Fergus, go back to Capp's and keep a tail on Farrow. I can outsmart him. And alert Stewart to back off and get his equipment out of here. No traces."

"I heard Farrow say he'd accompany the plane to London. I'll now have a chance to thoroughly go over Farrow's room, maybe find Bradley's original piece—the Stamford coin. It excited Dodds enough not to give it up," Fergus said.

"My instincts said not to trust Bradley the first day he was a drunken sot, bumping into us at the Bluebird. Dodds was too gullible and didn't take the time to validate the man's story. I don't trust him, I'm convinced it's a plant."

He clenched his teeth, but not in defeat. "The Grinkle site only finds pottery, but I know there'll be silver and gold coins. The emblems under the crocks match some ancient coins that I've seen with Dodds from the Silverdale Viking Hoard a few years back," Hennie said, louder than intended. "We'll need Darby to get here from Harrogate."

Descending toward the small aircraft field at London City Airport, the small aircraft circled the royal docks in the Borough of Newham, and over the Thames and Big Ben. Gabe was reminded how he'd missed the thrill and pulse of a city of a larger population, where no one knows your name.

The precious cargo was strapped securely but with the slightest shifting, he glanced back.

Every time I remove an artifact from its resting place, I feel like I've exhumed a grave. Tonight is no different.

He turned back from the window to face Nichols.

"You will stay with the crate yourself until it reaches the museum, right?"

"Indeed, Sir. That is my assignment. A car will meet you at the airport to take you directly to Great Russell Street. Mr. Davis will be waiting for you."

"Thanks, Nichols. Have you heard any update about Mr. Turner?"

"He's at Whitby Hospital. The doctor anticipates a full recovery, but it could take time as he babbles—he claims to have seen an apparition. Myself, I say it's a wild imagination."

Gabe nodded. "Under the circumstances, when he is able, can we have him escorted to London for questioning? We should restrict local authorities from questioning him before anyone interferes there."

"We'll give it a try."

Nichols called right away and spoke in soft tones to Whitby police.

"Gabe, it seems that his father is on his way from Harrogate now to see him."

Within minutes of touching down, Gabe and the crate were dispatched to the Museum. He watched as it was loaded into a black Hummer with seals and crests on the door.

Gabe's cell rang, with Davis on it.

"Just arrived, Davis, and we'll go directly to the Receiving bay. Meet us there."

Speeding through London with an armed escort, he dealt with a series of questions, replying to each with a yes.

Along High Street, local gossip buzzed about the Runswick excitement. By the time Troy heard the news, dusk was settling over the village. He ran breathless to the tavern.

"Ma, ma! Have you heard from Gabe? He was involved in a cave-in at the old railway tunnels off Port Mulgrave."

She dropped her tray on an empty table, breaking a cup. "Is he okay?"

Simultaneously, her phone beeped an incoming text.

'I'm fine but have gone to London to attend to business. Keep my location tight-lipped. Thanks, Gabe.'

"Troy!" M.J. raised her phone beckoning him to come. "Read this."

"I should have been on lookout," he said sullenly bearing the burden of guilt.

"Bless you, Troy. Thank goodness you weren't with him. Now put your bike around back and go up to the loft," M.J. said.

Troy started to the back. Before he felt anything, he heard heavy breathing, then a dirty hand over his mouth.

"Let go . . . let go!" Determined, Troy kicked and fought.

Hennie spat close to Troy's ear.

"Shut up, kid."

"Mr. Farrow warned you to keep your hands off me!"

Troy twisted Hennie's arm and spun around. With two full strength kicks to the shins, Hennie was knocked off balance. Troy was all of eighty-five pounds, the maximum weight the back trellis could take. Scampering up the lattice, his feet flew out of range of the henchman's reaching grasp.

"Stay away from me."

Troy reached for a terra cotta flower pot from the second floor sill and threw it directly at his attacker's head.

Hennie was barely conscious when Fergus arrived. Troy was now safely through the third floor window to his loft, pumped by his escape leering down at his foiled captors.

After texting M.J., Gabe sent one to Niles asking for the next day off, knowing his boss would agree.

The driver slowed as the car approached the museum gates and Gabe's attention was diverted to a pair of waiting guards.

The back overhead door was up at the museum, and Davis was standing outside, waving the customary documentation. The parking lot had a news vehicle from a local TV station, running toward Davis with a microphone, and a cameraman in tow.

"Glad you made it, Gabe. Any problems along the way?" Davis didn't bother for an answer.

The TV woman pushed through to Davis. "Word is out in the seaside villages of Yorkshire that a hoard has been discovered. Can you confirm it? We need a story."

"We're not able to confirm that today. But we've beefed up security on sites in the moors." He walked away with Gabe.

"Excuse me! Excuse me . . . a few quick questions," she pleaded.

"No comment for now," Davis repeated, leading Gabe inside.

"You can't imagine the Staithes grapevine. My landlady knew all about me before I even met her. And that was the day I arrived. The phone lines are buzzing constantly, and I became a local curiosity within minutes."

Davis laughed. "I had an aunt once that loved being the connecting piece. Come on into the loading dock, we have a team ready to unpack."

"Do you have a tap on Dodds' telephone line?"

"We do, but with no activity this evening."

A curator met them inside with flat packages. "Gentlemen, please put on these paper shoes and smocks."

More examiners in surgical guise waited around a table, all experts or understudies. Two archaeological scholars from universities attended—one from Oxford Medieval Studies and the other from Leeds University, Norse & Celtic History and Culture.

A glass rectangle sat over the Dragon head box. Two team members with gloves opened the access doors on the sides of the glass, to insert laser tubing. All eyes watched the tubing as it barely touched the surface of the box with pointed sponges. 3D x-rays then moved at rotating angles, producing a hologram inside the box and above the artifact.

The x-ray image stunned everyone, and no one dared to breathe. Suspended was the hologram outline of a golden arrow.

"It is it!" Davis whispered through a gasp.

The image continued to rotate showing a skull in remarkable condition and the arrow through the cavern of the right eye.

"Unbelievable!" Gabe muttered with satisfaction.

After ten minutes of silence at the rotating image, Davis turned to Gabe.

"We will work on acclimatization overnight before we can gather specimens. A room is booked for you at the Imperial Hotel in the Square; meet me back here at nine in the morning. I'll have an update from the archaeology team and we'll be in a better position to make a plan. I'd like you to return to Staithes right away, until we catch Dodds' gang red-handed."

The drizzle didn't stop Gabe, and the night air was fresh to walk to the hotel. Within blocks of Fitrovia, north of Soho, he would pass Madame Tussauds, the Palladium, the University of London and British Reference Library. On Hampstead Road, he was cautious on the wet, shiny cobblestones, then turned up Tavistock. In his sight was the neon light burning over the Imperial Hotel.

"Do you have a Sundries shop in the hotel?" he asked at reception. "I have no luggage."

"Take the elevator to the Colonnade level; a few shops are still open, Mr. Farrow."

Gabe's room was a single, turned down, with a view of Russell Square. He slid the curtains aside to allow nighttime London into his room, including the beeping of sirens and flashing of emergency vehicles.

The newspaper was too wide for the small table and hung over the edges. From his pockets, he retrieved his camera and cell phone.

There was so much today to take in all at once.

The camera's focused on the parallel land depression at the outside entrance of the railway tunnel, and he stayed on the image to think on it.

It has the same sensation as the tunnel picture in Milner's Gallery.

Gabe scrolled on, with images darkening as he set foot in the first cave. With the helmet's flashlight turned on, a video focused on the floor and walls as he entered the second cavern on the heels of Bradley.

At that moment, Bradley became visibly frenzied with emotion at the sight of the carved box. The video's sound then played the eerie words in a Viking dialect as the camera panned the room. Up in the corner, Gabe saw for the first time a narrow shaft of light and movement. He froze the panel and enlarged the background behind Bradley. Something fluttered.

If this cavern had been sealed for a thousand years, there'd be no signs of life, not even a bat. Is that possibly a protruding wire from the ceiling? And the tire treads . . .

It was late and Gabe checked the time. He logged the pictures with notes, and closed the camera.

A newspaper article on an open page captured his interest. J.K. Rowling was venturing into a new series, with filming to commence in London, then back to the seaside villages of the North Moors.

"Horace! The Odds & Sods! The movie sound and visual equipment in his boxes!" Gabe exclaimed aloud.

Gabe crawled out of the bed at six to a warm, low-pressure shower. In a half an hour, the sun would rise over the Thames.

The Breakfast Room hostess offered him the London News and coffee or tea. "It's a full English breakfast, Mr. Farrow. How would you like your eggs?"

He folded the newspaper into a manageable shape, creased around an item and photo of official vehicles arriving at the museum. The columnist conjectured the discovery and existence of a new hoard, without any evidence to substantiate the breaking news. It concluded that the Museum would hold a press conference at 10:30 a.m.

Wiping the last of his runny eggs with a whole wheat slice, Gabe took a dollop of Marmite to finalize the toast. He reminisced about the comfort of home-cooked breakfasts in town and wondered how they would be taking this news.

With a brisk ten minute walk back, he was back at the side door of the museum. A few eager reporters were already back, standing in wait, and he bypassed them to ring the staff privacy bell.

"Gabe Farrow to see Mr. Davis," he whispered into the intercom, and the lock was released.

"Glad you're here, Gabe. Who would have thought so many complications could arise from a wooden box with a golden arrow?" Davis lamented.

"It's a thousand years of complication. Do you want to give it to me—best to worst?"

Davis motioned toward his private office, and Gabe settled across from his desk. The wall was crowded with elegantly-framed credentials, certificates and awards. On the credenza was a family photo on his estate, and sundry political pictures. One showed Davis standing with Jarvis Turner, shaking hands at a charitable reception where Jarvis gave a sizable sum.

Gabe cringed.

Something is out of place. Is it Davis . . . or Turner? Something about the pair nags.

Shaking it for now, he waited for Davis to begin.

"Jarvis Turner arrived in Whitby last night and signed his son out against the doctor's wishes. The security demands at the site didn't give us leeway to have the Turners followed, and I'm afraid we've temporarily lost track of them. Well, Bradley anyway. I'll send a man to Harrogate to meet with his father."

"If you agree . . . when we've finished here, I'll return to Staithes. I am better used to investigating in the field."

He knew Davis would agree, and just continued. "I saw in the morning paper that the Museum will give a statement at 10:30 today. What will you say?"

"That's deferred to the curator, but I've informed the Secretary of State of the significance this could be to British history. Brief and simple—there'll be nothing further at this time, beyond confirming the approximate vintage of the trunk, and that Hardrada's dragon emblem coincides with the helm of a circa 1066 sword found near Stamford in the late 1800s. The arrow won't be mentioned."

"Last night, I regurgitated every detail of yesterday's recovery. Unfortunately, I have reason to suspect intervention within the last few years. I'll leave a copy of my video with your recovery unit. There is a shadow of light unaccounted for."

He paused, before his bombshell.

"Could there be a possibility that this has been faked? The first clue will be if the arrow is genuine solid gold. Then the age of the skull needs to be examined—it didn't look large enough for a Viking king."

Davis looked appalled. "What the Sam Hill are you saying, Farrow?"

"I've already said too much. I'll keep my further conclusions to myself until I have undisputed evidence. I'll track Turner and keep surveillance on Dodds' gang.

"If the box and arrow are indeed authentic and this is the burial site of Har's skull, it's logical that there'd be a hoard of significance nearby. It's good for the tourist business to keep legends alive, even the pretense of haunting and ghosts. I've learned from folks in Staithes about the filming of Diagon Alley. With the right equipment it isn't all that difficult."

"Farrow, you can have as much latitude as you need. Keep your eyes and ears open to all possibilities, including a deliberate deception."

"Thank you, Sir. I'll keep in touch. If you haven't heard from me for a while and need to verify my well-being, there are two ways. First contact is Niles Cobb at the craft mill on the cliff road. Also, at the Blue Cove, Room 3B, there's a loose board under the bed. A long metal box is there, where I'd stash anything in jeopardy."

"Fair enough, Gabe. Please tell that to Delia before you leave, too."

"Sure . . ." A new thought hit Gabe. "I could stop off in Harrogate myself on my way back north. I'd like to set eyes on Dodds and I could check on Jarvis Turner at the same time."

"Good plan! But I've got to go now. The curator's biting his nails."

"I'll leave right after the press conference."

Scanning the museum foyer, Gabe videotaped the audience for later review including a conglomeration of media cameras and reporters. The meeting was brief with Davis at the podium, ending with his promised, 'No further comment at this time'.

A man with a fedora leaned up to a marble pillar, holding a cell. Gabe noticed him, considering him as one of the media snapping pictures. On the stairs to the door, Gabe turned back in time to see the fedora man taking his pic.

Two can play this game.

His pace was fast to King's Cross and he arrived early for the train to Harrogate. The terminal air was heavy with the smell of diesel.

He lingered at a concrete pillar as red caps and porters passed. The terminal smelled heavily of diesel fuel, and on the overhead beams, doves contemplated dives at discarded food and floor crumbs.

On a suspended board, schedules clicked and changed as trains arrived and departed. Gabe dodged around wheeled suitcases and prams to get to the board, for Harrogate's gate.

"Platform 43," he said.

With time yet, he joined the coffee queue at a kiosk, and watched for a newspaper to read onboard. Behind him was the same fedora hat, and Gabe took a second glance.

Besides following me, something isn't right about that man. The fedora is a diversion, as his shoes are old and unpolished. It's not consistent.

Dodging into a mob of arriving passengers, Gabe swung around to approach him from behind. Up close, the man smelled of beef jerky and Old Spice, and Gabe smirked to watch him stretching his neck to search the crowd.

"Well, if it isn't my old friend Darby."

Gabe poked the offender in the back without a face-to-face. "No need to turn around. Who sent you to follow me?"

"I don't know what you mean," Darby said with a stutter.

"Of course you do. My guess is that your Harrogate boss wonders what we found and how you can get your hands on it. Everything is for profit, right?"

"I've nothing to say to you."

"I see it differently. Show me your train ticket."

Fedora man reluctantly pulled a boarding card from his inside pocket.

"Ah, ha! Harrogate! Isn't that a coincidence, I'm going that way too. Shall we sit together, Darby?"

The finger poke in his back became firmer.

"No thanks!"

"Oh, Darby, it's no bother. Join me. Platform 43. They're calling it now. Let's go."

Gabe nudged his opponent while keeping a firm grip on his elbow.

"Here we are, Car No. 13."

Darby was directed to the window seat so Gabe could block any chance of retreat. "Here, take part of the newspaper."

"No thanks." Darby's confidence was eroded to simple words.

"Well then. Why don't you catch me up on what happened at Runswick last night?"

"I'm not looking for trouble. I'm simply a lookout man."

"I know that, Darby. What did you 'lookout' at? I insist on details."

"I guess there's no harm in saying that Hennie called me to observe the security around the cave-in, if that's what the Museum has decided to call it."

A pellet of sweat started on his cheek.

"Get used to it, Darby, we have a ways to go. Who told you to track me to London?"

His nerves had overtaken now. "D—dodds."

"What did you expect to find out by following me?"

"I don't ask the reasons; I just do as I'm ordered."

"What is Hennie doing at the Grinkle Mine? Has your gang recovered any gold coins?"

"You don't understand, Mr. Farrow. Mr. Dodds is obsessed about finding gold. It's all about greed. They know you're looking for the same thing. That's why the heat is on you."

"And have you had dealings with Jarvis Turner?"

"No, Mr. Dodds threatened us with strict warnings not to have contact with him. But you must know that Bradley double-crossed us. We're supposed to keep tabs on him in Staithes—we know he came back. He thinks he outsmarted us with his disguises, but Hennie has gadgets to track people. One is in the sole of Bradley's shoe. We give him leeway and let him get overconfident, then he exposes himself."

"Did you know his father discharged him from the Hospital?"

"No . . . but I'm sure Hennie and Dodds know."

"What threat is Bradley?"

"He knows the system and he's seen documents. Most of all, his father can be dangerous."

"How do you mean 'dangerous'?"

"There are two ways in life, Mr. Farrow. On the table and under it. Jarvis Turner and Ian Dodds don't agree on what method their firm should be using. In spite of Jarvis Turner's 'holier than thou' persona, he's not at all what he seems."

"Darby, you're more perceptive than I gave you credit for. Do you give pause to your morals while working for those men?"

"You might find it hard to believe that I was raised in an Anglican church-going family. I was taught right from wrong, and if you do good deeds you will get ahead."

Darby was wringing his hands and stopped. He watched the scenery going by, and wished he could change his words.

"What happened?"

"My parents were in a London market on a Saturday morning, a beautiful day with the sun shining. I was just a teenager when my mother kissed me goodbye and said they'd be back in a few hours."

Distress on his face changed to pain, then anger.

"Go on . . ."

"That morning, a terrorist suicide car bomber blew himself up right where my parents were standing. Outside Harrods store. My life was taken from me, and I had to beg on the streets to survive. So you see, good deeds don't account for anything."

"Darby, I can see a good man behind the façade you project. Perhaps you can find yourself and return to the life your parents hoped for you."

"No, it's too late. One thing that stuck with me from my father was to choose my battles wisely. I choose to survive."

Gabe hadn't expected to feel this compassion. "Darby, there's more to that adage. The number of times you stand up to fight is not a measurement of life. You have a chance at any time to look in a different and better direction."

A painful silence ensued that was pivotal for both men.

"Darby, what can I do to earn your trust? I can help you turn your life around if that is truly what you want. Your father probably also told you that life is short.

"My own father walked out on my mother and me when I was six. I determined that I'd do the best I could for my Mom, but the fire inside to even the score with my real father will never die. Fortunately, I've allowed good people to help guide me. I have a promising career and folks who care about me. You can too."

"I don't know. You're confusing me."

"Darby, I doubt that you've done anything really criminal in your life. These men are using you. If I can recruit your support in exposing Dodd's crime ring, I can assure you a decent job."

"Hennie is keen and he'd detect my deceit."

"Speak the truth, but in different words, so you don't give yourself away. Everyone has a sore spot, you need to find Hennie's."

"It's more complicated that you know. Dodds is obsessed with the golden arrow. He says a Chinese collector will pay him three times the value. This shuffling in mines is a façade, waiting for someone like you to lead them to the trove. He and his partner also make millions in counterfeit gold futures and scams . . . I have proof. I'm supposed to pick up a package from Dodds to take back to Hennie. He expects me at the Kilt & Caber at four."

"Here's a transmitter. Affix it under the table, and retrieve it when you leave. You do that, and then come back to Staithes. If you ever need to flee Hennie, I know a place to hide." Cobb's back room crossed his mind.

"Is Fergus fiercely loyal to Hennie and Dodds?"

"He's hard to get a handle on. But he does as he's told without complaining."

"I'll need to see your proof about the gold smuggling and counterfeit scam. Actual documents and fingerprints. Are you willing to give it a try?"

A handshake sealed it, but with misgivings by both.

"And a sample of the silver and gold coins," Gabe said.

"What if I get caught by Hennie?"

"A fire escape ladder extends up to my window. It's always ajar, so you can get in. Under my bed are a couple of loose floor boards. You'll find a spare burner phone there that rings to Mr. Davis in London. He'll make sure you get help."

10

DARBY AND GABE parted at the Harrogate Terminal. They agreed to meet in two hours, and Gabe relayed the news of his new recruit, back to London.

Gabe's lorry took him to Harrogate Town Centre to an address next to McCormicks, a prestigious law firm once referenced in the Fortune 500.

Schmooze with the big guys and their reputation wears off on you.

The century stone building stood four floors high, with chrome lettering on the top showing Turner & Dodds as the chief resident. A doorman inside the revolving door directed Gabe to a fourth floor reception.

On the counter, a brochure rack would lure investors to precious metals in the gold mines of Ghana. Mr. Ian Dodds' name was imprinted, as the representative for the appointed UK clearing house. Gabe opened a brochure.

The enticement to invest in solid gold at a discounted price was the carrot—why invest in fake gold from Africa that could be a scam, when you can buy a bonafide security here in the UK without having to deal with Dubai Customs.

An eyebrow-raising list of credentials and experience for Dodds would convince almost anyone.

"Hello, how can I help you?" Gabe pocketed the brochure and turned toward a freshly permed, mature lady.

"I would like a moment with Jarvis Turner. I have come on behalf of Mr. Davis of London."

"His appointments are fully booked for today. Would you care to leave your card and reschedule for another day?"

"No, I have come from London this morning to meet with him. Relay my message." Gabe handed her a calling card sans the British Museum.

Loose lips sink ships. Receptionists know way too much about their bosses' lives as it is.

A private secretary arrived to take the card from reception. "Please wait, Sir. I'll see if Mr. Turner can squeeze you in. What may I ask is this about?"

"It's personal. Mr. Turner will understand when you mention Mr. Davis."

At this point the receptionist and now the secretary were completely snubbed.

Phones rang, couriers came and went, and customers with appointments were received, while Gabe remained seated in the lobby.

"Mr. Farrow?" An impeccably groomed, silver-haired man with a pencil mustache came from a long hall. His grey suit was sleek, from a bespoke tailor on Savile Row.

"Yes. Mr. Turner I presume." A strong business handshake was exchanged.

Jarvis Turner's office had a corner window overlooking the East Parade. Although the curtains were open, dim bankers' lamps were on about the room, exuding the effect of a quiet library.

"Please have a seat at the table. Coffee or tea?"

"Tea with lemon would be nice."

"Myrna, bring a pot for two. Lemon and biscuits." The intercom clicked on and off.

"Mr. Turner, may I inquire about the health of your son, Bradley?" Gabe's eyes searched the office for family photos, particularly of father and son.

"Bradley will be fine. Took a few good blows to the head, but he's young and resilient."

Jarvis Turner had not studied the man in the visitor's chair and was now scrutinizing his every detail.

"I understand Mr. Davis has spoken with you. I am the field investigator in Staithes and my mission is to intercept a clandestine mission in the Yorkshire Moors. It appears to be orchestrated from these offices, but Bradley has given me enough background to remove you from suspicion."

Jarvis's curiosity was peaked. "I'm glad to hear you've come to that conclusion."

Turner reached for a manila file on the corner of his desk.

"Here are photographs and courier logs that you'll see are out of line. My esteemed partner, Ian Dodds, is front and center in pilfering silver and gold coin, taken from fourteen holes excavated near Whitby Abbey. You might know he's been appointed to the British Treasury Board, giving him autonomy over the books. He is free to change the logs and weights at his pleasure. I am wise with silence, yet rich in observation. I play the part of the naïve partner that lets thievery go on under my nose."

A wise man is silent, not to make a confession to a stranger of his nobleness.

Jarvis was smug with superiority. He raised his chin high and looked down as he spoke.

"However, I am agreeable to do my duty to the crown and become a witness for the prosecution should things go that far."

Gabe's eyebrows raised. "You are willing to testify?"

"When I have assurances of my son's safety and immunity. The Turner name is respectable and should receive due respect from the courts. I will not turn on my partner for any vindictive reason, but I know that innocent people have been defrauded through Dodds' dealings. For that, I will not allow him to stand behind my good name."

"Have you broached Mr. Davis in that regard?"

"We've had discussions."

"Mr. Turner, I'll be returning to Staithes this afternoon. I have a network of trusted folks and accomplices, however Hennie and his gang are astute. I have from a good authority that Bradley is being tracked in the moors. Perhaps he should change his shoes."

Turner looked startled by Gabe's comment. "Shoes?"

"Yes, shoes." The words were followed by a sense of dawning and a knowing smile.

Gabe removed a transmitter tester from his pocket. "May I, Mr. Turner?"

"Of course. I check it myself every few days. I can't imagine what they would expect to find out from me. I find safety in being the old goose."

Quietly, Gabe checked all corners of Jarvis's office looking for an active microphone.

"All clear."

Gabe reached for the manila folder. "May I take these for review, Mr. Turner?"

"Certainly, I don't like having the file here frankly."

"Don't expect any contact from me, Mr. Turner. The British Museum will be in touch and will relay any instructions they deem necessary. However, I'll need Bradley's ongoing cooperation. Where can I find him?"

"He's laid up at home for a few days with a headache. He is your best contact in Yorkshire to keep tabs on Dodds' men."

Turner opened a desk drawer and triggered a hidden compartment.

"Take this. I was able to get it from under Ian's nose as evidence from the hoard they are currently depleting from the British government. My understanding is that they are working on land belonging to the National Park, therefore, there are no farmers' rights to tread on."

Gabe opened a brown evidence envelope from his pocket and Jarvis Turner dropped it in.

"You haven't met Ian Dodds yet, have you?"

"No, I haven't. Why?"

"Today is Friday and he goes round to the Kilt & Caber after work for a pint. That's where Bradley and I staged our falling out. Perhaps you'll catch him today."

"Thanks for the information, Mr. Turner. If you would like an update in future, feel free to contact Mr. Davis."

Gabe was about to depart Turner's office but stopped, overwhelmed by what he really came to say.

He closed the door again and spoke to Jarvis Turner for an agonizing ten minutes. When Gabe left, Jarvis was agitated and sweating. He paced back and forth across his window, then stopped to watch Gabe exit the building and turn out of sight at the corner.

Preposterous, I can't recall who Patricia would be.

The Kilt & Caber was a typical English Tudor-style tavern on the next block. Gabe helped himself to a corner table anticipating that Darby and Dodds would arrive shortly.

Darby arrived first and scouted out Gabe. Attaching the transmitter to a table by the main hearth, he ordered two pints of the house Black Sheep Ale—one to await Dodd's arrival.

Dodds was an obtuse, balding man with a Dustin Hoffman nose and a chip on his shoulder. He wore a proper business suit with a satin vest and stuffy bow tie.

"Darby? This ale for me? I can't stay more than a minute. Do you have anything for me?"

Taken aback, Darby was empty-handed.

"No, Sir. I wasn't asked to bring anything. Just to meet you and collect a packet for Hennie."

"Relax kid." Dodds looked over his shoulder out of habit, suspicious of everyone and everything. His eyes briefly met Gabe's, then summonsed the bartender. "This is warm; bring me a cold one."

He turned sharply to Darby. "Tell me what you know about last night. I heard the Turner kid was in a cave-in and significant artifacts were recovered. Was it the staged set-up that Stewart orchestrated, or is this something different?"

"I really don't know anything about Stewart or a set-up.

"Were precautions taken to cover our tracks?"

"I saw them bring out a stretcher. Apparently there was a second man, but I didn't see him. People in contamination suits went in with armloads of equipment. When they came out they carried a wooden crate on their shoulders as if it were Gandhi. One of the workman whispered about a golden arrow."

"Tell Hennie I want the second man found," Dodds said matter-of-factly, disguising his excitement about the arrow.

"Yes, Mr. Dodds."

"Well then, get on your way!" Dodds rose from his chair as the bartender arrived with the cold ale.

Darby eyeballed Gabe on his way out, then took the road to the train terminal. His keen reflexes as a lookout man told him he was being tailed. "Hope its Gabe."

It wasn't. Footsteps kept pace, but he didn't dare to turn around. As they closed in, he accelerated his pace, then took off in a sprint. The chase was on. He heard two men now, and stopped in a dark alley to flatten himself against the wall as they passed.

Gabe dove at the other man.

"Bradley, you don't have to lurk in the shadows. We have a pact, remember?" Gabe straddled over a downed ginger-haired bobby in uniform.

"I thought you had a headache. Seems you're right as rain. I was just about to tail Darby when I see you pop out of a car onto the street dressed as a bobby, no less."

"Get off me!"

Bradley struggled to his feet and reached for his flat cap. His green eyes darted back and forth between Gabe and Darby's alley.

"I had a visit with your father," Gabe said. "I was concerned about your health."

"I borrowed the uniform, and I've been watching you since you arrived in Harrogate. Fine way of showing your concern."

"Come on, Bradley, I'm headed for the train terminal. Are you going that way?"

"What about him?" Bradley nodded toward Darby.

"Darby is an excellent lookout man. We may be able to use him in the moors."

"You trusting' a turncoat? He's thick with Hennie."

Bradley was crazed at losing control of the situation, and wondered what Darby might say that could change everything.

"Everyone has their faults," Gabe said, "but Darby knows more than we do about where and what Hennie is up to. Even more so now that you've distanced yourself. I pledged my assistance to Darby in getting immunity when the scheme is exposed. He gave his word. Everyone deserves a second chance. Haven't I given you one, Bradley?"

"If you say so, Gabe."

"Northern Rail doesn't run to Whitby until tomorrow morning, so I hired a car. It will take an hour and a half, then we won't have to bus it to Staithes in the dark. We're to wait outside and the driver will be along in a few minutes. I'll bring Darby for the ride."

Everyone seemed at ease with the new travel plan. Taking the turnoff to A1, they drove up through Thirsk and Thornaby. The roads skirted the North Moors National Park until they joined the A171 direct to the ocean and Staithes.

"Ah, looks rather lovely." Gabe and Bradley shared a joke over their first meeting. "Who would have thought two unlikely bus passengers on their way to a quaint seaside village could end up like us, Bradley?"

"Where should I go? Hennie won't be pleased that I'm returning empty handed," Darby said.

"Blend in—I'll find you when I need you, Darby?"

"You can drop me at the hostel in Runswick," Bradley said.

The next morning, the Vauxhall stopped at the Runswick excavation site at 9 a.m. The entrance was surrounded with plastic sheeting and a tent-style decontamination unit. An officer approached the car for a security check.

Gabe opened his identifying documentation. Who is in charge of the excavation?"

The team's site supervisor welcomed Gabe, and he was taken aback at her sight.

I remember her . . . Clay.

"Come in, Mr. Farrow. We've recovered numerous items this morning. I'm not one to jump to conclusions, but from the age of the petrified wood on the carved box, it's easy to claim it instantly to be for the illustrious Hardrada, just because his Dragon head emblem was present."

Rebecca Clayburn had long golden curls, held back with a scarf. Even in field overalls, Gabe thought she looked magnificent.

Blue eyes and blonde hair, about my age. What more could I ask for? She doesn't show the slightest recognition, but I'm sure it's her . . . from the New York symposium.

"But you have your doubts, Ms. Clayburn?"

"The golden arrow has been transported to London, however, I retained a fleck of metal for my own testing."

She held up a clear vial containing a solution and a tiny speck that glittered in the light.

"My first assumption was that the arrow is authentic, however the environment doesn't agree with the thousand year timeline. The surrounding soil should have evidence of ironstone, but I found shards of metal encrusted with soil from another site."

She stared directly at Gabe as she spoke.

"The Dragon box was relocated at some time—there isn't a symbol of royalty on the box. We're not finding the significance of artifacts that we should expect if it is a royal vault. And you said something to Davis that rings loud and clear. It's the size of the skull. Hardrada was an enormous man more than seven feet in height. The skull in London belongs to a man less than six feet and the deterioration coincides with the 1800's. Add that to your smokescreen."

Yes, I see it in her eyes. She remembers, but for some reason she is denying our acquaintance.

"I had my suspicions last night," he said. My photos in the cavern show a slight glow behind Bradley in the upper corner. We both heard groaning and a Viking dialect warning us off."

"I saw a suspicious footprint," she added, "but because the soil is loamy, it's difficult to extract footprints so we need other evidence of outside matter.'

Gabe said, "I have another angle to pursue and I'll check back later tonight."

As an after-thought, he scrolled through his pictures. "Ms. Clayburn, before I go, do you remember seeing any of these men near the site? Is it possible any could be using a disguise?"

"Yes. This man, Bradley Turner. He came back with his father late last night. They didn't stay long at all."

She hovered over the images. "This one stood and watched from the parking area. His stare made me uncomfortable. Who is he?"

"He goes by the name of Hennie. Whenever you see him, alert your security and ensure he doesn't come on site."

Gabe started to pull the cell away, when Ms. Clayburn objected.

"There's another one there. Him! A really nice man but he asked a great many questions."

Niles Cobb!

Becca moved closer to Gabe enticing him with her delicate fragrance. He didn't move remembering the scent of Dior that his grandmother wore.

Gabe idled the Vauxhall outside the boarding house, and Bradley saw him from the window and vaulted down, two steps at a time. Gabe turned the engine off.

"Where's Hennie gone?"

"Back to the Grinkle Mine."

"Won't that be restricted due to the cave-in?"

"Apparently they're collecting a pottery field at Mulgrave. They have a self-made vault concealed in the railway tunnel where they deposit their goods then bring the boat round from Seaton. Whatever they find is sent to Dodds from time to time. Hennie is a stickler for the tiniest detail so Darby doesn't have room for error."

"Bradley, find out what you can from the recovery team, I'm going to the archaeologist's office where the mine office used to be. I'll meet you at the car in an hour. I need to see Horace at the Odds & Sods shop on High Street."

"There's one here in Runswick, I can check out." Bradley offered.

"Alright, inquire about old movie equipment the productions companies left behind when they finished filming Harry Potter."

"Movie equipment!"

"Yes. Remember when you were in the cavern we heard a roar and a gust of wind. That situation wouldn't have happened in an isolated hole. Either there is another way in and out, or the cavern was connected to a staged area that would explain the aerial view of track marks. It's possible the theatrics were triggered by a motion detector. Keep it casual we don't want to alert anyone. Do you know anyone by the name of Stewart?"

"Do you want me to buy equipment?" Bradley ignored the query about Stewart keeping his back turned so Gabe wouldn't see deceit on his face.

"No. Just curious tourist type enquiries."

"Alright, in an hour." Bradley walked downhill toward the seashore with his brown small-brimmed fedora hat announcing him.

"I don't know what you're getting at about old movie equipment, Gabe. I came up empty. But there was a kid helping to unload a delivery truck. He pulled me aside and told me he'd seen a bloke a couple of months back with a red pickup. The tarp over his load was flapping in the wind, and he saw an industrial fan and a smog inducer."

"Are we so lucky to have a name or description of the driver?" Gabe asked.

"Afraid not, but he does a lot of deliveries and saw it again a few weeks ago, parked at the lower beach in Robin's Hood Bay. The equipment was gone, but he's certain it was the same truck, with the word 'Bluebird' painted on the side in white."

"That brings up a lingering question, Bradley. What does the serpent tattoo on your hand mean?"

"In college, I ran with a gang, mostly up and coming football players. One summer we spent in the moors, being beach bums here, free to do as we like. One of the lads burglarized a cottage up on Boubly Cliff, taking valuable heirloom jewelry. Without witnesses or clues to follow, the Bobbies let the story disappear. The six of us made a vow of secrecy.

"Part of our pledge was that each of us have a snake tattoo on the right hand. One of the boys was planning on going to London to visit relatives and agreed to pawn the gems there. We each got about £50, which did nothing to appease my conscience growing up. I've only seen him in the last five years and he'd had the tat removed. Left a nasty red mess of aggravated skin. Stewart . . . Stewart Arbuckle."

"It's unlikely we'll cross paths with him here," Gabe pondered. "First appearances seem harmless, but the dragon head box we found was *not* in its original location. Those warning groans and winds were meant to scare us off. And what can you think of that could duplicate those sounds?"

Bradley shrugged, with no answer.

"Can you get your father to spot you enough to book a room at the Fox & Hound? It's a bit out of the way and they don't ask questions. The matron's name is Vera."

Bradley leaned into the car window. "I'll consider that, pal. See you Saturday."

At the Cleveland, Crystal seemed extra cheerful to see Gabe tying his service apron in the kitchen.

"Nice to see you, Gabe. We just seated a busload of Japanese tourists. Do you speak the language?"

Gabe laughed. "Konichiwa for hello . . . welcome. Sorry, that's all I know, but I'll try to use it today."

"Cook is trying to make sticky rice, and a herring and seaweed dish with ginger and oyster sauces for tonight's special," Crystal joked.

The group caused congestion and noise in the restaurant, and by mid-evening the crowd was starting to thin, queuing up outside for the return of their coach.

Hennie, Fergus and Darby pushed through the Japanese customers on the sidewalk. Hennie swung the door open, irritated at the wait for service.

"Crystal! Over here," he yelled with sarcasm.

Pretending not to hear, Crystal whispered in Gabe's ear. "My feet are tired and I can't put on another smile, especially for that kind. It's not your job, but would you take their order. The specials are on the chalkboard."

"Hello boys. Hungry tonight? North Sea Mackerel with mushy peas and rosemary potato is the special, with or without salad."

Darby tried too hard not to look Gabe in the eye.

"Can't you afford Mrs. Capp's rent increase?" Hennie said.

Gabe forced a congenial reply. "As a matter of fact, it *has* created stress to my budget, so a nice tip will be appreciated. Where have you boys been today?"

"You asking us? It's you that disappeared from Runswick last night. Mind telling us what you and the turncoat found?"

"The National Parks have full authority over anything found or comments made on their behalf. Sorry I can't oblige. Now, what will your order be?"

Hennie considered toying with Gabe, then relented, tossing the menu on the table in annoyance.

"Three specials and the on-tap around the table. Make it quick, we're starving."

"I'll let the cook know."

Gabe cleared the nearby tables, hoping to glean some useful information. Darby spotted him and speaking to be gently overheard, he asked Hennie. "The coins we planted in the Runswick cave-in area today, think they'll be seen by those museum folks?"

"Shhh, boy. They ain't figured nothin' yet. Setting a bait trap will keep them from the real source at Mulgrave where we found that old trunk. Looks like they can't tell yet."

Hennie sneered in the direction of Gabe, and returned to Darby.

"At the dawn of first light, take the ATV to Runswick and set a transmitter in the excavation hut before their crew turns up. Time yourself to get in and out during the guard change."

"Sure, Hennie, I can do that. No problem," Darby said.

"Fergus, have you located Bradley's hangout? The GPS tracker is dead—he either found it or changed his shoes. Find another way to keep tabs on him."

Between mouthfuls, Hennie's incoherent bits made no sense to Gabe.

It wasn't until closing that Gabe had a chance to strike up a conversation with Theo.

"It's good you get to work with your wife, Theo. Often working families, like the one I grew up in, rarely see each other except for Sunday dinner."

"Yes, Mandy and I celebrate twenty-five years in the fall."

"Do you have family nearby?"

Theo put his hands on his hips. "No one asks anymore about my family." He appeared both puzzled and embarrassed.

"I'm sorry if I've trod on something you don't wish to talk about."

"No. You just reminded me that I do have a family, albeit I haven't seen them in a while."

Gabe waited, letting the silence urge Theo on.

"Two boys. My oldest son died in the military."

"I'm so sorry, Theo, I didn't know. I didn't mean to poke old wounds."

"Naw, there isn't a day that goes by that I don't think of my boys. We have a silver cross to remember Kyle, but barely a phone call out of the blue from the younger boy, Stewart."

"Stewart . . . Stewart Arbuckle. I've heard or seen that name recently."

Theo's eyes lit up. "Is he in town?"

"Does he by chance drive a red pickup truck? I made a delivery for Niles in Robin's Hood Bay a few weeks back and I had to ask a fellow they called 'Stewart' to move his truck."

"By golly, could be. He avoids us, but I heard once that he bunked down in a shanty near Boulby Cliff. What about you, where's your family?"

Gabe had withdrawn enough from Theo to conclude that the father and son were not a conspiracy. But the query about his own family stuck like a dagger.

"Me? I was raised in the United States. I use my mother's name since my father disappeared when I was in primary school. Haven't seen or heard from him in years . . . but my mother said he was somewhere in England. So if I'm lucky, perhaps I'll run into him."

"Gabe, don't put life on hold waiting. It isn't any good."

On the way to the Blue Cove, he passed half a dozen pubs with their front doors propped open, some with boisterous tourists hanging outside or meandering in and out.

The Odds & Sods was locked, with a sun shade pulled down over the door pane. Looking inside, he saw Horace working in the back storeroom. A silhouette was with him and their voices were raised.

Gabe moved down the side and took cover behind a cardboard dumpster, within feet of the back door. The screen door was ajar with the evening's heat, and the spring had not snapped back into place. He opened it for a line of vision through the cracked window, then placed his ear to the wood.

Horace was pacing. "I filed off the numbers. There's no way to trace the pieces here."

The other man lashed at Horace and grabbed his collar. Gabe could see the offender's hands with its red scar but not his face.

"Stewart, I can bury the rest somewhere where it can't be found. The alum mine is condemned and no one in their right mind would go there since Axle died."

"Just see that it's done. If Hennie comes back on me about the agreement to haul equipment—you know who I'll be looking for. I've heard it's difficult to eat with broken arms."

The front door slammed and Horace dimmed the storeroom. Gabe moved behind a bin and watched Horace lock the back.

11

ON SATURDAY, Gabe woke to a lone rooster crowing and an iridescent sun rising over the Garth. Springing upright, he remembered the words 'dawn of first light'.

With yesterday's pants and shirt, he shot downstairs in bare feet with his socks in his back pocket. He opened the screen door, careful not to let it creak, and stepped onto the porch.

"Morning, Gabe. I was afraid you'd forgotten me in all the fuss about the relics."

Troy was sitting cross-legged on the dew-covered veranda steps with a gunny sack slung on his shoulder.

"Are we ready to go?"

"Did we have an arrangement for this morning?"

"No . . . but we did have one for Friday after school, but you were busy in London and Runswick. I thought we should reschedule for today."

Troy searched for a reaction and was bucking up for rejection.

In a flash, Gabe put himself in the place of the freckle-faced boy pleading to be accepted. The recollection of his own father walking out and leaving him behind flashed to him. He had desperately wanted to play before him at his championship baseball game. He couldn't do that to Troy.

"I was about to come and get you, but I thought your Ma might be enjoying a sleep-in, after working last night."

"She is. I left a note and made her a lunch. See, I've got lunch for us too." Troy raised his sack.

"First, working men need a full breakfast in their stomachs. We'll take the car and go to the Fox & Hound. They run a bed and breakfast and the cook's sure to be up by now."

Vera was setting out plates on the patio. "Ah, my disappearing tourist. I was hoping you'd come back. Take a seat wherever you like. It's sunny enough if you'd like an umbrella outside.

Instead, Troy led the way to an isolated table inside.

"Well if it ain't M.J.'s boy," Vera said. "You sure have grown."

Troy squirmed with the compliment. "Yes, Ma'am."

"Don't worry, kid. I'm not party to the gossip circle, no one will know you've been here."

Gabe winked at Vera. "Two of the Fishermen's Breakfast. How do you want your eggs, Troy?"

"Just half runny, not too dry."

Gabe agreed. "Me too."

"Gabe, I'm glad you didn't get hurt in the cave-in. Perhaps if you'd had me on point, it could have been avoided," Troy smirked.

He sensed something imminent on the kid's mind, and waited for more.

"I heard the mine had voices, roars and wind, and it got me thinking. You know how when there's a lot going on, the big people forget about the little people? That don't mean we don't see or understand." His eyes widened. "So, remember when I told you about the wizard at Roxby Beck?"

"Yes, what of it?"

"With wizardry, muggles, hobs and goblins, people say the explanation is the overactive minds of magical children. Maybe the mythical shapes are actually real people, but the mind doesn't want to admit that. Adults dismiss the differences between a child's imagination and the real world. Watching them film, I remember the Harry Potter folks using wind tunnels, echo chambers and even something they called a seismic aggravator."

Gabe felt like a child being explained the facts of life.

"By golly, Troy, I'm all ears."

"When the movie filming was going on, our school did a series of plays, with scripts and even sound effects. We borrowed some abandoned equipment from Horace's shop." Troy hushed to a whisper. "I found out something I know will help you catch the people that did this.

"Yesterday, riding my bike along Roxby Beck, I saw the ATV. Don't worry, I was out of sight but saw them bringing sacks from a tunnel opening. I can show you where it is. Let's say for the sake of adventure that it was gold from a hoard. They loaded it on the thingy and took it to a boat they hid on the other side of the rocky peninsula."

Vera arrived with breakfast platters, a pot of clover honey and a jar of marmite.

"Tea or coffee, men?"

"A pot of tea would hit the spot."

"Do you believe me, Gabe?"

"Of course, Troy, you're my lookout man. You'd never lie to me."

"I'm not finished my story about the movie equipment yet." He stuffed a slice of bacon in his mouth. "My teacher let us hold a science fair and build our own studio out of everyday things we found around town. I had an electronics kit my Da sent me one Christmas. If I hook it up to the copper plumbing pipes behind the toilet, I can get reception. It's called short wave and only goes a certain distance. I got it working and went to test it out on Main Street."

Troy leaned on his elbow for a big confession. His whisper became so silent that Gabe had to read his lips.

"Gabe, my transistor went wild at the back of the Odds & Sods, picking up the frequency. Yesterday, I got a ride to Runswick with a friend of my Mum. She wanted me to get a parcel from the post office there. My kit was in my backpack and while I waited for her to pick me up, I checked the back of a few shops. A red truck was parked on the upper beach like at Horace's place, and the static got really loud. I recorded the readings and I think you'll find they match up with the stuff from the Foley sound company."

"I am impressed, Troy. You are a born detective. Do we pick up from there today?"

"Not exactly. When I got home, I researched radio frequency. There's no end to how RF controls the world, Gabe. On expensive equipment, like the stuff the movie company had, the RF monitors are cryptically embedded at the point of design according to certified standardization and conformist protection guidelines. It's like each piece has its own fingerprint."

"Wow, boy. You're getting ahead of me. Slow down."

"It really doesn't matter whether or not you understand the RF, what is important is that it's a modified electronic gene. The equipment belonging to AC/DC Production is marked electronically, and you can trace it with a frequency tracker."

"Incredible, you're telling me that the stolen equipment can be tracked, even to the cave-in by its own calling card."

"Right! And that's how they create wizards. Priority protocol 2400 MHz."

"You are grossly underpaid, kid."

With the end of the rye toast, Gabe signaled for the bill as Bradley Turner came through the front door. He walked directly to their table.

"Hello Gabe."

Gabe looked up at the disguise and made a frog face. Bradley wore a Justin Timberlake newsboy cap and dark rimmed designer glasses, sporting yesterday's growth of beard.

"Bradley, so you've found us."

"I see that you're finished. Stay now and have a cuppa coffee with me."

Vera arrived with the coffee pot in hand. "Coffee's on the house. What'll you have, Turner?"

"Same as them, Vera, but get rid of the Marmite and bring me Scottish Marmalade. Marmite gives me bad memories."

Bradley began to rearrange the table in symmetrical alignment.

"You know, Bradley, by doing that you are leaving your calling card."

"Oh that, I can't help it. Things out of place drive me crazy. Even the salt and pepper shaker has to be exactly spaced and facing the same direction."

"Then you're the chap to answer my questions about the cave-in. What was out of place?"

Bradley's eyes shifted between Gabe and Troy. Closing his eyes, he backtracked to Thursday night.

"I'm entering the cavern and you are behind, telling me something. I couldn't hear you clearly because . . . because there was a hum from somewhere, maybe fifteen feet north."

"Great, keep going Bradley—sounds, sights and senses."

"Then a flutter . . . like a bird flapping its wings. No, like curtains flapping in an open window. Yes . . . I felt a light breeze." Bradley opened his eyes. "Wow!"

Gabe said, "We are making excellent progress men. Troy and I were discussing abandoned movie equipment and its capabilities. Capable of creating a wizard."

"Well, I'm sorry I was late."

"You're not, we have a full day ahead of us. Do you have any leads about Hennie's gang?"

He shook his head. "By the way, thanks for the tip about the shoes. It was embedded right into the tread, I never would have noticed. I haven't seen nor heard from Hennie since I returned from Harrogate."

"When we've finished here, we'll go to the Runswick site. We can accomplish more if we split up. Bradley, you set sights on the Grinkle mine. It seems they found some artifacts and are stashing it in the alum mine. Then we'll check for radio frequency signals at the cave-in. I overheard a conversation at the Cleveland last night that Hennie's gang plans to sabotage Becca's excavation site, so keep your eyes peeled.

"Bradley, I had a talk with Mr. Arbuckle from the Cleveland, and Stewart's name came up, the one you told me about. Keep an eye out for him, and follow if you see him. But don't approach him. He might recognize you and get scared off."

"Hello, Ms. Clayburn. This is my young partner here, Troy. He'll help me with measurements today if you don't mind."

She extended a hand and pretended not to notice his size.

"Not at all. It's refreshing to see young blood with a taste for detective work."

"Thank you, Ma'am. I'm particularly good with mathematics and Mr. Farrow was kind enough to include me today. Is it okay if I look at the items on the table?"

"Of course, but please don't touch. Here's a pair of disposable gloves to use in the tent, and shoe covers."

"Mr. Farrow, a friend of yours was here. He asked what we'd recovered and I turned him away. There isn't anything yet for novice eyes. I pressed for his name and he mumbled 'Mr. Henderson', but I have my doubts." She watched Gabe's eyes but didn't see any acknowledgment.

Gabe asked, "Did the gold fleck from the arrow match with carbon dating from the period of 1066?"

Becca grimaced. "Actually, it's not even 10 carat, and an alloy was added from a recent smelter. London is doing luminescence testing and radio carbon dating to track the gold source. The lead content is too high. Perhaps it's from a 1997 hoard between Harrogate and York. That one was investigated by Treasury, and a portion paid to a Harrogate precious metals firm. Every goldsmith leaves his tooling mark.

"One more thing, Gabe, a report came in that some graves at Whitby Abbey had been disturbed in recent weeks. I suspect that's where the skull came from, that the museum has."

"I suspected as much. Troy and I would like to make some measurements today."

"Go on down. Someone is working there now but go ahead and measure away."

Ms. Clayburn was smiling more this time.

"Thanks." Gabe gave her a thumbs up.

The second cavern was now supported with beams and joists. Inside, Troy knelt and opened his backpack, placing his transistor detector on the covered floor. Right off the bat, the needle was fervent, detecting the radio frequency he identified as part of AC/DC Productions.

"That's the same code I found at Odds & Sods, Gabe. It's back here. Careful, the soil is soft but on the left side there's a piece of wood. Look at the ceiling—tape is flapping."

Gabe nodded. "It's a fake wall."

"Listen," Troy said. "A faint hum from behind where the machine was installed. Why wouldn't the excavation crew have found it yet?"

Gabe said, "They move a square inch at a time with a metal detector. Why wouldn't this affect the signal of a metal sweep?"

"The production company's frequency is embedded with a cryptic code that wouldn't activate search equipment. But Scotland Yard or the Museum would know of its existence."

Gabe brushed the soil, exposing another wall opening, the ceiling with indentations from a wind machine and monitor. "Let's look directly outside the walls for clues or tire treads."

Gabe paced the same distance outside. "Troy, check these! Tracks from an ATV."

Behind, covered in a camouflage tarp, soil and grass grew over a large cargo crate, staked into the ground with a wayward section of cable protruding.

"That's been here a long time, long enough for grass. Get a fishing line from my pack and we'll thread it from between those oaks. We'll set up to photograph any movement."

"Troy, remember anything special about the first day we looked for tunnel entrances?"

"Yes, Mums says I have an excellent memory and sometimes it annoys her—so I don't always talk about everything out loud. But Gabe, I remember the stone slab."

"Right. The slab seemed out of place and you detected readings. Let's check the topography better. Pack our things back in the car; we're returning to the scene of our first crime," Gabe teased. "You remember where that was?"

"It was the first placc I took you. There was a scratch on the slab from a stone, remember? There were carved indentions making an odd shape, I meant to show you."

"Troy, treat me like an old man. When there's something important, make sure I'm paying attention. And if I don't acknowledge I heard you, nudge me and say it again louder. You're a walking encyclopedia, Troy."

"No, I pay attention in history class. I got an A plus."

"Did your history teacher ever talk about sites in the moors with ancient meeting houses or chambers?"

"There's nothing like that in Staithes, but the old Whitby Abbey might be a likely place. Of course, from time to time old burial caverns are found near Roxby Beck."

Troy was already climbing into the front seat of the Vauxhall.

"Ma is working tonight and said if you asked, I could have dinner with you."

"Thanks, buddy. We'll see. Bradley will meet us at Seaton Garth for a rehash today. Remind me to pay you at the end of the day." Troy smiled with self-confidence and belonging.

With Davis's maps, Gabe stepped through the terrain. Near the mossy slab was a trickle of a creek running through the metal grate.

"Let's leave the tunnel access for now. I'm interested in this slab."

Gabe ran his fingers around the circumference then dug with a trowel. "This is solid with a lot of depth. If it is indeed an artifact, I don't want to mar any part of it."

"How about building a wedge from another heavy object? Like the way you jack up a car when the tire's flat," Troy suggested.

"Look around for something to do that, like a Boy Scout." Gabe checked the museum documents for underground chambers, for possible secret societies in the medieval period.

"Gabe! Help!"

Troy was hanging on to a black, stone pillar projecting from the bank with his feet kicking in the air, not six feet from the limestone slab. A sequence of crunching groans sounded up from the earth.

"What are you doing?"

"I tried to see if this rock would move, and when I tugged, it shifted . . . like a lever. Hear that sound? It's from inside. Should I let go?"

Gabe reached his hands over Troy's. "I'll push it."

Adding his hundred and eighty pounds of body weight, the soil around the black pillar began to crumble, and the earth shed itself of about two feet of black rot.

"When I was your age, I remember a movie with relic hunters searching for a route to ancient treasure. There was one giant slab, like ours, and another rectangular rock with a key hole. This doesn't have that, but there could be a mechanism to open or move the slab. All of today's great inventions can be traced back to ancient superior civilizations and mathematics."

"Awesome! But it's heavier than we both are, how can we get it to open?" Troy was now wiggling with excitement, leaning over Gabe's shoulder.

"I have a friend in London that might be able to give me advice. Let's pack up for now. Bradley will be waiting at the Cod & Lobster."

While Troy loaded the car, Gabe called Davis.

12

THE LONDON MUSEUM saw more lines of tourists than a normal Saturday. Rumor had hit the press that the mysterious golden arrow of the eleventh century would become an exhibit in honor of the Battles of Stamford Bridge and the Battle of Hastings.

Without relenting, the most demanding of the reporters, the one from the Evening Standard, pushed for an interview with the curator of medieval antiquities, creating enough ruckus to frustrate the receptionist.

"As a citizen of Britain, I'm entitled to information. My taxes contribute to this building and the exhibits! I insist on just five minutes with the Curator."

"I'm sorry, Sir. It's Saturday afternoon, and he's no longer in the building."

Davis happened by, stopping at the commotion. "Hello, Dennis, I remember you."

The clerk moved some papers around on her desk, satisfied the man was no longer hers.

Davis provided his handshake and a smile. "We're delighted with the curiosity about such a significant time in our history, and we'll gladly share details with you later. As our clerk said, the Curator is not available, but if leave your card, I will give you a heads up when we have a further announcement."

The journalist backed down as Davis turned away to take a call came from Staithes.

"Mr. Farrow. I'm glad you called. We have a conclusive report that the golden arrow is indeed a fake. The detail was remarkable. Such precision would require either exclusive drawings or the real item. It's unsettling that a counterfeiter might actually put his hands on the genuine arrow."

Gabe said, "I have a box of history books of the Yorkshire Moors and I saw a sketch, an impression, of the golden arrow or a reproduction. It's possible the arrow was crafted from such a picture. I was expecting that, unfortunately. Today, however, I'm calling about a different matter."

Gabe relayed his discovery about the titan limestone slab. "I'm sending you a photo of the etching on the rock. Have the forensic lab people enlarge it and give an opinion. It's possible it is an outline of a dragon head."

"Gabe, we're ready to modify the Runswick sector to become a regular excavation—but if you would like Ms. Clayburn to consult with you, go ahead."

"I believe the limestone slab is a chamber doorway, but we'll need some muscle to move it. If it proves a viable theory, then the site security should be moved to Roxby."

"Yes, yes, of course. It's your call. Two security fellows are there that are strong and able to help. I'll go ahead and open the door with Clayburn, and you can get them whenever you need."

"Davis, one more thing. Bradley Turner has been on surveillance and suggested that Hennie might be the ringleader and Dodds the patsy. We won't concern ourselves with that right now, but keep it in mind."

"Will do. For now Dodds is on light surveillance."

Troy pretended to be drawing in the dirt, but had moved close enough to hear Gabe's end of the conversation.

"Does Mr. Davis know about me?"

"It is likely that the Museum would frown on me putting you in a precarious situation. They might even assume it is dangerous. So, no, I haven't said anything yet. Sometimes it's wiser not to say anything than get an answer you won't like. But be assured there will be a finder's fee. I'll make sure any reward is placed in trust for you, Troy."

"Yes, I agree, Gabe. Mr. Davis will meet me in 'due course'. Does in trust mean that you put your trust in me?"

"You amaze me, Troy. For your years, you are a wise old man. Yes, I do have trust in you, but when it comes to money 'in trust' means it is saved for you until you are of an adult age and better able to make financial decisions."

"Okay. Can I use your phone to let Mums know we're going to Cod & Lobster? Just so she doesn't worry."

Gabe walked to the back of the car and secured the trunk with the rest of their equipment. He could see the road up Boulby Cliff.

There goes the ATV. I wonder if Bradley is following one of them.

He and Troy jumped in the Vauxhall. He fell into a pace on the road parallel to the ATV, knowing they were headed for the alum mines.

"Troy, take as many pictures as you can."

At the silo depression of the mine, Hennie and Fergus removed the yellow tape and pried open a sheet of plywood over the entrance. With a shoulder check, they unloaded three small boxes. Darby was on point for them, smug at seeing a distant glint of sun reflecting on Gabe's binoculars.

Bradley was nowhere to be seen.

"Stay here with the car. Here's a micro receiver. I'll keep an ear bug with me so I can talk to you from wherever I am. Keep low." Troy delighted at gaining custody of another piece of transmitting evidence.

As Gabe neared the mine, Darby signaled to move to the huckleberry bushes, within twenty feet of the entrance. Hennie and Fergus were out of sight.

"Darcy, what's in the boxes? If it's part of a hoard, I need to document it with photographs."

"No . . . not now. Not if you want to catch them red-handed. They just yanked on the recovery lead and are coming up now."

"We're out of here then. See you at the mill tonight."

Bradley waited on the patio at Seaton Garth. He brought the Northern Echo newspaper to show Gabe.

"Gabe, a crime advisor named Harrison from North Yorkshire says artifacts have been disappearing in the last week from a suspected hoard near Whitby. A witness saw men digging at night, and another produced a dark picture of a vehicle at the Abbey the same night. Maybe that's where Hennie gets the stuff he buries in the mine."

"Is it the ATV, in the picture?"

"Maybe your London forensic detectives can tell," Bradley suggested.

"I'll pass it on. Did you learn anything about Hennie's caper today?"

"Darby stayed on lookout, then they took off with three boxes. When they left, I went in and found a lot of debris and fallen rock, leaving a pit."

Bradley held up a gold coin. "But they weren't too careful. They left this behind in the dust."

"Whoa! Is that real gold?" Troy leaned across, hoping to touch it.

"There's an emblem on one side, Gabe. Will Ms. Clayburn be able to examine it?"

"No, Bradley. We don't say a word to anyone. Got it?" Gabe's eyes darted between the two.

"You are both under an oath of secrecy. Any hoard discovered needs to be amassed. If it exceeds fifty percent in gold it is a trove. The Secretary of State determines the right of ownership. Either way, the coin doesn't belong to us. May I take a look?"

Gabe turned it over to see if the Hardrada triquetra emblem was stamped on the obverse. A chill from history overwhelmed him when he saw the imprint of a Viking king.

"I could use it as bait to tempt Dodds into the open," Bradley said.

"First, we'll assess the amount and source. Troy and I were at the alum mine when Hennie's gang came by. They had the boxes you mentioned. Troy needs to go home after supper, but Bradley, you and I will go back to the alum mine."

A waitress brought three large plastic bibs, pots of melted lemon butter and a variety of tools to dissect the lobsters.

"Holy cow!" Troy marveled.

"Have you ever had one of these before?" Gabe asked.

"Not a whole one to myself, just bits of meat in a salad."

Bradley said, "Watch me kid, there's a knack." He laughed at himself and his pretense to Troy to be a culinary expert on the mechanics of lobsters.

"We'll draw the rich, luscious meat from the claw. Then dip it in the butter and stuff it in your mouth. It's okay to let the juice run down your chin. That's what the bibs are for."

The three were fully involved and Troy was the first to see Becca at the door.

"Ms. Clayburn, over here. Would you like to join us?" he asked.

"That's dear of you, Troy, but I'll keep my distance while the shells are flying."

"It's alright. My Mum will be expecting me home. Gabe, I should go." He jumped to his feet. "You can sit here, Ms. Clayburn."

Troy went around behind Gabe's chair and leaned in to whisper. "You can pay me later. Tomorrow's Sunday, will we go out again?"

"Why don't you sleep in? I'll check with your Mum about noon."

Troy skipped off, whistling. The waitress cleared away shell buckets and lobster remains while Becca perused the menu.

"The river trout with lemon tartar," she said.

"Gabe, I received a call from Mr. Davis. It's too bad about the arrow deception as I hoped it would be a clue in Yorkshire history. I consulted with the Archaeology Council and a Heritage Monuments group as it would have helped to appeal for excavation funding. There's always a next time, right?"

Bradley quickly added to the conversation, to stay visible.

"Someone went to great effort on this deception, with movie, sound, and special effects to simulate haunting. What a farce—it's nothing more than a smokescreen to put us off track."

Becca said, "We will be packed up by tomorrow and turn over the site to a local study group."

Gabe nudged Bradley. "I expect we can trust Ms. Clayburn with your discovery."

"First of all, call me Becca. Ms. Clayburn sounds like my grandmother."

Bradley carefully revealed the gold coin, wrapped in tissue.

"It has a peculiar symbol on one side. Another party was digging in an abandoned mine, and as they were removing heritage goods, this was inadvertently left behind. But it could be deliberate."

"May I?" Becca held out her hand.

Her fingers trembled slightly. She tucked a wayward lock behind her ear.

"I've seen this once before. I believe it is from the same period as the original golden arrow. Could it be?"

Gabe said, "Since Davis has already spoken with you, can we arrange for some muscle to help move a rock slab? It must be close to a thousand pounds."

"It needs more than muscle, but we can't draw attention to the site. It'll turn into a circus. But I see two choices. If you hire a truck to bring out a crane, you'd become a news item.

"A more discreet way is to manoeuver it by chain and lever. Using the center of gravity, we can distribute the weight until it moves. The principle of a weigh scale."

"So excavation is your other area of expertise. Obviously chain and lever, I'd say," Gabe surmised.

"What would we need?" Bradley asked.

"Not much . . . a chain or straps to secure a load on a pickup, a center joist of metal or wood, and a beam about eight feet. That should be all."

"I don't know where, but we'll find them," Gabe said. "Bradley, can you commandeer your red pickup friend? We don't need the goods delivered directly to the site. The petrol lot will do fine and we can take it from there."

"Stewart . . . I suppose I could give him a try."

Gabe was content to sip coffee as Becca ate, and became conscious that she was taking nervous glances his way. He also bristled a bit noticing Bradley's interest in her.

"Where are you staying, Becca?" Bradley said.

"I had a cottage at Runswick, but if we'll be here a while longer, I'll move to Staithes. I saw a quaint row of cottages in the upper Beck. That way I can walk to most things."

Gabe said, "I have a car, Becca, if you need to go anywhere someone can drive you."

"I'll keep that in mind too, Gabe," Bradley said. He turned back to Becca. "I'm staying up the road at the Fox & Hound. They have cottages for short-term rent. It would be easier to coordinate transportation from there, right Gabe?"

Gabe poked Bradley with his shoe.

"I'm at the Blue Cove boarding house a couple of blocks up from High Street. My landlady, Mrs. Capp, had a sign in her window this morning with a room to let. It's up to you where you want to headquarter yourself."

Becca showed a modest smile at the chivalrous competitors vying for her attention.

"I'm sure both have unique advantages. Perhaps I'll take the morning to check out my options."

Leaving her at Seaton Garth, Gabe and Bradley drove to Cobbs' mill where Darby was to be waiting.

It looked undisturbed as Gabe expected for a Saturday night, with the loading bay's night light and motion sensor the only signs of habitation. They idled in the parking area and waited.

Darby finally tapped on the window. "Gabe, I hope you brought something to eat."

"By golly, Darby. Just a survival kit Troy put together. It might be juice boxes and granola bars."

"Hennie is suspicious. He whispers to Fergus, making sure I'm not close enough to hear. What good am I to you under these circumstances?"

"Do you have anything for London at this point?"

"I can vouch that pottery and relics were stashed in the silo."

Darby looked inside the car at Bradley, and stopped. Gabe sensed an unspoken communication.

"There's nothing else I can tell you," Darby said.

"Darby, we need something concrete to tie Hennie to Dodds or vice versa. What if we gave you some gold flecks from the Runswick vial. You could tell Hennie you overheard someone in town and followed them to the cave-in. A break-in is sure to placate Hennie and secure your loyalty."

"Worth a try, I suppose."

"I'll take you back to the Blue Cove tonight, Darby, but first I'll arrange for the bait for you."

He texted Becca and got an immediate reply.

"Hop in, Darby. We'll go by the Fox & Hound and I'll get you the sample. It tested positive for some level of gold combined with a modern alloy."

Mrs. Capp was knitting on the veranda under the moonlight when Gabe finally arrived for the night.

"I see your 'for let' sign is still in the window, Maude. I met a tourist in town that was looking for a place. I'll let her know you have a room."

"*Her* . . . it would be nice to have another woman around here. Put in a good word."

"Sure." Gabe turned to light patter. "It's a beautiful sky, isn't it? As a boy, I loved searching for the Big Dipper and Orion's Belt."

"I enjoy the stars twinkling over our little town. I knit afghan squares for the Ladies Auxiliary that sews and sends them to refugees . . ." She stopped. Neither could ignore the sudden raised voices from upstairs.

"Don't you dare cross me! I'll kill you . . . do you hear me? I'll kill you."

Gabe knew it was Hennie, but the intensity was alarming. Gabe and Maude were on their feet, without a plan. Suddenly, the screen of a window blew out from the third floor, and crashing glass shards rained down over the porch.

A shriek and pleaful cry for help was followed by a body tumbling through the open window from the third landing. Everything happened in seconds.

"Lands sake!" Maude was in a panic.

Gabe rushed to the body, fearing it to be Darby.

Hennie glared out the same window without a sign of concern.

Gabe leaned over the lifeless body in the yard. "Does Staithes have an EMS, Maude?"

"Just the lifeboat station. I'll call. Who is it?"

"I don't know—he's face down."

The front door flung open and Hennie, Fergus and Darby rushed past. Darby's face was white with fear, and looked frantically at Gabe as he was being pushed on by Fergus, holding something to his back.

Who the heck is this, then?

Rotating the body gently on its side, he recognized the ginger curls and the freckled face smeared with blood. He was clammy and cold.

"Bradley!"

"It can't be Bradley Turner. He went back to Harrogate weeks ago," Maude pleaded, her hands to her face.

A Hummer with flashing red lights wheeled into the courtyard and two men rushed out.

"What happened?" the driver demanded, apparently the sole EMS authority of Staithes.

"Maude and I were sitting here having a chat. There was a brawl of some sort on the third floor, then he came flying out," Gabe summarized.

"It's Saturday night and I'm understaffed. It's me and the kid with medical training. Mr. Farrow, will you call 101 and get an ambulance chopper from Whitby, this looks bad—his neck could be broken but he has a faint pulse."

Leaning over the stretcher, Gabe was relieved at Bradley's breathing. He retrieved his friend's cell, but it was too late to check his pockets for the gold coin flaunted at dinner.

I've got to find Darby. Was Bradley a double-crosser or did Darby turn him in to save his own skin? What's Bradley doing here?

In spite of the hour, Gabe texted Becca and Davis.

Becca was back in Runswick, and replied she'd meet Gabe in the morning to make a revised plan. Gabe said he'd pick her up and they'd load equipment to bring to Roxby Beck.

She was outside listening to the morning sparrows when he pulled up for her. Becca felt a twinge when Gabe stepped out of the car and she was relieved to see him.

"Becca, did Bradley say anything else about the coin?"

"When a person is nervous, often deception shows. His hand kept touching the right pocket of his jeans, and I assume the gold coin was there. I took detailed pictures of the coin—the markings are unique and I'd know it again."

Gabe said, "Davis will follow Bradley's condition and communicate with Jarvis Turner. He says you're an excellent field agent, by the way."

She blushed. "That's a rare compliment, and I'll take it."

"And he says you can stay on while we examine the new site. I'm pretty happy about that." Gabe glanced to see a pink tinge flush her face.

"I took Turner's phone," he said. "His messages say he arranged for Stewart to supply cable and a beam. They were to meet at the petrol station at ten today. Stewart hasn't gone through our vetting, so I'll keep my guard and pay whatever he asks."

"Gabe, can you make arrangements with your Mrs. Capp for the flat on my behalf. Under the circumstances, it will be best if we stay in close communication."

"I agree." Gabe felt an intense reaction. "Maude said she would really enjoy some female company for a change."

"I can do that. Sometimes old ladies know more than you give them credit for."

"Yes, old ladies and young boys."

13

DAVIS RECEIVED a cell call at seven the next morning.

"It's Jarvis Turner, Mr. Davis. I'll be bringing my son home from Whitby this morning. He passed away last night. It wasn't worth it for him to expose a greedy man. Bradley was a good kid and only wanted what was best for his family."

"I'm so sorry, Jarvis. What can we do?"

"Make sure Dodds pays for this. Besides being an embezzler, now he's a murderer."

"There was something in his personal effects. Something unusual."

"Was it a medieval gold coin?"

"Yes. What am I to do with it?"

"I'll send an envoy from the Treasury to take custody of it."

"Was this the price for my son?"

Davis was silent, searching for the right answer.

"If you and your family don't mind, we'll send a surveillance team to the funeral. Human nature often brings the guilty back to the scene. It's possible someone has reason to gloat."

"Go ahead, but I'll not mention it to my wife."

The funeral was scheduled to be in Harrogate on Tuesday afternoon. Davis sent a text to Gabe and Becca.

High Street was reverberating with rumors of the tragic events of the previous evening. When Gabe and Becca arrived at the Seadrift Café, M.J. was outside sweeping.

"Gabe, I'm so sorry about your friend."

She looked at Becca, and her face was pleasant but showed confusion about Gabe's new companion.

"Thanks, M.J. I'd like you to meet Becca Clayburn. She is the excavation site supervisor for the Runswick collapse."

"Pleased to meet you, Ms. Clayburn."

At Gabe's voice, Troy bounded from the Garth. "Ahoy, matey, have you come for me?"

M.J. grabbed his backpack and pulled him in. "Troy, I'm afraid I have is bad news." She looked to Gabe to explain.

"Hey sport, Bradley had a terrible accident, he's . . . gone. I'm sorry, Troy."

Stunned by feelings he had not dealt with to this point in his ten years, Troy looked forlorn.

"I'm sorry too, Gabe. He was your friend."

"Thanks, pal. I have business to take care of, but I'll call for you sometime after the funeral on Tuesday. I'll need to go to Harrogate."

"Sure." Troy brushed some dirt off his shoes, expecting it would conceal these strange new feelings.

M.J. put her hand on Gabe's arm as he turned to leave. "Gabe, you have no idea how much you mean to him. His face lights up at night when he talks, telling fantastic stories. You're always the hero; please don't change that for him."

At the Seadrift, Gabe felt the eyes of the town on him wanting to ask gruesome questions, but he held his head high. Darby was on his mind, but he'd committed to keep the relationship secret.

Darby, what have you done? I hope you are safe.

"Why don't we buy some pastries for Mrs. Capp? That will cheer her up," Becca suggested. Her selections were put into a pink box and tied with ribbon. "We'll drop this off on our way back up the hill."

"You go ahead, Becca. I need a word with the Arbuckles. I'll meet you on the porch."

Becca's long curls gathered in a clip at the back, and she wore sneakers and blue jeans with a soft, baby blue tee. Gabe watched her halfway up the hill.

Maude lit up as Becca neared.

"These are for you, Mrs. Capp."

"Bless your heart dear. Call me Maude. I was telling Gabe how I missed having a female in the house for a change. I had a lady with a young lad in your flat a few months ago, but she kept to herself. I'm usually outnumbered with young men, mostly gentlemen like Gabe, but those three from upstairs were totally unpredictable."

At ten o'clock, Gabe and Becca neared the petrol station and stopped beside the red pickup. Stewart was a quiet, young man, the same age as Bradley, but nervous at the first meeting.

"Hello. Stewart?"

"Yes, Mr. Farrow. I was sorry to hear about Bradley. We were pals a while back. I must have spoken to him only minutes before the accident." Stewart was kicking at the ground not wanting to make eye contact.

"Thanks. I see you were a member of an old club," Gabe said, pointing at the red scar on Stewart's hand.

Stewart turned away with a look of fear. "How do you know about that?"

"It means nothing to me, Stewart. Bradley mentioned that you'd be able to get us the supplies we need. Cable and beams."

"Right. I have them in the back under the tarp. Do you mind helping me unload?"

"The cable can go right into my trunk. The beam will have to remain here for now."

"I can move it wherever you want."

"No, this is fine." Gabe pulled an envelope of currency from his jacket. "Here's the price we agreed. Thanks for your help."

Stewart didn't bother to count the money, and was glad to get out Staithes.

Gabe unloaded the equipment at the Roxby Beck gully. Wrapping the end in discarded cardboard, he towed the beam as close as possible behind the Vauxhall.

Becca said, "I've checked out the slab again. We can move it, the two of us."

"You're the supervisor," he grinned. "How do we get the cable around the circumference?"

"It's like wrapping a parcel. The soil is soft enough to clear away with shovels. We can dig to the depth of the slab."

In next hour, Becca secured the cable from east to west and partially from north to south. The hiss of hot air balloons approached overhead, and Gabe covered the Vauxhall with branches and leaves. The pair hid tightly together behind the slab, staying out of sight as the balloon baskets brushed over the treetops.

Following a YouTube video on weights and pulleys, they wedged the end of the eight-foot beam under the center of gravity on the slab's bottom and rolled a joist under the mid-point. The limestone slab eased away from the bank, enough that they got their hands behind.

"Watch your feet, Gabe! This would crush them."

"Becca, if you guide the cable, I'll rotate the beam."

"It's working!"

With a two foot opening secured behind the slab, Becca shone the flashlight inside. It was dark and hollow. She turned on a sound recorder for their progress, and counted step measurements and descriptions out loud.

"The air is stagnant," she said.

"I still have oxygen tanks in my car from a previous search."

"Great. I'll wait."

Wearing the breathing masks, they eased down a slanted floor. The flashlights followed a path of debris and fallen stones from the sides of the tunnel, then a staircase led to a large chamber, with stone and wooden arches spanning the room.

Gabe lifted his mask enough to speak. "This is incredible, Becca. Etchings on the stone walls . . . am I right to guess that *this* is the eleventh century vault?"

"First impressions—yes. But it's too early to jump to conclusions."

"Look here. Old torches." Gabe lit a match to two stubs wrapped in oiled animal skin and hair. With a poof, the quiet chamber was a blaze of light.

"Incredible!" Becca shouted. "Ceremonies and rituals must have been here in the center, with these bones and lava ash. Maybe wild boars."

A ring of stones and stumps surrounded the fire pit, and a chamber opened to a narrow passage guarded by stone pillars. On each side, a symbol painted in dried blood depicted a dog with a skull and crossbones.

"This means the area has been blessed and that death or the black dog may not pass," Becca interpreted. "It must be the opening to the burial vault. They are all indications of pagan rituals."

"Over here . . . a handprint on the wall. Shine the light. Is it an ancient ink or beast blood? It has similarities to a large human hand."

"If this isn't Hardrada, it could be one of his sons. This is a truly monumental find, Gabe."

"Shall we continue to the vault?"

"First, inform Davis, and I'll bring in a decontamination unit. Every single sign, mark and location is a clue to the mystery unfolding here."

Sean Davis sipped a Sunday morning coffee at his Bath estate, a stone's throw from Whitechurch station and thirty minutes from his London office. Compensated well, he received frequent bids from institutions and universities based on his experience and degrees, but his loyalty stayed with the British Museum. At forty-eight, he presented an ageless air of dignity, with never a hair out of place.

"Yes, Davis here . . . why are you calling me on a Sunday morning, Gabe?"

Gabe was almost breathless in excitement. "We've found the motherlode, Davis. Ms. Clayburn's early conclusion is that we have indeed found the vault of Hardrada."

He stood to talk. "Blimey! Is that the truth?" Gabe waited in silence for instructions. "Let me talk to Ms. Clayburn."

A brief conversation followed. Becca nodded and repeated 'yes' numerous times, and at the end, turned to Gabe.

"A high security alert will be in force as soon as you relay the coordinates to Davis. He needs it instantly, and I'll put a security team and excavation technologists on site."

"Becca, take the Vauxhall to Runswick if you need to go. One of us should remain until the area is secured."

"I'll take you up on that. Don't venture further into the cavern until I get back." She peered up at Gabe as if whatever she said would matter.

Gabe spent the time in photos of the area and recording calculations for London. In less than an hour, a bronze Toyota Land Rover rumbled up to the open area near the cavern with a utility trailer in tow. Gabe assumed it was Becca's people and went to greet them.

"Hello, did Becca send you?"

The driver, a burly Anglo-African stepped from the vehicle. "Becca who?"

"Stay where you are," Gabe demanded raising his hand to halt. The driver continued to approach regardless, and another man with a threatening demeanor stepped from the passenger side.

Minutes later the Vauxhall arrived.

"Gosh, guys—you gave me a start. You didn't say you were with Ms. Clayburn?"

"We *are* with Ms. Clayburn, but you asked if we were with Becca. Who's that?"

Still ruffled, Gabe barely saw the humor, but Becca laughed at the confusion.

"I'll introduce William and Charlie with the security unit. Gentlemen, this is Gabe Farrow, the lead investigator."

"What about permission to access the site?" Gabe queried.

"Davis said he'd take care of that. Roxby Beck is part of the North Yorkshire Moors National Park. Archaeological finds supersede district authority, and I can't see a problem. The area doesn't obstruct any thruway or access to farmer's fields."

"How do we keep this confidential? If word gets out that this is Hardrada, the press will swarm us like ants."

"My security team has been with me for years. I trust them with my life."

"While you set up, I need to find a friend who has gone missing. I'll be an hour, I expect."

Gabe parked on the crest of the hill, and paced down toward the silo, sensitive to everything he passed. He inspected the soil as he walked, finding no discernable footprints as the morning dew had already evaporated.

With a branch of leaves, he swept away his own footprints near the mine. At the plywood sheet, he photographed a smear of dried blood.

Gabe stood to listen for a vehicle or any movement. A pair of birds called from the sumac trees, and the shape of a balloon vanished on the horizon. He scanned in every direction, but stopped to squint at the far-off green fields, dotted with grazing sheep.

The sun is reflecting across the field. It's a mirror . . . or a photo lens. Someone is watching.

Creeping to the car trunk, he removed a rifle that Davis had loaned him as a precaution. It had never been fired, but Davis kept it even after the English population was restricted from owning firearms.

From a position hidden in the thicket, he focused again on the reflection. A high-powered long-range rifle was aimed his way.

Who is it that has such a prohibited firearm? Military?

Gabe zoomed on his target. The man was suited in camouflage, with a three-headed serpent tattoo on his hand. He wondered if they made eye contact.

Bradley's gone. And the military rifle? A single shot would alert farmers and tourists across the county."

Crouching on knees, he moved forward through the field. He spotted a camouflaged military helmet to the side, and took cover in the high, sweet grass. Still no movement from the target.

Gabe stayed put until his cell phone vibrated. It was Becca, and he was about to answer when someone rose nearby in the bushes.

The assailant stood over him with the cold rim of a rifle touching his right temple. "Get up, Gabe Farrow. The hide and seek is over." The bright sun was blinding from the assailant's back.

"Stand up! Turn around with your back toward me."

The opponent kicked Gabe's rifle into a gully.

Gabe didn't know the deep, garbled voice, and assumed it was a deliberate deception. "What do you want with the alum mine?"

With his head down, Gabe observed the man's Hi-Tec hiking boots, dusted and damp from the dew, with a blob of white paint.

A bandana was then tied over his eyes, and with his hands yanked behind, plastic ties were tightened to dig and cut into his wrists.

When he'd had enough, he shouted, "Enough!"

"Do you remember the military march?"

"Yes."

"Step exactly as I instruct you. One, two, three, four . . . One, two, three, four. Bigger steps now!"

The rifle barrel was jammed into his back.

No one knows I'm here. I wonder how long before Becca looks for me.

Gabe counted the distance at a yard a step, and when he slowed, the rifle butt burrowed deeper.

"Halt now! Hold up here! Now, slowly back up until the back of your thighs feel a hard surface . . . Sit down. You won't fall."

Gabe felt the metal panel of a pickup truck bed and sat back. His feet were tied with the security straps, then swung around into the cargo area, and his body was covered by a tarp.

"This is what you get for sticking your nose in other folks' business. Why couldn't you accept the myth and legends of the moors and let our theatrics be?"

He heard the driver's door, and when the engine turned over, he knew it wasn't Stewart's. More like an older vehicle, with smells of diesel fuel and sounds of a leaky muffler.

They traveled for twenty minutes at normal speed, and Gabe contemplated the route. Either back toward Runswick Bay, or toward Whitby. Along bumpy roads, Gabe heard the splashing surf.

The North Sea. I could be on the upper bank along the cliffs.

Two hours after Gabe left the vault, Becca attempted the first call to his cell, then intermittently for another forty-five minutes.

"Mr. Davis, I'm sorry to disturb you. Mr. Farrow left some time ago and hasn't returned. He mentioned Boulby Cliff, but I don't know the reason. I've tried his cell repeatedly but I don't get an answer. It rings, so it's turned on. Did he say to you where he was going?"

"No, but I'll have security in London trace his number. They'll get a location."

Minutes later, she read a text confirming a live signal from his phone at Runswick Bay in the railway tunnels—'Two men are dispatched to find him. We won't resort to bringing in local authorities.'

The Land Rover sped onto the Hinderwell road with William and Charlie of Becca's excavation team destined for the coordinates for Gabe's phone signal.

Still blindfolded, Gabe wasn't sure of his directions in the tunnel. His foot straps were released for his walk from the truck into the old railway tunnels. The rails and rotted ties made for unsteady walking.

"Here, stop!"

"Mr. Farrow, we'll get better acquainted later, but for now you'll remain here." His assailant pushed down on Gabe's shoulder. "Sit down, there's an infested blanket to sit on." He spat as he spoke.

With a two-handed shove, he was on his knees in the mud. His guard placed a call keeping his words muffled by his hand, but Gabe heard enough of it.

"Mr. Henderson, the package is in place and the alum mine is ready to close up. They'll never find Darby there, buried with the movie apparatus. I could smell the methane, and he won't have long. It will be an 'accidental' slide."

The guard listened for ten minutes to Henderson's scolding.

"Yes, Sir," he said. The man's voice wobbled in fear from Henderson's intimidation.

Gabe closed his eyes under the blindfold.

I should have told Becca what I was doing. If Darby stays low, he'll buy time. Gases will rise to the ceiling with longer viable oxygen on the floor.

"Well, pal, you're on your own for a while. Take my word that it's best to stay put. These old tunnels harbor secrets galore—and vermin, snakes, and ghosts."

Gabe's waist was chained and locked to the wheel of an ancient cart, languishing on a rail. He knew his cell could be traced. The man had taken it from him, but he guessed it could still be in the tunnel, as it had vibrated when they had entered.

With the slack in his chain, he found a trickle of water from a natural, rocky fountain in the wall, and licked at the drips. He knew the urgency of the throbbing and numbness moving up his arms to his shoulders. As its swelling progressed, the plastic straps tightened even more.

If I can find a piece of shale or a spike, I could cut these, then look for my phone. A cell lockout in the mine is likely, but I could get outside.

A hundred thoughts raced through his mind including his threatening conversation with Jarvis Turner.

In a few hours others will look for me. I'm due at the Cleveland at five. Tomorrow, Niles will think I've left town, but he knows the situation I've got myself into. I should have told Becca about Cobb and his gem.

With a dull flint, he hacked at the straps, only creating nicks and cuts that drew blood, but without breaking free.

His blindfold allowed no difference between day and night, and he kept his wits by marking his estimate of the passage of time with marks in the dirt. Recalling details from past hours over maps and routes, he visualized his probable location.

At the excavation site, Becca continued to wait at the perimeter as the museum team began analysis of the outer chamber. She was becoming increasingly anxious for Gabe's return.

"Reynolds, no one is to go beyond the first room. We'll wait for Gabe to come back and we'll make the findings together."

She stood, filming the activity as she observed the progress. Numerous forensic markers were placed from the slab door, down the limestone stairs and around the ceremonial pit.

A document photographer scoured every foot with continuous rapid shooting, alternating his cameras and lenses. Becca's mind alternated between the reverence of the chamber and the worry about Gabe.

"I'm sorry gentlemen—I'll leave you to your examinations. I'll be in the site tent."

She moved outside, wondering if Gabe had acquaintances other than the boy.

Her instincts said Troy was the one to talk to.

14

WILLIAM AND CHARLIE followed a pulsing blip into the railway tunnel, and walking straight, they dodged piles of rubble from a recent collapse.

William raised his hand and they froze to listen.

"I hear water. Trickling. Shhh. It's straight ahead, there's no further access. Farrow is either trapped beyond this cave-in or in a parallel channel. Can you open the mine route blueprint?"

"I've got it," Charlie said pulling up the map on his cell. "We're in the southeast arm. Another tunnel is ten meters to our right, and a structure ahead appears to have a route into the west arm. That must be the area with the water."

"Put on your air filter to be safe. The ceiling has a few old ventilation fans to circulate the air; I wonder if we could find a power source and reboot."

Charlie crawled the length of the floor, following a heavy-duty, twisted cable wrapped in old cotton duct tape.

"I found a floor switch."

They listened. It cranked, then groaned and rumbled. Then a purr.

A fluster of dust and debris collapsed from the ceiling, but the ventilator still hummed.

Do you hear any sound that could be Farrow?" William asked.

The two yelled out. "Ahoy, Farrow! Ahoy, Farrow!"

Gabe, still gagged, tied and blinded, was stunned at a muffled sound of his name.

Gas must be getting to me. I was sure I heard someone call my name.

Kneeling on the damp floor, his hands felt for something heavy to make a noise. Finding an old pipe, he crawled until he bumped into a rusted jigger.

I'll bang three times and listen. No use wasting Morse code on the bats . . . bats! There must be a fresh air intake.

William turned his head at the faint clank. He called again and listened at the wall.

"I'll double-back and try another lane," Charlie said.

Bang . . . bang . . . bang.

"Listen!"

"Farrow! Farrow!"

Three more resonated in reply.

"It's him. Now how do we find him?"

Becca raced on foot to the Endeavour to find Troy, helping M.J. on the patio.

"Good morning, M.J." She didn't waste time and blurted out, "I need Troy's help."

"Oh, no! But what can Troy do?"

"I'd like to talk to him and get any locations where Gabe has been with your son. Everything must be checked."

"Of course," M.J. replied, but Troy was already at her elbow.

"Troy, can you tell me all the places that Gabe took you. Secret or not."

"When a man makes a pact of loyalty, it isn't meant to be broken." The ten year old boy stood firm like a man.

Becca looked surprised at the wisdom of the freckle-faced lad. "How can we work with that, Troy? Gabe has been missing for quite some time. We fear he may have crossed paths with the wrong people or met danger."

"Can I talk with Mr. Davis?"

"Mr. Davis? What do you know about him?" Becca wasn't sure if she should laugh or come down with a heavy hand.

"Which is your question?"

"From my agreement with Mr. Farrow, Mr. Davis was in charge."

"It's Sunday, Troy. I don't want to disturb Mr. Davis at his home if it isn't an emergency."

"Have it your way, Ms. Clayburn."

Troy turned back to the umbrellas, tight-lipped.

Becca helped herself to a chair and dialed London.

"Mr. Davis, I have an accomplice of Gabe Farrow here. He insists on speaking with you before giving up information to locate Gabe."

Troy, standing erect, straightened his hair and his shirt and took the cell from Becca.

"Mr. Davis, my name is Troy Duckworth. I have been a scout and guide for Mr. Farrow for the last few weeks. He has trusted me with information that I promised not to tell. I understand he might be in danger and would expect me to help."

Whatever Davis said brought a smile to Troy's face.

"There are three sites that we investigated—the alum mine at Boulby Cliff, the Port Mulgrave arm of the old railway near Runswick, and the gully at Roxby Beck. He didn't let me go in the excavation site of the old Viking in Runswick. Would you like me to take Ms. Clayburn to those locations to see if we can find him?"

Banter back and forth continued until Troy was happy with the reply and handed the phone back to Becca.

"Well, Ms. Clayburn, it seems you have a new recruit. He's a local boy and knows the terrain like the back of his hand. He will be better than a map. Makes assurances to the mother," Davis said.

"Let's go, Ms. Clayburn. Gabe won't mind if you use his car. He showed me how to hot wire it if I found myself needing an escape from danger. Part of my Boy Scout training." He winked.

M.J. looked both appalled and amused.

"The Vauxhall is missing."

"Well, that's your first clue. Tap into his GPS and we'll find it. Hop on my Mum's bike and keep up."

Troy stood at the top of the hill on High Street and took his bearings.

"If this is where he was, he would've been looking toward Boulby Cliff. The old alum mine is there that Hennie's gang often went to. If he saw the ATV or Hennie's men, he would have gone closer."

The uphill climb was a bit much for Becca, but she wouldn't allow a ten year old boy to show her up.

"There it is, Ms. Clayburn. There's Gabe's car. We can put the bikes in the hatch and go closer."

Checking the ground behind the car, Troy picked up an empty shell casing. "No one around here uses guns except for the clay pigeon shoot, and those would be rubber bullets. He walked up this way until he got to the huckleberry mound. From here he crawled on his knees or stomach. He must have seen something unusual."

Becca noticed too that the long grass was depressed for some distance. "Yes, this happened in the last few hours. You're an excellent Boy Scout."

Keeping pace along the path, they came within reach of the mine entrance.

"Look at the ditch—this depression. He took cover here, I'd say." Troy got down into it for the correct vantage.

"His head was here, so he was looking over there—see the indentions from the toe of his boots. Toward that Sumac tree. Something or someone must have been there. But he didn't go that way as another set of tracks is over here. Looks like a kafuffle of some sort."

Troy was on his knees feeling the depth of treads. "Here's a big hiking boot; from the tread it looks brand new. The imprint is deep enough for a heavy man."

Becca spied the wood butt end of a rifle on the ground on the next ridge. She snapped a picture and tagged it for evidence.

"It's loaded but hasn't been fired!" Davis's initials were on the barrel.

"Maybe anticipating danger," Troy replied. "Two people went this way." He paced fifteen long steps to the tire tracks.

"Here, Ms. Clayburn, there was a vehicle. From the width between wheels and the tire size, I'd say a truck."

"Well, Troy, I went to Girl Guides at your age and I never learned to do tracking like you."

"Gabe showed me how. I'm his lookout man."

Becca suddenly realized Troy was a ten year old boy and not a grown man. He had genuine fear on his face. "Don't worry Troy, we'll find him."

"I know." Troy kicked at a small rock.

The trail of tire marks led back to Boulby Cliff Road where the Vauxhall waited.

"We can't do anything more here, Troy. You did really well."

Becca's phone beeped with a message.

"Great news, Troy. My security guys have picked up Gabe's cell at the Grinkle mine. I'll need to meet them over there."

"I'm coming."

There was no room for discussion. "I usually spend Sundays with Gabe anyway." Troy ran ahead to the Vauxhall and was sitting shotgun when she got in.

"The air vent must have an intake and output point. Look for a buried ventilation shaft, Charlie."

Starting at the wall by the entrance, their digging and picking accelerated and uncovered a length of tubing. Their spirits were high, bolstered by the taps with Gabe, now louder.

Finally, Gabe had a breakthrough by severing his wrist ties, and he ripped the duct tape from his mouth. With strips from his shirt, he wrapped tourniquets around both bleeding wrists.

"Hello! This is Gabe Farrow? Who's there?"

Unsure if they heard him, he kept it up, echoing on the stone wall. He found his cell, but the battery had died.

With no light, he felt his pockets for anything that could help, and laid out some Cod & Lobster matches, a penknife, a gas receipt and an Odds & Sods business card.

From the mine, he scrounged for loose articles and gathered some shards of rock, driftwood and oiled railway ties, a twine, a tin can and sundry other scraps.

His best find was an axe head, and with two swift chops to the chain, he was free. Exploring further, he found a glass insulator on a broken EXIT light. He pounded a hole in the side of the can for air, and built a tiny tinder fire from debris into a makeshift lantern. He held another match in the air hoping for a breeze, then another match until a flicker came from his left.

In the tunnel's southeast arm, William and Charlie were in a parallel line to the noises, then the ground shuddered a warning and chunks of mud slid down the walls from the ceiling.

"Farrow? Stay where you are."

"Okay. I have light now."

"Do you see a ventilation shaft?"

"No. But a partial railway track with a jigger on three wheels. I have an axe and can dig if I know where."

"The jigger . . . that's good. We have a bit of track here too."

Gabe froze at a shuffling sound behind.

Is it the guard?

The Vauxhall arrived at the Mulgrave entrance of the railway tunnels, and Becca parked it out of sight.

"Follow me, Ms. Clayburn. Something you should see before we go in."

Climbing a man-made bank to an upper ridge, they stopped by the decrepit shack of a long-ago manager. Troy shuffled his feet to feel below the thistles. "I know a trap door up here, somewhere. Billy McGuire and I found it a few summers ago. Then Gabe and I saw Hennie's men lift equipment from the hole."

Becca stayed close, poking and circling her shoe through the grass.

"Ah! Here it is." She tugged at a heavy iron ring.

Inside the wide hinged door was a ladder descending about ten feet.

"I'll go first, Ms. Clayburn. I'm smaller . . . it's all clear, you can come down too." They left the trap door open for light.

Troy shone his flashlight onto a collection of movie equipment piled at the base.

"They look similar to the sound machines in the fake chamber," Becca said.

A tag was on one. "It says Odds & Sods," Troy said. "Horace is a good guy; he couldn't know that Hennie's gang is stealing from his shop."

"We'll find Gabe, then come back. Does it lead anywhere?"

"It was an air raid shelter in the war as this was a flyover for German bombers. There's a bedroom, stove and toilet, and boxes of tinned food and glass bottles of water. Someone could stay a long time and set up hauntings of the tunnels to keep folks out."

Becca fought silent urges of claustrophobia, and needed to move on. "Is there access to the Mulgrave arm to find Gabe?"

"Over here."

Behind two stacked wooden crates was a four foot refrigerator door that opened into the wall. "You'll need to duck and stay hunched over for about six feet before the opening. Use your flashlight, Ms. Clayburn."

Troy raised his hand. "Shhh. A noise."

"I heard it too. What is that?" she whispered.

"A pipe banging. And a breeze from this ventilation shaft." He put his head into an opening. "A distant purr, maybe from one of the tunnels."

His small voice echoed. "I can fit in it. In that direction I'd be obstructed by the fan but this one is okay. You should wait here."

Troy pulled at a lever, and a flap door dropped from the ventilation chute. He hoisted his eighty-five pounds up and wriggled inside.

Becca said, "Take this rope. And call to me so I know . . ."

His feet disappeared, and he hollered as he crawled. "Gabe! It's Troy."

Troy's voice was clear through the vents, and Gabe called back into a metal manhole in the center of the arched brick ceiling.

"You're close! I see your flashlight moving."

Directly above, Troy released the vent maintenance door and dropped to a cross beam. His arm reached down through the wide manhole and he looked across the room.

"Gabe, take my hand. Quickly!"

Then his voice raised abruptly. "*Now*, Gabe! You don't have time to argue about it," he yelled. "Remember the pulley system? Gabe!"

From Troy's eyes and voice, Gabe knew something perilous was behind him.

He turned to see the shooter in a black hooded mask, and recognized the long-range lens from the alum field.

Troy lowered his rope for Gabe's arms, and pulled with all his might with his feet anchored on a rafter. A bullet zinged off the ceiling inches from his head. Gabe jumped straight up about three feet and braced his arms above the manhole, then flung himself clear as two more bullets fired in the darkness. The pair collapsed onto the brick floor above the manhole.

Troy was in command. "Jam a pipe in the vent hatch and no one can follow us. Becca is waiting at the other end."

Minutes later, they burst through the other end, falling through the trap drawer to the floor of the air raid room. Gabe looked up at Becca, then at the sound equipment, with speakers teetering on the top.

"Is *this* the haunting source for the Runswick excavation? Why the ruse?"

Becca texted William and Charlie. 'Gabe is safe, get out of the mine. There's a shooter. Meet at supervisor's shack.'

The refrigerator door was latched and the trio pulled through the upper door to daylight. Without looking back, they fled inside the manager's shack, and Becca radioed for security. Two more shots pierced the air, and William and Charlie burst outside.

They all clustered together for cover in the tall grass. "We were almost through from the other tunnel," William said. "How'd you get out?"

"I have my own Guardian Angel." Gabe tousled Troy's curly locks. "You were really brave. If your Mum knew what you did, she'd never let me see you again."

"That's not true, Gabe. She talks about you like you're my big brother."

"I knew M.J. was a smart woman." Becca slid one arm around Troy and the other on Gabe. "Troy and I need to fill you in on today. Davis okayed the new recruit."

"Becca, take Troy with you to the car. William and Charlie—come with me. A man in the tunnel was firing with a hunting rifle. Check for a pickup or anyone around the mine entrance."

Becca found binoculars in the glove compartment and braced herself on the hill with Troy. "Do you see that? A pickup speeding toward the Hinderwell Road."

Gabe ran to her with the same observation.

"Too late, he had a good head start."

"Becca, if you're here with William and Charlie, who's guarding Hardrada?"

Becca picked up her cell.

"Thank goodness, Reynolds. I'm on my way back right now."

Troy studied Gabe's face without a word until halfway back to Roxby Beck.

"Are you sending me home now?"

Becca listened to Gabe's silence, then spoke up. "I need to check-in at the site office, then it's *my* treat for a steak dinner. We have a lot to discuss and I need to fill in a few reports."

"Are you in, Troy?"

"Yes, please. Do you mind if we eat at the Endeavour. It's not just a pub, but has a great steak. If you don't like that, the Royal George across the street has the best baron of beef."

M.J. was relieved when they entered. "So glad you're all safe and sound."

"Mum, they know the Endeavour makes the best steak dinner. We're a bit peckish from roaming around the countryside."

"Peckish?"

"You know . . . hollow."

"Shall I bring you ale or wine with your dinner?" M.J. asked.

Gabe looked sheepishly at Becca. "How be we celebrate with a bottle of burgundy?"

"I'm in."

Troy started the discussion, recounting his scouting and tracking, and assured Gabe he'd provided lookout services for Ms. Clayburn.

Gabe said, "When I was taken, the sun blocked my vision and I didn't see who it was. Just a silhouette. But I noticed his shoes."

"Steel-toed hiking boots, right?" Troy boasted.

"How'd you know? The treads, they were new."

"Yes, new, but the right foot had a spot of white paint. It isn't easy to get paint off hiking boots without leaving a mark."

M.J. overheard the chatter. "A lot of tourists come through here. I'll pay more attention to boots; sooner or later he'll be wanting a drink."

"Good, M.J., but careful—he's dangerous."

"M.J., where could a man buy a pair of Doc Marten's in town?"

"Naw, you'd need to go to Whitby for that."

By the time the plates were clear, Gabe was ready to level with Becca and Troy. He lowered his voice.

"When I was put in the mine, my assailant phoned someone named Henderson. He said that Darby crossed the line and was 'taken care of' in the alum mine. No one could survive for long without oxygen. It's full of methane and I think Darby was murdered."

Troy's mouth dropped with alarm. "You don't think Mr. Henderson could be Hennie do you?"

"By golly, Troy. I didn't connect the similarity. Of course, that's possible."

"If that's the case, it's not safe for you to return to the Blue Cove," Becca cautioned.

"It's a small town, Becca. Half the residents already know we're having dinner here and what we ate."

Becca laughed, assuming Gabe was joking.

"No, Becca, it's true," Troy added.

"If it's not safe for me, it's also not safe for you."

"M.J.? Do you have room for Ms. Clayburn upstairs for tonight?" Gabe whispered.

"Yes, a room is available. Anything you need, you can borrow from my closet. I'll get you a key."

Becca waited, then asked. "What about you?"

"I have a place to go. Niles has a spare room at the mill. In the morning, I'll stop at the Blue Cove to check in with Maude. I'm curious whether Hennie or Darby have shown their faces."

"I'll come with you, Gabe," Becca said. "I'll need a change of clothes."

"It has to be before breakfast so I'm at work by nine. But Maude has morning tea early."

"Gabe, we need to go into Hardrada's chamber soon, before you go to Harrogate. Davis will want the goods delivered to London as soon as possible."

"Okay. Roxby Beck tomorrow after work."

When the grey Vauxhall pulled up to the boarding house, Maude ran from the porch.

"Good gracious, Gabe, you wouldn't believe the stories I've been hearing about you."

"We're fine, but there are unseemly activities going on. Have you seen Hennie or Darby since Bradley had his accident?"

"Hennie and Fergus stormed in late last night—they were drunk as skunks so I kept a distance. He has scratches on his neck from the episode with Bradley. The Whitby police came by and did some measurements and asked more questions."

"Did anyone else come to see Hennie?"

"Funny you ask. A truck stopped out front yesterday morning and those two from upstairs jumped in and they were gone. It was noisy taking off; a bad muffler I think."

"Did you recognize the driver?"

"He made a point of me not seeing him and held a newspaper near his face, but my gut says he's been here before."

"Did you catch a license number or model?"

"Gabe, you know I pride myself on the accuracy of my information. Gossip is a skill, not a habit." Maude laughed at her joke, and rifling through her apron, she pulled out a napkin from the ice cream shop. A partial number was scribbled on a corner."

"Pure genius, Maude. I'll need to take this and check it out."

Gabe stopped. "I'm sorry I missed the eclairs this week, I'll make it up to you. I'll be working at the mill most of today. Then tomorrow I'll go to Harrogate for Bradley's funeral."

"Yes, dear boy. I'd go myself but I'm no good at that sort of thing."

15

DODDS WAS IRATE that Gabe escaped from his grasp. Chasing the trio toward the manager's shack, he felt a new murderous surge in his veins. Shaking with anger, he aimed and shot three times, each over Gabe's head. Fleeing the crime scene in the black pickup, he sped to the boarding house.

Dodds cursed and blasted the horn for Hennie.

That busybody landlady! She's watching me. I should have clocked Farrow good and I wouldn't be in this predicament. Jarvis is fanatical about getting that golden arrow and Farrow is my ticket into the museum.

Jarvis's private cell rang above the East Parade.

"Dodds. Why are you calling me?"

Dodds allowed himself to ramble. "I could have cleaned up the threat by killing Farrow here. What is your issue—that we must keep him alive?"

"I told you, it's complicated. There's some history I need to resolve."

"History! The golden arrow is more history than you could ever hope for," Dodds said.

"It's personal. Don't press me on that—it's between me and Farrow."

"Whatever. I've spared your boy for now," Dodds said, "but Hennie and I need leeway to proceed with the heist. Word is that the museum exhibit will move to London soon, and I've sent Fergus ahead to get hired into their security unit. A fellow there owes me a favor."

"Right. No one will recognize Fergus, not even me," Jarvis grimaced.

"I pulled strings with a Treasury board member and got the museum's blueprints for the exhibit area. The security firm has details of the alarm system. Some magnetic fields to deal with, but we'll take counter measures."

Jarvis said, "And you think you can walk in and pick up the golden arrow?"

"Hear me out, Jarvis. I've learned a bit about Farrow's habits from Bradley and Hennie. He has two weaknesses—the kid that hangs around him, and the girl from the excavation site."

"Go ahead, I'm listening."

"Two ways to handle this. We could take the boy, and Farrow could deliver the goods as ransom. Or I could just make a threat of that to Farrow. He can't take care of the kid when he's in London."

"The longer the scheme drags on, the more attention is drawn to our company and ourselves. The museum theft must be swift and without a footprint," Jarvis said.

"Alright, I'll proceed with Hennie about the details and get back to you." Dodds softly added, "We didn't mean to hurt your boy."

With more pints than they could handle at Smuggler's Boathouse, Hennie and Dodds blubbered about the genius of their scheme to let the excavation continue, then usurp the goods under the noses of the hoity-toity at the museum. Both delighted in setting Fergus up as the inside man.

At a table for two with his fisherman buddy, Niles Cobb hadn't taken any notice of Hennie, but as they grew more boisterous, he lent an ear.

"Ha-ha," Dobbs bragged on. "My contact with the museum's security unit has specs to disable the exhibit. We can trip the second set of lasers with a higher magnetic field. It's a sophisticated system, but none too clever for me and my men. Farrow will have to oblige or we threaten to kill the kid."

Hennie hooted with overconfidence and slammed his mug on the table. "Waitress, another over here."

Dodds tried to muffle his slur. "When should we snatch the kid?"

"As long as it's even trade. The kid . . . for the golden arrow and the gold and gems that were left in the coffin. The museum heist will take them off guard. Makes me feel like a pirate." The pair were now in drunken stitches. "We'll let one of them walk the plank," Ferguson roared.

The restaurant manager came to their table.

"Gentlemen, it seems you're having a good time. But this is a family establishment so I need to ask you to take it outside. We won't be serving you another pint."

Dodds' faced reddened with a response, but just as quickly he forgot what it was he wanted to say. The pair eased out the door supporting one another in laughter.

Gabe heard the back door latch. "Mornin' Niles. Coffee's on."

Niles had a pained look in his eyes. "My mind has imagined terrible things, Gabe. I'm glad to see you safe and whole."

Gabe put his an arm on Cobb's shoulder in a gentlemen's hug. "I knew I could trust you. The tale is now complicated. You know about Bradley Turner and the discovery of a fake golden arrow. Now the thugs are coming out of the woodwork and I'm doing my best to stay in front. I took advantage of your invitation and stayed here last night."

Stirring double cream and sugar, Niles weighed up how to say it best.

"Gabe, I don't want to heap onto your list of oddities in Staithes, but I walked my dogs in the upper sheep fields yesterday. A large, black truck was near the mine, and I know I've seen it before."

"Anything you remember about that will be helpful."

The order basket was full and Gabe regretted neglecting Niles and his duties at the mill.

"I see you can't get along without me," he joked, and thumbed through the papers. "What's my priority today?" Gabe came to an abrupt stall, seeing Niles' distress.

"What is it? Are you alright?"

"Sit down, Gabe." Niles moved the glass buoy to the side.

Niles clenched his hands and Gabe knew something vital was about to happen.

"I was in Robin Hood's Bay with a pal last night. Lo and behold, Hennie was there with that stranger fellow. I'm afraid they're no good. They are scheming to kidnap Troy to make you give them the golden arrow. They were drunk so I'm not sure how accurate the plans are, but the gist of it was that they would let you take the find to London.

"Fergus, the hop-along fellow, is an inside plant and they would walk right out the front door with the goods. They said you would have to oblige or they'll threaten to harm the kid."

"By Jove, Niles."

"I can't be certain if they decided to kidnap Troy or just threaten you with harm to him. If not him, then Becca."

Gabe was stunned and speechless for a few moments.

"Either way, this is incredible."

His troubled eyes looked back. "Niles, I'll need to ask for your help. I can't always guard Troy. When the exhibit goes to London, can the boy work here so he is supervised?"

"Of course, of course. I've known M.J. and Troy since he was a babe."

"I need time to think this over."

Gabe then jolted himself back to reality, and neither spoke as Niles passed him some work orders.

"Here, take these two and I'll work on the third. I guess you'll be going to Harrogate tomorrow for the day."

"You know the funeral is important. I assure you I'll be back on Wednesday."

"Yes, yes. Do what's right. When you leave today, can you take those boxes to the Cleveland? They already sold out the last of them."

Gabe was to meet Becca at 3:00 p.m., and she waited inside. His heart was pounding when he finally arrived at Roxby Beck, delayed by the Cleveland delivery. Hearing Cobb's suggestion that Hennie was possibly planning harm to Becca, incited him.

The contamination system was functional and he was screened and prepped with a dust jacket and shoes before entering.

She lit up at his sight but stopped abruptly at the concern in his eyes. He was intense but said nothing.

"Hardrada is waiting for us! Hurray! I've been on pins and needles all day for you." He picked up a portable floodlight to take inside, then put it down.

"First, there's something I need to take care of."

Gabe inched closer until he could smell the lavender scent in her hair. As he put his arms around her waist, she raised onto her toes. In a moment of surrender, they came to a new understanding, with a long, soft kiss and lingering embrace.

"There, that's settled. Now we can get to work." Gabe felt a burden of relief.

Niles' news will spoil our moment. No need to worry Becca now.

"Definitely." Becca scanned the words on her chart and watched Gabe from the corner of her eye, enjoying the tingling his embrace had left.

"Gabe, are you ready to meet history?"

"Absolutely."

A pile of pre-numbered rocks was removed from the entrance to the burial vault. A single slab stepped down into the lower chamber, with the roof low and arched, showing few signs of age.

"It's hard to focus on the attributes of science, when we are the first humans to step into this chamber in a thousand years," Becca declared.

A pair of fragile wall scones enhanced the entrance, and they inspected them without touching. The room was barren, except for a raised, limestone platform and a bronze rectangle in the middle. Her technicians spread a plastic contamination curtain over the entire area, and Becca confirmed a satisfactory humidity level and the absence of foreign matter.

"The trunk is sealed with animal wax. I'll need to photograph this thoroughly." After a prolonged examination, she felt ready to raise the lid.

"So little rust or decay has taken place. The cavern has been uncontaminated for so long."

The lid groaned and creaked from the initial attempt to wedge a gap, before raising it all the way. As it cleared, Gabe took one end of the rectangle, and Becca the other.

Becca led. "One, two, three . . . heave." The two technicians at her elbow took possession of the lid.

"Oh, it's incredible!" she cried out.

Before them was the massive skull of Hardrada. Some neck vertebrae were intact and a solid gold arrow pierced the right eye socket of the substantial skull. Pouches of jewels, precious metal and gemstones were in the corners.

"It was a ritual, to be sure, that Hardrada could buy his way into the hereafter. This certainly confirms he was a man of great esteem and financial status."

Becca snapped pictures from all angles, stills and video, and texted them to London.

Davis called back right away about the discovery. "This time, there seems to be no doubt about the authenticity. Well done."

Becca gave Davis a spontaneous, verbal report of facts, measurements and opinions. He taped the call for the record, then spoke briefly with Gabe.

"You're going to the funeral in Harrogate tomorrow? What time is it?"

Gabe said, "The obituary listing says it's the Co-operative Funeral facility on Knaresborough Road. The service is at 2 p.m. Are you coming?"

"Yes, I'll have Lloyds meet us in Harrogate and they'll transport the skull chamber to London. Can you bring it with you? Ordinarily I wouldn't ask, but you have security staff at your disposal and I understand you have your own car. Ms.

Clayburn will take the appropriate measures to ensure the safe transfer."

"Under the circumstances, I'll borrow Becca's Land Rover and take William and Charlie. Will that be enough protection?"

"Why don't you bring Ms. Clayburn too? She has access to a .22 revolver, should there be a remote chance of an ambush. We're on a secure phone line."

Becca had been listening and nodded, ready for Davis to wrap it up. "We'll meet at Lloyd's Bank on Cambridge Crescent in Harrogate at noon. Ask for Mr. Reid, the bank manager."

At the outskirts of town, the drive to Harrogate in the Land Rover became eventful. Gabe was in the passenger seat looking for anything unusual, and spotted a black truck well behind them. He advised William and Charlie, who were in front in the Vauxhall, leading the way.

Several blocks from Cambridge, the truck moved closer, and nudged their bumper. The Rover veered to the shoulder and back onto the pavement. The crate shifted, but Becca kept control. Gabe alerted Davis by text.

Becca switched on a portable emergency siren she placed on the roof of the vehicle.

"That should scare him off. Can you see their faces yet?"

"Afraid not."

The undue attention deterred the truck, and it pulled off at the next exit.

At the Lloyds Bank, Becca stopped directly behind the armored security vehicle at the curb, opposite the front doors. Davis was waiting and marched quickly to the car.

"Glad to see you've arrived right on time. Looks like you avoided a radical driver."

"Radical, Davis?" Gabe said. "The truck followed us from Staithes. When he realized our destination, he made an attempt to intercept. Can you put an all-points bulletin out on this vehicle?" Davis examined the phone photo and the zoomed scratchy scrawl of a plate.

"This shouldn't be difficult."

Two armed guards opened the Rover's hatch and eased the rectangular box into a metal crate with a seal, as Davis signed the documents of value and limits of authority. Another pair of guards waited at the bank door to receive the transfer.

"There, we're free of the cargo for now. It should be at the museum by the time I return to London," Davis said.

Mention of London worried Gabe.

I wish I had specifics of Dodds' plan. For now, we're lame ducks.

Becca wore a finely tailored, navy suit with a crisp, silk, ivory blouse. Gabe was cleanly shaven, in a dark charcoal suit that Mrs. Capp had insisted on pressing. Silently, he admired a pin on Becca's suit.

Sean Davis, Becca Clayburn and Gabe Farrow took seats together in the mid-section of the funeral chapel. A closed oak casket was at the front surrounded by floral tributes, and Jarvis Turner and his wife stood next to it, receiving guests who opted to approach. Davis and Gabe took turns to proceed separately with condolences.

Gabe's handshake to Jarvis was firm and their eyes met, with no words yet. Gabe leaned to whisper, and Turner's face reddened as the acrimony of their last meeting was still fresh.

"Your accusations are absurd, Mr. Farrow. You've made a mistake, but this is not the time nor place."

Returning to his seat, Gabe's face was flushed too.

Davis said to Gabe. "I can't help but notice a lack of grief from the family. Jarvis said they were totally stricken by Bradley's demise, but I've never seen such a flamboyant, grief-stricken mother. Everyone handles it differently, though."

"Did you know it would be a closed casket, Davis?"

"No, but I didn't know of the extent of the boy's injuries."

"Nor did I."

The service was Anglican by a parish priest. The eulogy was by Jarvis Turner, with tributes from a cousin and old friends, and a beautiful prayer, sung by his sister.

A reception was hosted in the basement hall. Gabe slipped outside. The black truck was empty at the end of the lane. He managed to pop the door lock, and planted a bug in the driver's seat.

Family and friends traded memories over tea and finger sandwiches, next to a display of family photos. Gabe was drawn to pictures of Bradley as a lad Troy's age, fishing and camping, then college photos, and family Christmases.

One photo stood out to him, of Bradley with his arm around his father; on the other side was Ian Dodds, with his arm around Bradley too. All three were beaming. The picture was autographed by Dodds as a 21st birthday gift, 'I will always be here for you, signed Hydra'.

His family dotes over him, but I could pierce their happy balloon in a flash. From what I know of Hydra, it's a three-headed serpent. So that's the link to the tattoo—it's a brotherhood.

Off to one side were two men in dark suits, cleanly shaven with fresh haircuts, both with sunglasses.

Davis pointed them out to Gabe. "The man closest to corner is Ian Dodds. His head has been turning to follow you since we arrived."

"It's almost funny, wearing sunglasses inside," Gabe said. I wouldn't have recognized Dodds anyway. I've never met him."

Gabe looked again at the two men, and nearly choked.

Incredible—the other man is Hennie. With a scruffy beard and work clothes, I'm sure that man is Mrs. Capp's tenant.

Sharing his suspicions to Becca, Gabe felt his own deep rage mounting.

Who's the boss? Hennie or Dodds? I've become a pawn for both.

He dug in his heels and stared back at Ian Dodds from head to toe, ensuring Dodds knew it. He wasn't about to be intimidated, but would play the game.

I wonder if he wears steel toed Doc Martens on the weekends.

Gabe watched as Dodds fidgeted, adjusted his tie and squirmed from the prolonged eye contact. Dodds whispered to Hennie, and both men glared back, waiting for Gabe to make the first move.

Gabe took long, confident strides across the room, scared but enjoying their suspense.

"Congratulations, Mr. Dodds, on your appointment to the Treasury Board. That will be more convenient for you to convert bullion and ancient coins."

Gabe neither smiled nor extended his hand. He leaned to talk and slipped a microchipped coin in Dodds' pocket.

"I'm glad both you and Mr. Henderson were able to come today. I never would have figured it out if you hadn't shown up as a couple." Gabe pointed at visible skin-toned bandages on Hennie's neck.

Dodds' eyes were steely-grey.

"My partner, Mr. Turner, would be surprised that you have come with ulterior motives, other than sympathetic. I really don't know what you're talking about."

"I'm not at liberty to give you advance warning. But your ruse with the golden arrow is up and your sound effects in Runswick are exposed. Yes, you succeeded in frightening the community with your labyrinth of theatrics.

"You should be shaking in your boots. I have a witness to Darby's demise, and the pottery chips you pass around to sites have your fingerprints. You didn't think Darby was dumb enough not to have collateral worth his life, do you?"

Gabe had lied, having no knowledge of fingerprints. He abruptly left and returned to Becca.

Hennie said nothing, and Dodds stood with his mouth gaping—then became flustered as he tried several times to call Gabe back over. His erratic behavior became embarrassing as others noticed it, including Jarvis Turner, who moved over to calm him.

"You're upsetting my family, Ian. This isn't the place for your dirty laundry."

In the lot, Gabe told Davis, "There's a bug in their truck."

"Let me know what comes of it. I'll be returning to London with my chauffeur."

"So Hennie *is* Henderson. I can keep up with developments in Staithes, but we need dedicated surveillance in Harrogate."

"I'll see what we can do," Davis said.

Half the vehicles had left, but in the far laneway, the black truck remained.

"Under the giant oak, Becca!"

She looked and nodded. "I feel we're standing in the midst of our enemies. I don't trust any of the Turner or Dodds affiliates." Over her shoulder, eyes were on her. She dropped the car keys on the ground.

"I've got it, Becca." As Gabe bent to retrieve them, he surveyed the lot. Hennie and Jarvis Turner were in intense discussion and Gabe turned up the volume of the receiver. It wasn't clear which man spoke first.

"You said you took care of it. What is Farrow doing in Harrogate?"

"I left him in the old tunnel with no hope of an escape. I returned last night to ensure he was out of commission.

Someone helped him through the roof and ventilation shaft, and he got away. Don't worry, Mr. Henderson.

"I followed him a few days ago to the old mill near Hinderwell Road. Fergus is preparing a car bomb for me to place under his Vauxhall. If that doesn't warn him off, he should run for his life."

"See it through. Farrow is a thorn, making it difficult to get the Whitby coins out of Yorkshire. Once the treasure is extracted, cover your own tracks and get out of Staithes. The community is far too nosey."

Becca and Gabe listened in alarm.

"If Davis heard this, especially the car bomb, he'd pull us off the case."

"See this lapel pin, Gabe? There's a mini cam behind the amethyst. I didn't get anything that you haven't, but I'll send it all to Davis's forensic lab."

"Becca, perhaps you should return to London. You will be safe there."

"No, I promised Troy that when he's in school, I will take over as your lookout man."

Niles' words about Becca were screaming in his thoughts but it was too much to dump that part on her today.

"Becca, it's time we warn M.J. to keep a closer watch."

"We'll finish crating in a few days and I'll complete the manifest. For now, I'll move over to the Endeavour and keep an eye on M.J. and Troy. Maude won't like it, but if she knew the truth, she'd insist on it."

"We have involved far too many good people. Archaeology is generally a safe occupation."

Becca said, "You didn't know what to expect when you came to Staithes. Davis was on a trail of stolen bullion, but he didn't know it would lead to murder."

"I'll be back at the Blue Cove tonight to see who turns up. My sound and visual mic is in their unit, and I set up a webcam where the sound equipment was kept."

"Gabe. About what we discussed when we met in New York—are we still on track? Whatever happens, I've got your back. Can I look at your news clipping once more?"

"Yes, nothing has changed that." He unfolded it. "It's either one or it's the other, but it's clear they're both Brits. Twenty years can change a person dramatically with hair loss, moustache, a few pounds and whatever."

"I have my woman's instincts, but I'll reserve my selection until we gather more evidence." Becca looked closely at the two men in suits. "I'll scan it with my phone if it's okay, and when I get back to London, I'll spend time in the newspaper's archives."

"First things, first. The truth is bound to come out on this."

Gabe's flat was cool, with his window open all night. He kept it dark, without running the water or the TV.

He checked under the floor mat in the dark and felt a fresh nick in the pine floor boards.

"The only other people that knew about this were Bradley and Darby."

He lifted the tin box. "It feels heavier." On top of the newspapers were an envelope and a wrapped instrument.

By his phone's glow, he read the message:

Gabe, if you read this, I may already be dead. Hennie's on to me. They concocted a scheme with Jarvis Turner to make you look foolish and intercept the Hardrada arrow. Mr. Turner was part of a ruse to leave egg on Davis's face and put him off their trail. I moved the Whitby coins and buried them in the alum mine in the wind machine. Also there's a file about the fake precious metals scam Dodds runs. Thanks for your faith in me.

It was 2 a.m., and he tiptoed down the staircase. He took the bike, as the Vauxhall would be heard in town.

Niles Cobb would arrive at the mill in five hours, and he'd ask for some days off. The mill was too isolated, and a kidnapping would be easy for Hennie. They knew Gabe would cooperate to save his friend, if it came to that.

A light rain left the cobblestone shining. He passed the Roxby footbridge and a few miles later saw the distant, tall, night lamp outside the mill. The sign 'Cobb's Mill' waved in the breeze.

At the far end of the turnout, a man got into a black truck.

"What has Dodds done now?"

Gabe hid the bike a hundred feet back, and waited in the outer garage for sunrise. Afraid of dozing, he stretched a low fishing line from a fence post to the garage, and attached two galvanized pails.

"That'll wake me up if anyone comes. They're talking about bombs now, and I wouldn't forgive myself if Niles suffered any consequences due to my involvement with Hennie's gang."

Tapping his Q-Pro phone into the bug on Dodds' truck, he found active vibrations, suggesting he was still within fifty feet. The signal locked on a site across the road at some abandoned tractor equipment. With a night scanner, he made out the shape of a man in the ditch, with the same long-distance rifle lens.

Gabe woke Niles by phone, warning him not to come to the mill due to the impending danger.

"Gabe, I'm not afraid of anyone. It's my mill and I won't be intimidated."

"Trust me, Niles. A sniper is fixed on the front of the building and it's possible he may have rigged a bomb to one of the doors. Stay at your home until it is clear."

"I'll not stand for this, Gabe. I'm going to call the police."

"Please Niles, let me arrange for undercover security to deal with it."

"Call me in half an hour, or I'll come," Niles asserted.

Gabe phoned Becca from the garage about security support.

"This is bigger than we can handle. It's time to bring in the Yorkshire Crime Unit. We need a swat squad to disarm the sniper and any possible bomb."

"My authority is limited, but I'll have Davis make arrangements right away. Stay out of view; we know what he is capable of."

"I don't have any weapons for protection, however, Niles had a hunter's bag hanging in the garage. I'm certain I saw the ends of a bow and arrow. My archery skills might need to be tested."

Rifling more, he found an ideal slingshot for his back pocket and returned to his point next to a galvanized rim of a drainage barrel. The man was still in the farmer's ditch, but there was no sign of his black truck.

There must be a second man to have moved the truck.

Through the amplified speaker, he now heard a different vehicle, with a quieter engine, close now to the parking lot. It wheeled into the mill yard, disrupting the booby trap pails, with a crash and clatter.

There are two black vehicles.

"Not a very sophisticated night alarm." Both men laughed.

Two police officers paced the outside and checked doors. An additional unmarked black police vehicle sped in behind.

Gabe saw no movement from the ditch, except the withdrawal of the rifle barrel. He ventured out with his hands up and approached the first officer. As he did, the shooter took a stance to fire.

"My name is Gabe Farrow. I'm the one who made the complaint about a sniper. He's behind you, across the road."

The warning came too late for a second officer who was stunned when a bullet struck his safety vest.

"Get down, Mr. Farrow!"

"He's armed with a long-range rifle," Gabe said.

The mist provided cover for Dodds' black truck as it skidded from the bush, with its tinted windows concealed the driver. Coming to a screech near the sniper, he slammed on the brakes and threw open the passenger door.

The second police vehicle tried to cut off its exit, but only slowed it slightly.

A traffic jam was converging near the mill, coming from the direction of Staithes. Gabe saw the Land Rover and Niles' delivery truck near the front of the line. The passing lane had sirens echoing in the distance, approaching at high speed.

Meanwhile, the criminal black truck was being pursued in the opposite direction.

Niles turned his truck ninety degrees on the road near the mill, and got out to redirect a parade of curious viewers to turn around and go back to town. Two unmarked cruisers in line were radioed to turn around and join the chase.

"He's headed for Saltburn. I phoned Jimmy at the Lifeboat Station and he's going to blockade the road at Cow Bar Bank. There's a limit to where they can go," Niles boasted with new authority.

"Does he know not to approach, that they are armed?"

Niles' face fell. "By golly, I didn't know that."

"Jimmy! Jimmy! Come in." Niles called on his radio.

For a few minutes there was no answer, then to Niles' relief, Jimmy answered.

"I've parked the rescue vehicle in the middle of the road, but I'm taking cover myself. I'll fire a flare if I see them."

For a hamlet the size of Staithes, everyone was on alert. Local shortwave and ham operators were broadcasting events. There wasn't a chance of the black truck leaving the moors without being noticed and reported.

As far as Gabe could see now, pickup trucks were parked sideways on the road, impeding access.

An insurance nightmare! Seems we've got our own army.

Gabe rushed to Becca and asked to take the wheel of the Rover. In 4X4, he mounted the ditch and gunned the vehicle across a sheep pasture to resume on a cow path lane. The Boulby Cliffs were in his rear view mirror, with the back drop of Beacon Hill coming up on his left.

The immediate terrain took him to unsteady hills and dales until he joined Cleveland Way. Bypassing lush green dales and moorlands covered in heather, he stayed in view of the stone walls marking the way. The black truck was still in his vision bypassing Staithes, through Port Mulgrave, Runswick Bay and Sandsend to the coast of Whitby where the River Esk joined the sea.

The truck, being a heavier vehicle, spun in the dirt on the route overlooking a link of coastal villages. His determination was focused, and the two men gloated as the 4X4 became distant.

Gabe said, "I know where he's headed. But I'll get there first." He recalled his first impression of the gang, when they motored by boat into an unmarked sheltered harbor.

"Becca, call the police to tell them where he's headed. Have someone in Whitby haul the red, inboard jetty ashore and anchor it well. That should stall them. Lobster trawlers will already be at sea, so their only option would be the fishing cobbles. We've got them!"

Looking back, Cobb's truck was forging its way through rugged terrain. "No, Niles, no. Old men don't chase criminals," he muttered under his breath.

Becca was on her cell for too long and turned to Gabe. "They said for you to back off; they will take care of it."

"No way! As an investigator for the British Museum, I have a vested interest in capturing the men. They tried to kill me, likely killed Bradley and Darby, and raided the grounds of Whitby Abbey." His voice had a fierceness she hadn't heard before.

"Remember Gabe, they're armed and you're not."

Amused briefly, he wondered how good his shot would be from approximately fifteen feet. "I once cleared a squirrel from two trees with a single pebble."

"I don't know what you're talking about, Gabe. Whatever you decide to do, I've got your back." Becca was glued to the GPS. "The Lingrow Cliffs are ahead on the other side, but there's no easy way to take the Rover down that incline. How be you hop out and jog the Kettleness footpath to the harbor, and I'll take the long way around and meet you at the beach."

Without a reply, Gabe threw the Rover into park and tore down the muddy path, with Niles' sack over his shoulder.

The slipperiness from a recent mist propelled him faster than his legs could carry him, and nearing the bottom, he was covered in mud, head-to-toe. "A better disguise than I could have thought up myself."

Behind a breakwall, dozens of lobster traps waited for use. It was close to the jetty, and would provide cover. Gathering a handful of suitable pebbles, he laid his ammunition in a row on the ground and set two arrows beside.

From above, the black truck careened out of control, sliding down a ramp and pivoting into a gully. They revved, but stuck deeper, then Hennie got out, followed by Dodds. Fergus was nowhere in sight.

Noticing the Land Rover pursuing them, Hennie took the rifle and fired at Becca, then chased behind Dodds to the beach.

"It's not here, Ian." Hennie pulled at his hair in confusion.

"It's over there."

Dodds pointed to the freshly anchored jetty. As he moved within range of Gabe, the distance police sirens echoed louder.

"Quick, get it into the water."

"I'm trying. This anchor took more than one man."

Gabe looked up the stairs to Whitby's Seacliff Hotel. Word was out, and the front balcony overflowed with spectators waiting for an impending capture, many pointing and laughing at the predicament of the jetty.

Gabe was now just twenty feet from Dodds. He removed the slingshot from his hip pocket, and with determination, fired a sharp pebble. Struck in the temple, Dodds stumbled, and rubbed his head, dazed.

Using Niles' bow, Gabe's first arrow was for Dodds. Taking it in the thigh, he yelped and crumpled to the ground, losing consciousness. His second aim would be for Hennie, but was too late, as the culprit was cornered by four policemen.

"Hands up!"

The crowd was delighted and the boldest ones cheered.

When Hennie saw Gabe, he was livid and blurted out, "I should have killed you myself, but Jarvis was noble and insisted you be spared."

Standing close, Gabe noted Dodds' hiking boots, with the smear of white paint.

Becca was laughing at Gabe's comical appearance. "Is that you in there, Gabe Farrow?"

"I guess I could use a shower." As he shook his limbs, clumps of mud fell from his clothing and hair.

At Cobb's Mill, a police sweep found a pressure bomb under the front welcome mat, and a search of the Vauxhall revealed an automatic detonator improperly wired into the starter.

Coinciding with their work at Hardrada's excavation site, the museum staked claim to any hoard at the alum mine. With the discovery of Darby's body, they called in Mr. Harrison again from Whitby's Crime Unit.

At first access in the mine, Gabe staked thirty feet down the silo decline, then turned north and shifted through mud and debris another five feet. A hollow space rattled in the base of the wind machine, hiding a heavy tin box. It was exactly where Darby had left it, with the remaining contents of the Whitby Abbey's scavenging by Hennie's gang.

Ian Dodds and Dwight Henderson took the Fifth Amendment, but the London and Harrogate newspapers flashed pictures and articles of national shame based in their own Treasury. Dodds and Hennie were promptly incarcerated, to wait impatiently for bail arrangements from Jarvis.

Jarvis resorted to confiding with Bradley. Profoundly fit for a dead man, he had been moving about conveniently as the gardener, while living in the Harrogate guest cottage.

"Bradley, you understand we *must* have the Hardrada cache—our Chinese buyer is getting impatient. Dodds and Hennie hatched the plan to intercept the exhibit when it arrives in London, and an inside man will handle the alarm system. You need to go back to Staithes and put the kid on hold."

"What do you mean . . . put the kid on hold?"

"It's our leverage so there are no complications in London. You have lots of hiding places in the moors to stash the kid," Jarvis said.

"He's a smart kid; it won't be as easy as you think."

Jarvis was in a rage at that. "If you can't do it, I have others who will cooperate."

16

POLICE TESTED and grilled Jarvis Turner, hoping for any lapses to help the case, and journalists from London arrived for press conferences and an inside scoop on Ian Dodds.

Jarvis managed to maintain his solid reputation through the scandal, staying steadfast in denying Dodds as a friend and peer.

"My relationship with Mr. Dodds was strictly business. He has a financial background and dealt professionally with transactions and precious metals entrusted to us."

A London News man badgered him. "What about the Silverdale Hoard years ago? It was reported you personally profited from that discovery, taking more than a finder's fee."

"As I recall, I was informed after the fact, and only shared in the respect that Mr. Dodds needed our firm as a vehicle for processing. We provided an arms-length service and maintained the highest integrity."

"Can you prove that?"

Turner's short fuse was showing. "Perhaps you should address your questions to my attorney, since you have resorted to challenging me about unsubstantiated tidbits twenty years old. For now, I have no further comment. I reiterate that Ian Dodds is no longer affiliated with this firm. We are in the process of changing the company name to 'Turner & Son'. I understand that the Treasury Board has rescinded Mr. Dodds' appointment and no one from this office will have future participation on that board."

As he made his way through the media throng, journalists kept peppering him. A young women yelled, "Did Ian Dodds murder your son?"

"Preposterous! Now out of my way, I have matters to attend to."

A member of the museum's surveillance team blended into the media, standing on the front steps of his firm. He taped and reported Turner's comment verbatim, noting the reference to 'Turner & Son', since Bradley was his only known son, and in spite of Jarvis's explanation of a posthumous honor.

Since Bradley's funeral, Davis had nagging concerns about the Turner family's behavior, and field agents were assigned to follow and report his activities.

Davis was equally deluged with media at the London office over the discovery of the golden arrow at Roxby. Historians from across Europe and America begged for interviews and consultations, defending their rights that history is not owned by any one country or generation.

Clara Perkins, a history intern, was appointed from the museum's PR Department to field inquiries and send press releases about the discoveries at Roxby Beck. Somehow the location was leaked, starting a rush of curiosity-seekers to the area, requiring an expanded security team on location.

Becca coordinated the Roxby and Boulby Cliff teams, until the bulk of Darby's deposit was moved to the British Museum. After that, the mine was sealed with concrete.

Darby's identity remained a mystery, and Davis ordered a search for next of kin, otherwise the state would assume expense for a simple cremation at Stonefall Cemetery in Harrogate. After seven days, no one came forward.

Davis moaned to Gabe in a call, "If we had declared he was eligible for the finder's fee on the Whitby Abbey find, a lot of loving relatives might have come forward—a significant sum to be sure. Darby's box had solid silver and gold coins, worth a tidy sum."

"We could do that and see what happens. Pilfering from Yorkshire has gone on by this gang for years. There must be others with knowledge. A picture might draw some out. We don't know for certain that Darby is even his name. Someone knows him."

"Agreed. I'll give specs to Marjorie and she can post an ad in Harrogate, Whitby and London."

"I'll be in Staithes until the weekend. Call with anything at all. The Whitby police still have questions about the beach incident."

"It's too tidy for Jarvis Turner to give up his partner and turn a blind eye to the goings-on. He's a cold man, and not to be under-estimated. Hennie and Dodds will transfer to the London jails soon. Whitby and Harrogate haven't objected. They'll be relieved."

"Davis—we need to talk."

"What, Gabe? You can trust me with anything."

"Reliable information says that Dodds and Turner have a plot afoot, that you and I need to discuss."

"Let's not trust the security of our cell phones. Is it urgent?"

"I'll come to London soon. I'll need to investigate more."

The voice message from Detective Harrison asked to meet today if possible in Whitby, and Gabe called right back, hoping for news.

"Mr. Farrow, we need your help while clues are fresh. In person is best—your phone could be tapped."

"It'll take me an hour."

Harrison was joined by the Captain and two officers. He was polite and straight to the point.

"Gabe, please tell us what's going on. This is a peace-loving country, and we haven't had bombs here since the war."

"What do you know about Viking history in the moors?"

"You can refresh our memory if it won't take long."

"Well . . . in 1066, England's throne was being fought for by two kings. Hardrada Godwinson, the King of Norway invaded Yorkshire from the North Sea, and his troops waited here before planning to attack an English blockade of Stamford Bridge. With so much piracy and pillaging, their treasures were buried in caverns and underground chambers, and are now being discovered.

"What drew me was a rumor at the British Museum, that thieves carelessly let a gold coin from King Hardrada surface in an unrelated hoard.

"That was a year ago, and I was assigned by the museum to find the thieves and intercept the hoard. The gang recovering these coins were processing them through the black market, with the bullion melting by the crown's own Treasury Board."

The Captain said, "Mr. Farrow, this sounds like an incredible fantasy, but can you get to these current crimes now?"

"The puzzle will fall into place soon. Ian Dodds, in your jail, masterminded the criminal bullion distribution, with Dwight Henderson, his accomplice, working the hoards. It's uncertain who's the boss, but both are responsible for the murder of three men—Axle, a gang member that died in the alum mine; Bradley Turner, thrown from a third floor window; and an unidentified man, Darby, who double-crossed them. He was buried alive.

"The museum has now excavated the site of Hardrada's burial, and sent the discovery to London."

One of Harrison's men asked, "Does the Yorkshire Heritage Society lay claim to a portion of the hoard?"

"I'm not involved in legalities; I work for Mr. Davis at the London Museum. You should take up those questions with him," Gabe summed.

Harrison said, "Since the arrest, neither of the men has given a statement. They refuse a comment and deny knowledge of any hoard."

Gabe looked disdainfully at the inquisitor for wasting his time. "These are conniving, murderous men. What did you expect them to say? You can call me any time to answer your questions, but if there's nothing else, I have business to attend to."

"You'll let us know when you have plans to leave the jurisdiction of Yorkshire-Hinderwell, Mr. Farrow?"

"Certainly." Gabe rose and shook Harrison's hand.

Davis called within minutes.

"Gabe, you made an impression on the Crimes Unit. They called to verify your credentials and then to challenge our authority. It's nothing for you to be concerned about, as Scotland Yard in Victoria is negotiating with the National Crime Agency for custody of Henderson and Dodds, in London's jurisdiction.

"Also, we're paying closer attention to Jarvis Turner. I'm sending you a picture of him at dinner with an unidentified man in Harrogate. It's the man with the fisherman's toque and turtleneck sweater. Zoom in on his right hand, Gabe—there's a serpent tattoo."

Gabe was alarmed at the photo.

"It's Bradley Turner! No wonder his parents didn't grieve—he's alive. And in cahoots with Dodds after all. His story was a total fabrication.

"Since the funeral I haven't been entirely convinced of Bradley's death. I researched the possibility of someone administering a drug to induce a physical state of appearing to be dead. Is it too late to test for tetrododoxin?"

"Can't rule out anything anymore, can we?" Davis added.

"It appears that Bradley is the walking dead, but who helped him is another question." Gabe concluded.

Davis was in stunned silence, waiting for more from Gabe.

"Just like it might have been Hennie in charge instead of Dodds—what if it's the same about Turner and Dodds? Is Turner the boss? So what else has he conjured up? We've assumed only that Hennie's gang is stealing hoards from the British people—but what if it were the reverse, that they are planting counterfeit hoards?"

"Scotland Yard is advising us," Davis said. "I'll test the coins that we know were processed through his firm. Can you gather enough evidence to support a search warrant for Jarvis Turner's office and any safes in their building?"

"Becca and I will get on it right away."

"One more thing. A seamstress from Leeds has claimed the body of John Darby as her brother, and arranged for his burial at Hunslet Carr. A small reward was granted to her.

Delia was newly assigned the tracking duties for every name in the hoard's file, and wasted no time running checks on Bradley Turner, Dwight Henderson, Ian Dodds, John Darby and Gabe Farrow. The findings produced a surprise—a Securities investigation on the selling of gold bullion certificates outside the country without substantiated assets in the UK.

Davis examined the reports over the weekend. First thing Monday, he removed a business card holder from the back of his desk bottom drawer. Folded in a square was an embossed certificate issued by a Florida gold scammer twenty years before. This was the first time he looked at it since arriving in England and investing himself in archaeology.

He closed the office door to read the report again in silence. He noted that Dwight Henderson and Ian Dodds were from Cornwall and moved to Leeds ten years before. Hennie had served five prison years for fraud and embezzlement from an insurance scam, then went under cover and worked on gold smuggling. A prior note was handwritten on the bottom—'suspect in Skytracker Investment scam in Sarasota, Florida'. It was twenty years before and no charges were laid.

"Insufficient evidence, my foot! It takes two to tango—they're both guilty." Davis's fury was mounting, hoping for vengeance. He put aside a plain folder for 'Gabe Farrow'.

Davis's Risk Management chief waited outside to discuss the counterfeit analysis of the gold coin Jarvis Turner had offered. His conclusive report confirmed that the alloy and dye cut was a match to the same hoard Dodds & Turner claimed before 2000.

"Enough for a search warrant," Davis said. "A thousand years ago, the odds were one in a million. Guaranteed we'll find a signature in the dye."

He called Gabe, and Becca was with him. "We need you both to come to Harrogate to consult in the questioning of Jarvis. Keep your eyes peeled for Bradley of course, as we don't know what part he plays or whether or not he's dangerous," Davis warned.

He asked to speak to Becca. "Do you have the ability to do a private confidential DNA test?"

"Yes, I can do that in my after-hours time."

"I'll send you an envelope.

In Harrogate, Gabe and Becca met Davis on the concourse of the East Parade for a briefing of the proceedings.

"Mr. Farrow and Ms. Clayburn, this is Inspector Knight from Scotland Yard. He will make the approach to Jarvis Turner and we will wait in the lobby until called. Turner is presently in a meeting in the company's boardroom. He's unaware of what is about to take place. No doubt, he will continue with his con," Davis said.

"Be assured, if he has gold bars or silver wafers in his safe, his eyes will shift directly to its location the moment you enter," Knight said. "I'll have men outside and close by, should anyone involved in the deception try to escape."

"Over there." Gabe whispered to Inspector Knight. "The man entering the elevator in the fisherman's toque is Bradley Turner. You're getting the whole family on a platter."

Bradley was nonchalant and oblivious to the unmarked police in the building. When he raised his hand to the elevator button, the serpent tattoo was visible.

"One at a time," the Inspector said. "I may allow the son to deliberately escape. We can tail him and see who he talks to or where he goes. We shouldn't assume that once Turner and Dodds are in custody, the entire scam comes to an end. This is an octopus with far reaching tentacles."

"You're in charge, Sir. We'll do as you ask," Davis said.

Inspector Knight and two officers took the elevator to the top floor, and a team of examiners waited for the next one.

The receptionist did her best to intercept, but a flip of the Scotland Yard badge stopped her, and the Inspector's entourage walked past with his eyes on the double doors ahead.

"Turner, I'm Inspector Knight of Scotland Yard."

Jarvis stood up, surprised and perplexed. "I beg your pardon. This is highly inappropriate. I'm in a meeting, Inspector, make an appointment with my Secretary." His fingers waved him away and he sat again, his eyes red with fury.

"That won't be necessary; I have a search warrant."

Knight produced a folded document and turned to the others at the table. "Gentlemen, give your names to my officers. Then you may leave, with the understanding that we may be around to make inquiries of you later today."

"This is not acceptable," Jarvis objected.

"Take a seat, Mr. Turner. You'll be more comfortable while we complete our examinations," Knight suggested.

Turner unlocked his private office and watched with Knight as an officer opened cabinets and drawers. A load of empty banker's boxes lined the outer office to be filled with suspicious documents and binders.

"Now, Mr. Turner, the search warrant includes the contents of your office safe. Would you kindly oblige by opening it."

Turner's jaw was clenched and his face twitched. "The audacity!"

"Sir, open the safe."

"I'll wait for my attorney to arrive."

"That won't be necessary, Mr. Turner." The inspector spread open the warrant document. "See this paragraph here, it gives us authority to proceed without him. Do you wish to comply or shall we cite you with interfering with police business."

From where Jarvis stood, he could see the commotion in the outer office, and caught a glimpse of Gabe Farrow, Sean Davis, and Becca Clayburn.

"How dare you bring those people here?" Turner was in the throes of slamming his fist into his desk and kicked the office door shut with a slam of his foot.

"The safe, Sir."

Turner angrily obliged, spinning the dial back and forth until it popped.

Knight poked with the eraser end of a pencil lifting documents and passed them to another officer wearing plastic gloves.

"List these on the manifest . . . what do we have here?"

With stacks of documents taken, it was apparent there was a false back within the safe, and a false bottom. "Do you have a key for this, Mr. Turner?"

"It's in the desk drawer."

Turner looked away, dreading the moment.

"Well, well, well," Knight gloated with satisfaction.

In an evidence box, they placed five cut dyes for eleventh century gold coins. From the bottom floor, they withdrew three tiers of small trays of gold ingots.

"Now, that we have sufficient information, Mr. Turner, would you now unlock your private bathroom and change room?"

"There's no need. There's no one there."

"What made you think we supposed a person in there?"

Turner made the decision not to say another word.

Light under the door provided the shadow of pacing feet, and one of Knight's officers removed a key from Turner's desk.

"You see, Mr. Turner, when we arrived, a young man got into the lift and went to this exact floor. He wore a fisherman's toque over his eyes, as though he were shielding his identity. But pressing the up button, the man showed a serpent tattoo on his right hand. Our information suggests that your deceased son had a similar tattoo. It represents something called 'Hydra'."

Turner raised his eyebrows at the mention of Hydra, but shrugged his shoulders in resignation.

Knight radioed for Davis's party to join them.

"This is Mr. Gabe Farrow. I understand you've met and know he was acquainted with your son, Bradley, at the Blue Cove in Staithes. He'll be able to identify the person in your change room, should it be your son."

"Bloomin' codger! Farrow, you have no idea what this means."

At that moment, Gabe was thankful Jarvis Turner was restrained. Nodding to Inspector Knight and Mr. Davis, their attention was turned to a second search warrant. On Davis's cue, they deferred the opening of the lavatory, to Jarvis's relief.

In handcuffs, Jarvis was led through the office, shielding his face. At reception, he said. "Lois, get my lawyer and demand bail immediately."

Inspector Knight remained on the upper floor, as the other warrant was served on Ian Dodd's office. No gold or plates were found in Dodds' safe, but it was the hidden files of the mail fraud and gold scam that satisfied Davis.

Davis invited Inspector Knight for a briefing with Becca and Gabe before they drove to Yorkshire.

"A good start, folks. Well done all," said Knight. "Turner is tight-lipped and has clammed up. The pair in Whitby will now be transported to the Curtis Green Building in London, and we expect the same stubborn lack of cooperation."

Gabe nodded. "Likely because they're protecting others. Their hopes lie in Bradley, that he'll deceive us further. Mr. Davis tracked Jarvis Turner's dealings offshore, with precious metals converted to bullion on the black market. The gold was certified, then exchanged for fraudulent certificates."

"Yes, it's only the tip of the iceberg. Our unit will check out smelters in the UK, and Bradley will never get out of our sight. If we're patient, we hope he leads us to where the gold is converted. We ask that the museum be a resource to help identify genuine and counterfeit coins, and signatures left behind."

"Absolutely, Inspector. Come by my office in London and we'll discuss this further."

"We'd like to keep details out of the press. They'll be like hunting hounds, eager to profit from those down on their luck, while digging up as many sordid details as they can."

Davis said, "Gabe, I suggest you now assist the detective unit in London—it's time to drop the curtains on this gold scam. Becca can handle the excavation site on her own."

The comment took Gabe off guard, not thinking about leaving Staithes this soon.

What about Becca and Niles . . . and Troy?

"Inspector, it will be helpful if Jarvis Turner makes bail. With Dodds and Hennie detained, he'll need to resort to others. We can't leave loose ends and have gold smuggled out of the country. And the information that Darby left indicates the scheme extends to mail fraud."

"I have yet to re-examine the Darby papers," Knight said.

Gabe still dwelt on the shock of leaving. "Whatever you require of me, Mr. Davis. However, I'd like to return to Staithes to clear up some personal matters."

Becca was silent and gazed into space. She'd become accustomed to Gabe being close, and glanced at him, thinking how handsome he was beside her.

His jaw was tight and pulsing. She came to know that was his reaction when upset, and she felt slight comfort. This was not a relationship she would let walk out of her life.

Gabe brushed the back of her hand discreetly, and she moved hers closer so they touched.

Adjourning the session, Davis gripped Gabe's arm. "I had a talk with your young lookout man. He's a hero, really—you might not have been found without his help. I'll see that he gets a finder's fee. Maybe there's a future in the detective field when he grows up.

"Oh believe me, he is grown up. Sir, there's another matter we need to discuss, that I mentioned on the phone. Are you leaving by car or train?"

"My chauffeur will come for me in about an hour."

"That's plenty of time . . . it's a sensitive matter." He looked toward Becca.

"I trust Ms. Clayburn implicitly," Davis said, and motioned toward the hotel lounge. "In here."

Davis and Becca sat in stunned silence as Gabe relayed the conversation that Niles Cobb overheard at Robin Hood's Bay.

"When and where?" Davis asked.

"It depends on the movement of the exhibit. Before it's on the road to London, I'll need protection for Troy. Maybe sooner."

17

BY EARLY AFTERNOON, Gabe and Becca arrived in Staithes, and Gabe chose not to go by Cobbs' Mill.

In these few months in the charming seaside village, he forged deep relationships in town. On the drive back, they both skirted the topic but knew it had to come up. He churned his dilemma over and over.

I don't have a fairy tale ending for Becca. After the tomb is closed, she'll go to London. My mission's done with the hoard. My father is still unresolved, and I'm angry about the scoundrel who stole from my family and took my father from me. I'm afraid of condemning the wrong man.

Becca played with her smart phone as if to read messages, but her eyes glazed without a focus. She was conscious of what she would say from her heart but feared the consequences. Gabe sensed her struggling as he stopped at the Endeavor. He got out and hugged her tightly.

"I'll come back later."

Tourists were flooding the town by Thursday afternoon for the long weekend, with most cottages and inns full. August first was a monthly changeover, overlapping summer visits, and another Monday Bank Holiday.

Gabe was chatting on Mrs. Capp's porch as a station wagon stopped in front, with suitcases tied on top. Two boys were hanging out the back windows.

"Mrs. Capp, I heard you have a vacant room on the third floor. We don't mind cleaning up ourselves; there's nothing else available. My family has looked forward to this the entire school year."

Maude looked at the family with compassion but wasn't ready to close up Hennie's room.

Gabe neared his landlady and put an arm over her shoulder and said, "Mrs. Capp, let me run and pack up the personals from 3C. We'll put the boxes in the basement. Hennie and his gang will not be returning—I heard that directly from Scotland Yard."

"Thanks Gabe. I'll get clean linens and towels." Maude looked both delighted and relieved.

The tourist gave his thumbs up to the boys, and received hoots of cheer. "Yeah!"

Maude returned moments later to see a second car in front, a yellow Fiat 500, with a young couple. They were early twenties and full of adventure. From the window, they asked about accommodation too. They were insistent and panicky that the town was full.

"Please Mrs. Capp, a friend sent me a picture of your boarding house and assured us you would have room. We've no place else to go." The woman was on Maude's steps pleading.

In a spur of the moment decision, Gabe took Maude aside again.

"Mrs. Capp, when I was in London, they talked about sending me to Harrogate on an assignment. You shouldn't turn away paying customers, when I may not be able to finish out the month.

A pained look crossed her face. "Gabe. No, Gabe—you can't mean that."

"Niles has a room at the mill I can use. If you could get me more linens, I'll pack up a couple boxes and you'll have plenty of room for these nice people."

He put his arms on her shoulders. "Sometimes we don't have control over what happens in our lives—this is one of those times. But don't think I won't come to take my girl for cherry custard ice cream." Gabe urged a smile. "Besides, the lady in the Fiat looks right for a cuppa tea on hot afternoons."

"Well, at least I'll have Becca for a bit longer."

Gabe bit his lip, not to speak on her behalf.

All in due course.

Gabe retrieved the tin box from the floor and the transmitter equipment from 3C and 3B. In two cardboard boxes, he packed all his personal assets to stash in the Vauxhall.

"Now that I'm homeless, I should check in on the Arbuckles about the weekend."

At the Endeavour, Becca was sipping an ice tea and was glad he'd come so soon. He leaned close and she closed her eyes in anticipation of a kiss. Leaning across the table he cupped her chin in his hand and caressed her lips with his mouth. As he pulled back, she blushed and looked awkwardly away yet sighing in contentment.

Gabe's spontaneous exit at the Blue Cove surprised her and she felt instant guilt for abandoning Maude.

"Should I take my room back? I think M.J. needs me to vacant the room here. They're overbooked this week."

She leaned her face close, with an enticing smile. "Will you join me for a drink?"

"You know I will. I was on my way to the Cleveland to check if they need me this weekend. I'll go later—being with you is much nicer."

"You're a popular man in town. I'm not sure they'll manage when you leave."

"I intend to spend summer weekends here. My roots just won't pack up easily."

"Don't be so hard on yourself. Folks will understand."

From the corner, Troy bounded to the front on his bike. "Gabe! Have you come for me?"

"I'm leaving for Arbuckles, but maybe you and Becca could have an early supper with me if I'm not working."

Troy hopped on his bike, with a brave 'okay' shielding his disappointment.

"We're alright tonight, Gabe, but we'll have weekend lineups out the door," Mandy said. "Theo's in Runswick for supplies, but come tomorrow at five."

Everything felt different to him now, concealing the deceit of his imminent exodus, and the danger facing the town.

Crystal rushed on seeing him and poked his shoulder in jest. "We've heard so many stories, we don't know which to believe. At least, it's good to see you're alright." She hoped for some news, but settled for a shared laugh.

"I can't stay now, Crystal, but I'm in the kitchen tomorrow."

Window posters for the weekend festival were on every store, and M.J and Becca taped an extra one at the Endeavor.

CORPUS CHRISTI LONG WEEKEND

Friday through Monday
9 a.m. to 10 p.m.
(Fireworks at dusk)
Milner's Art & Heritage Festival on High Street and Church Streets
Grand Prix Boat Racing from Staithes to Runswick Bay
End of World War II celebrations & parades (1940's)
Old Jack's Boat – the return of Bernard Cribbins
Garnett Sisters (1 p.m. & 3 p.m.)
Fund Raising (Silent Auction) for Disabled Miners – Marathon over Cleveland Way
Clay Pigeon Shoot off Cow Bar Bank
Short Film Festival at the Fire Hall
Chili Cook Off at Lifeboat Station
Pie & Cake Competition at Cleveland Corner (2-4 p.m.)
Three-Legged Races on Seaton Garth 10 a.m. daily
Beach Kite Regatta
Hiking Tours available at Lifeboat Station
Harry Potter movies on large screen, Cowbar Flat

Gabe was back quickly to see Becca again. M.J was on a stepladder with Becca holding the poster flat to the wall.

"Hi, M.J. I told Troy I'd take him and Becca for dinner tonight. No surprise he chose the Endeavor."

"He'll be tickled. I'm on the late shift—but I could sit in on dessert." Her eyebrows rose with a teethy grin.

Gabe asked, "How did Troy take all this commotion? You know he was the key to my discovery?"

"He was silently proud, and rightly. He's a humble tyke. I'm just glad everyone is safe and sound, and I'd dread the day if you ever left Staithes."

Becca put a hand on Gabe's arm, understanding his awkward situation. Her recovery was quick. "As Gabe will be at museum business away from Staithes, could Troy come with me to the excavation site? It will be a rare educational experience. Tell him I need a good lookout man."

I should have seen the deep compassion in her before. What a nice thing for Becca to do for Troy, and for me.

Walking uphill to the Blue Cove, Becca slipped her hand into his, without a word.

Troy burst into the Endeavor door, out of breath.

"Did you order for me? I caught a bucket of clams for Mrs. Capp as the tide started out to sea. I've gotten on to checking up on her when you're out of town, Gabe. Isn't that part of being a lookout man?" he teased.

M.J. joined the trio for lemon tartlets and a pot of tea. "It's gratifying to eat with friends for a change. I see why Troy likes you both so much."

Gabe was reticent, with his secret departure looming. After dinner, he walked Becca to the boarding house.

"Tomorrow, I'll put in a decent day's work for Niles, then stop here to see you before the Cleveland tomorrow night. I feel like I'm in no man's land."

"I've decided to stay at the Blue Cove," she said. "It settles things down a bit."

Her arms wrapped around his waist to pull him close. "Mr. Farrow, I might not sleep tonight, thinking about you. Although the changeover to Harrogate is unsettling, everything will sort itself out."

On her toes, he thought her lips were never softer and as he pulled her close he felt her heart beating against his.

"Ms. Clayburn, my dear Becca . . . do you feel a twinge in your heart as I do?" They kissed again at the door.

"Remember, Becca, you're my date for tomorrow's fireworks on the beach." He walked away backwards not wanting to take his eyes off her.

Niles was at the shop an hour before opening. He'd heard from Maude that Gabe would be sleeping in his back room, and arrived with a bag of pastries, warm from Saltburn.

"Mornin' Gabe!"

"Niles! Glad you're here early. The coffee started brewing a minute ago."

Unshaven and in yesterday's tee shirt, Gabe pulled up a milk stool to the antique hardware desk.

"Niles, I noticed you tried to be a hero when the sniper was set up across the field."

"I'm older than you, Gabe. But my years of experience give me equal standing. I knew you'd cut across field and it'd be safe to follow. But I never expected you to play out the David and Goliath slingshot scenario." He snorted in a burst of laughter.

"Pretty good shot, right?"

"It's been good for business. After the arrest, streams of tourists drove out from Staithes and Whitby to ask about the glass blower. Your buoys from last week sold out fast. Glad you autographed them."

"Good then that the kilns are fired up. I didn't mean to leave you in the lurch, but I knew you'd understand."

"Of course! I keep in contact with Maude. I know what's going on in your life before you do."

"I have something to tell you that even Maude doesn't know about. Sorry to bear bad news, but I have to confide in you as my deputized agent."

"Shoot, Gabe!"

"Bradley Turner is alive and well in Harrogate."

"That can't be true, Gabe."

"There's no question. He deceived us into thinking he was on our side and helping, but the entire time he was feeding bad information to distract us. My boss, Mr. Davis, has asked that

I consult with Scotland Yard in Harrogate next Monday. I'll be gone until Thursday.

"Niles, I told him about the conversation you heard at Robin's Bay. No one knows the timing of Dodds' plan, but the London Inspector indicated he'll get bail this week. The museum sharpened their screening of security staff, but it's Troy I'm mostly worried about."

"We're a small sleepy town, Gabe. Life goes on. Don't fret yourself. David Milner's son finished high school and wants a summer job before University next month. I'll bring him on as a helper, along with young Troy. We'll get by."

Gabe sighed, with the weight of Judas off his shoulders. "Now that's out of the way, what smells so good in the bag?"

"Cream cheese Danish or a chocolate croissant. You pick."

"Niles, do you know of any precious metal craftsmen? A novice that would melt gold coins into bullion?"

"Years ago, as a hobby, I bought one of those do-it-yourself melting kits. A couple of boxes are in the store room or attic. It came with a crucible, tongs, molds, and a ten pound furnace. It just needs Borax from a supermarket or hardware store. Other than that—no, I haven't heard of anyone so foolish."

The afternoon ground slowly for him, missing Becca and imagining sleuthing the moors with her. At 3 p.m., he cleaned and polished his bench for the night.

"I'm working at the Cleveland tonight, Niles. Is there anything to go there? I have my car today."

"Yes, yes, a single special order on the back desk."

Davis sent a new dossier to Gabe with Jarvis Turner's known travel routings of the last six months, with frequent crossings at Portsmouth to Le Havre on the overnight ferry.

Gabe phoned Davis. "I've read it. But what's it mean, and how did you get it?"

"Unfortunately for Jarvis, the UK opted out of Europe's Schengen Agreement, so all travelers need customs forms. Jarvis no doubt thought he'd beat the system, but there are records of his crossings and shipments.

"Jarvis or Bradley then shipped a suspicious box of Marmite tri-paks from Portsmouth to China. It's a unique British souvenir, in demand there. Photos of Jarvis and Bradley were sent to the Customs Office for ID, with interviews of nightshift officers. We suspect gold in the Marmite boxes.

"The quality of precious metals leaving London is superior to local resources in countries like China. They liken it to the Greek myth of Hydra—if you cut off one head of the serpentine, he regrows more to replace it. I'm becoming convinced that Jarvis Turner is the kingpin, with a long-time association with Dodds."

"Hydra. I saw a movie of it as a kid and it scared me to death," Gabe said.

"It's an analogy."

"You think the three heads are Jarvis, Dodds, and Bradley?"

"Does that surprise you?" Davis asked.

"No, but if so, that must plague Hennie. It would explain the trio in a photo I've seen. How do we set a Customs trap?"

"I doubt it will come to that. Becca comes to London next week with the exhibit, and we assume Turner's group still plans to rob Hardrada from under our noses. We've beefed our screening of museum employees, and narrowed our suspicions of employees. Only a select few have access to alarm blueprints, and photos of Stewart, Fergus and Bradley have gone to Inspector Knight's forensic facial reconstruction specialists.

"What have you decided for the boy, Gabe?"

"It won't be easy. I'll recruit Niles Cobb in Staithes and I'll need others to watch him. I'll let you know as soon as possible."

Hanging up, Gabe was distressed. It seemed an impossible task.

How can I protect Troy?

On the way to High Street, he took a detour to the Roxby excavation site. At the first chamber, he listened to Becca's explanation of the history to her new protégé.

"Awesome, Ms. Clayburn, Troy said. "I'll remember this experience for the rest of my life."

Becca caught sight of Gabe and smiled her approval of her new co-worker.

"Hi Gabe. Come to check on us?"

"I couldn't stay away from you," he laughed. "Hey, Troy, thanks for filling in for me. I'm wondering if the two of you can meet me at Seaton Garth tonight for the fireworks. I'll be finished work about nine."

"Sure, Gabe. If Mums isn't working late, can she come?"

Becca winked. "I'd like the female companionship."

It felt to Gabe like a boy's last day at camp, with misgivings after a great time, but having to move on. Checking his watch every thirty minutes or so, he couldn't wait to see Becca.

Have her eyes always twinkled like that, or maybe I was slow to notice.

At the end of his shift, she was waiting outside in an indigo crepe sun dress that flowed with the breeze. She stood with Troy, and a blanket under her arm.

"Gabe, Mums says to save a place and she'll find us in half an hour. She won't miss too much of the show."

"Great! Let's get a spot."

He reflected back to the May long weekend with the last fireworks, when the faces were mostly strangers. Now, ten weeks later, he could put a name to half of them.

Gabe surveyed the lawn chairs and blankets. At the beach, the honeymooning couple from the Fiat were lounging with soft drinks. Further near the beach, he caught a glimpse of the red pickup.

"I still haven't sorted out Stewart's role. Maybe the adage is right, to keep friends close but enemies closer," he said.

"I don't agree with that," Becca said, snuggling closer. Troy was twenty feet away with a beach ball, and Gabe used the chance to test some thoughts.

"Becca, who do you trust most in Staithes? I mean someone other than me? An extra lookout . . . you know." He whispered, "For Troy."

"Niles of course, and Maude has a heart of gold. Reg and Anne Firth are noble, and the Milners keep to themselves. M.J. is wise, but too close to the situation. You know more folks that I do."

"Niles and Maude . . . hmm. If we remove brawn and strength as factors, a collaboration or ruse might be the way. Whatever the plan, it's fair and time to talk to M.J. and Troy of the possibilities."

"I'll come with you for moral support." Becca tucked her arm in his. After the fireworks, the foursome walked up High Street, all of them still looking to the sky.

"Why are you so quiet, Gabe?" Troy asked. "Are you unhappy?"

"Troy, I need to have a chat with you and your Mum."

M.J. stopped in her heels, in alarm. "What is it, Gabe?"

"Somewhere quiet." His heart and Becca's both beat faster.

"Come up to the flat, we'll talk there." At the side of the Endeavor, she unlocked the door to the second floor.

"You're scaring me, Gabe," M.J. said, breaking the silence.

"I didn't mean to do that. I've been grateful to both of you for letting me spend time with Troy. He's an amazing boy."

Troy's voice was steady. "Gabe, spit it out. We can keep a secret."

"Yes, I know you will both keep a secret. This is a big one, I'm afraid."

"Shall I make a pot of tea?" M.J. didn't wait for an answer and returned right away.

"You know about my work with the museum. Troy has not only been a helper to find the tomb, but a good friend. Unfortunately, criminals are after the golden arrow and its booty. Niles Cobb overheard a plot by Hennie and Dodds to rob the museum when it all arrives. They plan to force my cooperation by threatening me with something very special."

"What is it, Gabe?" Troy asked. "What's more special than the golden arrow?"

Gabe could barely swallow the guilt in his throat. "You!"

M.J. gasped and reached for her son. Becca laid a reassuring hand on Gabe's back.

"Gabe, get away from my son. Stay away. I knew there'd be trouble when I first set eyes on you."

"No, Mum, I wouldn't change a thing. You have to trust me, I've learned how to take care of myself." Troy was calm and cool and his words cut into M.J.

"I always tried to be both mother and father."

Gabe said, "M.J. you're an amazing mother. I've been honored to have your trust up to now and I'll do everything in my power to see that Troy stays safe."

"If you could do that, this wouldn't be happening."

Becca interjected, "M.J., let us tell you what we know before you jump to conclusions."

"Alright. I'm listening."

Gabe started. "They're scheming to kidnap Troy as leverage for my cooperation. Of course, I'll agree to cooperate. The London police are involved and it's no longer up to me. If it happens, it would be after the exhibit arrives in London—but we have to devise a plan to see it doesn't happen.

"Troy, you're the best person to ensure they can't take you. Starting today, check in every hour with your Mother. At the slightest sign of anything suspicious, call Niles Cobb or Jimmy at the lifeboat station."

Gabe pulled a transmitter from his pocket. "This goes everywhere you go. The best place is in the bottom of your shoe. Niles Cobb wants you to help at the mill while I'm in London. He'll drive you both ways and your Mum can go on with her day."

"I'd like to help at the mill. I heard the Milner boy will apprentice there for the rest of the summer."

Troy examined the new toy. "And my own tracker."

"I have a plan," Gabe said, "but it needs your help. Get me some paper and we'll sketch it out."

M.J. was at first speechless, then rose and clasped her hands with a roar of laughter and approval.

"The very concept of the townsfolk doing this—what an idea!"

Becca added, "Everyone will be vigilant to ensure Troy's safety."

Troy asked, "Vigilant. Is that like a vigilante group?"

"Not exactly, Troy. Vigilante groups might take it upon themselves to retaliate. *Our* group will be watching and reporting."

Finally, a reason to laugh. Troy remained perplexed but joined in anyway.

In the morning, Gabe met at the mill with Niles Cobb, carrying the notes from M.J.

"Niles, this may sound outlandish. But the town is going to be the boy's guardian."

"The town?" Niles asked.

"Well, not the whole town, but a contingent of Staithes townsfolk. They're not aware yet, but we know who we can trust. We drew a list of twenty who would step up.

"This is curious indeed, please go on."

"Gabe said, "Tonight, I'll need your help. I'll also invite Captain Harrison, Becca, M.J and Troy."

Captain Harrison and Niles Cobb arrived on cue at the Endeavour for the proposal. M.J. and Troy held a table, and Gabe and Becca came together. Most knew each other, but formalities still dictated introductions. Gabe led the meeting.

"It's a plan to keep Troy safe, and every hour he'll be under a watchful eye." It's unconventional, but we'll enlist folks we trust.

Harrison interjected, "You realize you are on your own with this, Gabe. I just don't have the manpower to run this."

"Hear me out, Sir. You'll only be needed in an emergency. We drew a list of the most trustworthy in town, for a meeting Saturday. Tomorrow we'll approach each one and get their agreements to confidentiality."

Harrison perused the names, and smiled at some. "They're from all walks. This just might work. I'll listen."

M.J. said, "Well, he's *my* boy, and I say we do it. In Staithes, we look out for one another. It's our best quality . . . and we also pass information fast."

"I can't deny that," Harrison laughed.

Niles said, "Remember when the Harry Potter movies were filmed here—everyone had a role? That's what we'll do, assign roles."

"M.J. will schedule Troy's daily routine," said Gabe, "with someone always within twenty feet. Niles will monitor shifts and anything suspicious."

Harrison stood and nodded his consent. "Thanks for the invite. I need your update after the meeting."

On Saturday morning, folks slipped through the front door of the lodge, in the pretense of a watch program for the school.

Mr. Marlowe, the postman was first; next Vera Robbins, then Pickersgill and on down the list. The twentieth and last was David Milner, and Gabe locked the door.

Troy, Niles and M.J. sat on chairs facing the noisy crowd. Becca sat with Maude. Gabe took the podium, and the chitchat hushed.

"Thank you all. You have each been selected as esteemed townsfolk, worthy of this honor and responsibility." Maude Capp smiled at being raised in status from gossip to confidante.

"You'll each have shifts and roles to protect young Troy here. You know he's become a local hero of sorts . . . shall we call this Operation Troy?"

With a resounding applause, Troy stood up half way for an awkward bow.

Adding prestige, Becca stood to outline the Hardrada discovery and thank them on behalf of the London museum.

Gabe said, "Niles Cobb will be our coordinator. For sake of demonstration, let's say Jimmy from the Lifeboat Station has a shift from eleven to noon. Troy would need to be within view on the beach during Jimmy's shift. We'll give Troy an exact timetable."

Jimmy's hand rose. "Can we pretend we're fishing?"

"Well, it isn't necessary to pretend, you may certainly fish."

Marlowe asked, "Can he help me deliver the mail?"

"Yes, yes, be creative. Troy will accommodate you. Won't you, Troy?"

With his hands locked under wiggling legs, he grinned broadly. "Yes."

"We have photos of suspicious characters—if you see any, tell Niles. Before you leave today, check with him for your block of time." As Gabe stepped away, the throng surged toward Niles and Troy.

The next morning, Gabe was astounded as he peered down High Street. Not only was Troy delivering mail with Marlowe, but a throng of half a dozen other assignees were mingling along within a few meters, as if extras on the set of a movie.

Pretenses had no limit—some sweeping the cobblestone streets, dusting strangers' window sills, or watering flowers in every garden. Heads watched from upper windows and shopkeepers rested on lawn chairs with coffee and old newspapers to play their parts. The chairs were remarkably repositioned every few minutes within the twenty meter arc. Troy was well guarded.

You'd think they're producing a movie on Main Street.

18

TWO DAYS LATER, Troy's assignment was with Becca at the excavation tent. He stood in her view at the edge of the site, watching for the arrival of the museum caravan on Whitby road. At the triple blast of a foghorn, he called to Becca, as the red roof of a transport cab peeked over the horizon. Three silver tractor-trailers made a marvelous sight, with the insignia crest of the British Museum.

Inside the tent, the crating was complete, with sheet-slabs cut from the ground and walls. Hardrada's tomb was fully dismantled for reconstruction in London, with ceremonial stumps, and numbered stones and rock slabs in precise order.

Becca was uptight, following her own strict rules, never wavering from the accuracy of the blueprints.

"Isn't this fabulous, Ms. Clayburn?" Troy spoke softly.

"Yes, yes, of course."

"What can I do to help?"

The moment of his gentleness caused her to weaken. She allowed her body to slump to the floor and cradle her arms around her knees. "I wish Gabe were here."

"What would he say to you then?"

She smiled at the youthful blue eyes. "He'd tell me to buck up and finish the job."

"No, Ms. Clayburn. He'd tell you that you've already done a fantastic job, but it's time to let others help."

Rising to her feet with renewed spirit, she pulled Troy in for a needed hug.

"You're right, little man."

Her hand waved in the air. "Reynolds! Reynolds, can you take over here. I need some fresh air."

"Yes, Ma'am, glad to help."

On a grassy knoll outside the chaos, Troy asked, "Will you be going to London with the trucks?"

"Yes, Troy, that's my job. But we'll bring you and your Mum for the opening gala of the exhibit next month. I'll see to it that you have a pass anytime you can come to the museum."

Loading continued the next day, and townsfolk came to watch with lawn chairs and picnic hampers, as if it were a traveling circus. A mobile kiosk served free coffee and donuts, and the hamlet of Staithes was in its glory.

Troy arranged a front row seat for Maude Capp. Crossing her swollen ankles, she sat back in her lawn chair, proud of her recent superiority and recipient of Troy's attention. Maude knitted for the Auxiliary as she socialized.

"My, he's a fine boy. He brings me clams from the beach and checks on me every day." Maude ensured she was overheard by others in her gossip club, behind her in the row of lawn chairs. "He's like a grandson to me."

The assembled onlookers included Counsellor Newman, members of the Heritage Society, the Yorkshire Moors Warden, and Jimmy from the Lifeboat Station. Local firemen set up a display at the road, and the Whitby radio station broadcast with a live announcer on site.

Twenty meters away and with his eyes on Troy, Pickersgill kicked stones in his assignment.

A rep of British Geographic was granted entrance to the tent, and Becca was inundated with questions about Hardrada's tomb. Troy remained at her side, fielding questions and spewing historical facts that would spin a novice historian.

"I've arrived in Harrogate," Gabe said. "I'm driving toward the Turner estate at Knaresborough. Is there an update I should know?"

"Bradley Turner visited Dodds and Hennie today at the prison," Davis said. "He was disguised with a touring cap and grey beard, and they communicated in sign language so our bug was useless. Our detective followed him from the family guest cottage and back. He's there now, on the estate."

"Anything from Jarvis?"

"We're watching every move. Mrs. Turner left yesterday for relatives in Scotland. Our unmarked car is outside the estate. Let him know when you're close."

The detective hid his car on a gravel access and crept to a vantage behind a lilac cluster to focus on the guest house. He snuck to the side and fixed a transmitter to the front door window panel, then attached a tracker to the car in the carport.

Back at his own vehicle, he watched for Bradley to come out. Minutes later, Gabe called. "I'm here and parked a quarter mile from the gate."

Within an hour, Bradley emerged from the front, in the image of an old man, wearing a green tweed flat cap, brown sports coat and the identifiable grey beard. He followed a stone footpath to the carport and started up a dated blue Bentley sports car. He placed a worn catalogue case on the passenger seat.

The detective dodged low in his sedan before Bradley was out of sight.

"There he goes, right at the corner."

"I've got it." Gabe tailed the sports car to a petrol station north of town, with the detective behind.

Bradley waited, parked outside the convenience store. Simultaneously, a red pickup drove into the lot, and Bradley and Stewart entered the store together. With binoculars, Gabe scrutinized the door from down the street, and the detective watched, facing the other way.

A few minutes later, Stewart and Bradley exited. After a brief conversation, they parted. The pickup continued toward Masham and the Bentley returned to Harrogate with the detective in pursuit.

Gabe kept pace behind Stewart, replaying the events in his mind. An inconsistency nagged at him—both entered the store and both exited—the tweed cap, but the jacket askew.

"Dang Turner! It was Bradley's green hat and windbreaker, but the man didn't have a beard. It was a switch."

Gabe radioed the detective tailing the Bentley. "They switched at the petrol station. You've got Stewart in the sports car. I'll stick with Bradley in the pickup. He got a head start but his tail lights are still in sight."

Gabe texted Davis. 'Bradley's in the pick-up ahead but getting out of sight in traffic. Can you watch him on GPS?'

The reply was instant. 'The pickup is stopping at a lane. It's a farmhouse in Nidderdale.'

Gabe watched as he passed the lane. "Two people are inside—both Bradley and Stewart. It was a triple deception! Who was in the sports car then?"

He continued to the neighbor's lane and reached the detective and Davis by text.

The neighbor came out the side door.

"Hello, I'm afraid I'm lost. My cousin Bradley Turner has property out this way. Do you know where I'd find him?"

"Bradley Turner . . . no, never heard the name."

"What about Stewart Arbuckle?"

"Stu . . . yes, he rents the old farmhouse down the road. My only complaint is that he burns something with a bad smell. Grey smoke comes from his chimney, then for days the smell of burnt eggs lingers and blows my way. If you find him, you could suggest he tone it down."

"Will do. I chugged into your lane low on petrol. Would you mind if I cross on foot to his place? Stu keeps a jerry can in the back of his pick-up."

"Naw! His truck is in the drive, so he must be home. If he doesn't have any, come back and I'll get some from my barn."

"Much obliged."

By the time Gabe reached the farmhouse, grey smoke puffed from the garage chimney. He phoned Davis.

"I'm on Bradley's property. They're melting gold in the garage. We need a search warrant, and it's too risky to go in myself without backup."

"Don't get too close, Gabe. Hold your position. Send any photos. Oh, and Hydra is the name they use for their operation. Check in again within the hour."

"Yes, Sir. I have a Zen viewer and Q-pro to zoom."

So Hydra has a deeper meaning. The photo signed by Ian Dodds simply extended a lie that it was an old gang.

By the time Gabe neared the garage, his hands were swelling with welts and a rash from a patch of stinging nettles. Frantic with irritation, he yearned for cool water or anything to alleviate the symptoms.

He spotted a stream and followed the fence that way, but spied an open rain barrel first.

It's risky to move out in the open, but this is unbearable.

The cold water eased the itch, and in the scraps of a wild garden, he broke open a cucumber to wipe juice on the areas, thinking it could help in some way.

On his elbows, Gabe came close enough to the garage for his transmitters. He stood on his toes to place a mic at a window that was angled open for fresh air.

He lowered to the ground to listen through an earpiece. It was Bradley.

"There's already an unmarked, black car parked in front of the house day and night. We shook them today, but sooner or later one of us will slip up. And the blighter Farrow is apparently moving over to Harrogate to keep eyes on me."

"You say the word, Bradley, and I'll take care of him."

"What do you mean, Stewart?"

"On busy weekends, he works for my Da. Every day, he starts his shift with a double-double coffee. A packet of saccharine will do the trick and it's untraceable."

"That's outright premeditated murder. Stealing and counterfeit is enough," Bradley said.

Gabe heard it, and it wasn't consoling. He moved to a laundry perch near the back door, beside a bigger garden. He reached for another cuke, split it open and slathered his hands with the juice.

A piercing sound broke the silence—a blow horn, triggered by a motion detector. As two Dobermans charged from the cornfield at breakneck speed, Gabe searched wildly for an escape. With a ladder from the ground, he started up to the farmhouse roof to take refuge behind the chimney.

Footsteps scrambled from inside, with Bradley yelling to quieten the dogs. Neither budged from the foot of the ladder, both claiming and pawing at the rungs. A crow's nest was disturbed as Gabe scrunched in hiding, and the incessant cawing was enough for Bradley.

"Quiet, Damian, it's those daft crows again." A scan of the lane and fields didn't trigger any further alarm.

"Pay no mind, Stewart. My dogs go crazy when the crows charge at them. We'll finish this last shipment. The outside cams will pick up any movement, even rabbits and birds."

"You know, Bradley, you could make a lot more if you added alloy in the base."

"I'm not taking those kind of chances in a foreign country. Get the coin plates ready from the floor safe."

Smelting gold and stamping the plates took their next hour, with the coins moved to a cooling rack. Stewart spread a wad of mail on the desk and gloated as he counted the checks.

"Folks are so easily duped."

Bradley said, "I'll make the deposit when I get back to Harrogate. Print the certificates and we'll put those back in the post."

Stewart opened the desk computer. In a few minutes they had pocketed more than £40,000.

After two hours, Gabe started down the ladder, as the pinschers were long gone to the corn fields in search of more crows. He froze at the thud of security bars falling in place on the windows of the farmhouse and garage.

Stewart checked outside that nothing was out of place, and stopped at a tall metal box, the type used for breakers and electrical monitoring, on a utility pole outside the garage. Gabe held his breath, back on the roof ledge.

A short while later, the pickup spun out of the driveway with the two men and turned toward Harrogate.

When they were out of sight, Gabe stretched up to examine the utility box and delicately erased some video footage. Scurrying across the field, he started up his car at the neighbor's farm. He glanced back at a black vehicle arriving in the farmhouse lane. An officer exited and paced the perimeter.

So the house has security patrol while the sots are away.

En route to Harrogate, Gabe slowed down to ease past the same petrol station. The pickup was there again, with Bradley working on something in the cargo area.

Gabe alerted Davis, who called back in minutes.

"Our man is on his way to pick up Bradley's tail. Park nearby till you see him."

At a gravel turnoff within sight, Gabe rambled a verbal update on the farm.

"It confirms everything, Gabe. Oh, and we also agree with your conclusion that Henderson is Dodd's boss. Dodds is simply the go man between Hennie and Jarvis.

"We taped a visit by Bradley at their jail. It was hushed, but we got enough to determine the hierarchy, with an admission that gold coins from the Mulgrave hoard fund their scheme. It's admissible in court."

"Hope it stands up for a conviction. What about the cash-for-gold scheme? Are the Turners connected?"

"Good news, if you think it's that . . . yes. That and a get rich scheme are both linked to them. For the cash scam, they place ads in small town papers, and collect mailings of gold and jewelry at a post box in Harrogate. The postal manager described a serpent tattoo on the mailbox owner. The payout to the naïve seller is mere pennies on the ounce, with no avenue to complain. And the melted gold goes to China on the black market for premium prices."

Gabe's mind had stalled on mention of the second scheme. "Tell me more about the 'get rich' part. People are gullible and believe in a slip of paper, like they did later in the Madoff Ponzi scheme. In the States, my uncle lost his entire inheritance to gold certificate scam . . . as did my own father when I was a boy. So many had their savings wiped out. My uncle lost his life, and I lost my father."

Davis was silent, as Gabe's words penetrated his own memories of the Florida scam. On that day in 1996 when his world crashed, he felt unworthy of being a husband and father.

Patricia had looked into his eyes with love and forgiveness, but he had nothing to give back. Commiserating then in his personal failure, he determined to leave what was left in the bank for his wife, and disappear, hoping she'd get a fresh start. As he found out later, Patricia Hermes resumed her maiden name.

My boy's name was Samuel Gabriel Hermes. Patricia must have legally changed his name to her own surname—Farrow. Could this be? His brown eyes and golden curls have haunted me over the years.

Shaun Hermes had become Sean Davis after arriving in Bristol, finding work in an investment company and vowing to track and seek retribution for the demise of his life in America.

Yes, those are the eyes. How could I have forsaken my own child? Vivian knows nothing of my past . . . how do I resolve this?

Gabe heard the lapse in Davis's voice, but said nothing.

"Gabe, I've always regarded your instincts as truth," Davis said. We'll take a step back and make sure we've dotted our 'I's' and crossed the 'T's'. We need solid evidence."

Gabe said, "With a false name, I used a London postal box to buy a gold scam certificate from their brochure. It's been forwarded to my Harrogate hotel, and should have fingerprints and be another trail to the fake gold."

"Courier it to Inspector Knight as soon as you can. The caravan is en route to London with the exhibit, and Becca will return shortly to oversee the unloading and prep for the opening. A date is now penciled for the gala."

Gabe clenched his fists, disturbed that he'd miss her departure. "I'll stay on stake-out in Harrogate till Friday, then go to Staithes to see Becca."

"How's your plan with the townsfolk about the boy?"

"Troy's in good hands. I have full confidence in the town. I have to go now. The detective is here to tail Bradley . . . we'll talk later."

Davis opened the 'Farrow' file that Delia had left on his desk.

In his room at the Majestic, Gabe brewed a coffee with the supplies on the nightstand. The stakeout vehicle had confirmed that Bradley was back in the Harrogate cottage, oblivious to the noose tightening on his father's empire.

At a loud knock on the door, Gabe listened quietly. "We have an envelope for you, Mr. Farrow."

With tissue to prevent his fingerprints, he removed a congratulatory letter from Jarvis & Dodds, and examined the gold certificate. It reeked to him of prosperity, with watermarked paper and a security hologram.

"This could fool England's best banks. How could my uncle or father be expected to know? They were doing their best."

He placed it back in the envelope and readdressed it to Davis in London.

"Room service, please . . . I need a courier pickup for the morning, and tape to seal an envelope. I'll come down for it."

At the farmhouse, Bradley's security man shone his light on the footprints around the electrical box.

"Mr. Turner, did anything unusual happen when you were here? A section of the tape is blank and there may be signs of an intruder."

"The dogs were upset, but I called them off as it was the crows."

Bradley was agitated at his suspicion.

"You don't know what's good for you, Gabe. I can set a trap as easily as you."

He dialed immediately to a long distance number.

Davis arrived at Inspector Knight's office early for their weekly case update. The Inspector had significant news this time.

"About six months ago, Jarvis Turner took a parcel out of the UK through France. Customs asked for a declaration of items, and he flagrantly claimed it to be jars of Marmite as gifts for his friends, and offered three jars as a gift. He was smuggling gold ingots and coins that we tracked from the farmhouse," Inspector Knight said.

Davis said, "Bradley is booked to cross on the ferry from Portsmouth tonight. No doubt he'll be carrying Marmite," he mocked. "I'll ask Farrow to watch for Bradley taking a parcel from the farmhouse."

"Also, Jarvis Turner is persistent in trying to get bail, so I have decided to play ball. He'll no doubt contact Bradley, and we're releasing Hennie and Dodds on bond awaiting trial."

"Alright, let me know where Jarvis goes."

"Another thing, Davis, I received an envelope from Farrow this morning with a certificate he bought to test. We also ran a DNA on Farrow from the records in our database. It's been right under our nose."

Inspector Knight knew he had Davis's attention.

"My suspicions have been confirmed that Gabe's vendetta against the Turners is personal. He is of the assumption that Jarvis Turner may be his father and wants to make him pay for childhood abandonment."

"Leave it with me . . . and Inspector, can we keep this under wraps?"

"Of course, Sean."

Instead of driving home, Davis returned to his office and pulled out the worn manila envelope.

"I never thought this would come back to haunt me."

19

ON MONDAY MORNING, the museum convoy rolled out of Staithes.

Maude was on the porch early to watch for passersby. Bart Marlowe, the postman, stopped her to see if she knew yet of any imagined sightings of thugs scouring the town. She shook her head.

"What's the last word from Niles?" Maude asked.

"Troy's gone to the beach to dig clams. Jimmy Reagan radioed five minutes ago."

"Land sakes, this must be suffocating for the poor boy."

"Have you seen anything unusual up this way, Maude?"

"The only activity here this morning was my newlywed couple asking where Troy gets the clams. I sent them to the beach."

"Are they the pair that roam the streets in the yellow Fiat?"

"Yes . . . yes. That's unusual isn't it, Bart?" Horror swept over her face.

The postman was immediately on his radio to Niles. "Maude Capp reports an inquiry about Troy's clam digging at the beach. Have Jimmy check it out. They ain't townsfolk as far as we're concerned."

Seconds later, Jimmy was on the beach where Troy should have been. Instantly, the blow horn alerted everyone to the possibility of Troy's abduction.

Mary Jane ran out from the Seadrift. "What is it, Jimmy?"

"The couple from the Blue Cove. They came to the beach to ask Troy about clam digging. Did you see them?"

On her tip toes, her hand shielded the sun from her eyes. "There, Jimmy. Over there. They're putting him in the yellow car."

Three blows of the horn and the entire population of Staithes was on the streets, a number much greater that those sworn to secrecy.

Jimmy announced over his speaker, "The yellow car has abducted Troy. Intercept! Intercept!"

Niles was surprised to see the red pickup truck ramming the Fiat as it headed for the Hinderwell road.

"Thata boy, Stewart."

"Ahoy, thar!" Niles stepped to the middle of the road.

"Troy, get out of the car."

The Fiat made a haphazard attempt to back up and make a run, but a mob of angry townsfolk had them surrounded. The driver jumped out to run, but a crowd encircled him, and his only hope was that the police would rescue him. His passenger stayed inside with her head down as townsfolk pounded the window.

Detective Harrison arrived in minutes to declare that it must remain a secret until all kidnappers were accounted for.

The couple was taken to Whitby and held in separate cells without communication. The woman was the first to request immunity and provided Hennie's follow-up instructions.

"I'm to text this number and say the boy has been secured."

Harrison replied. "Send the text."

In the late evening, Gabe was phoned by the Harrogate detective, that Bradley was on the move. "Mr. Farrow, the suspect left his property with Jarvis Turner, and I followed them to the A661."

"Did he have anything with him? Like a package?"

"Yes, he did. It was a small carry on."

Gabe left the Majestic in a hurry and took the rental car to the outskirts of town, waiting for sight of his tail. The red pickup was headed toward the farmhouse, and as dusk descended, Gabe closed the distance on him.

Cruising past the farmhouse, Gabe observed new yard motion security lights. Two vehicles were in the lane and the garage lights were on. With his cell, he activated the transmitter on the garage window.

The driver's door was open on the black truck. As Gabe crept up behind, he heard their muffled discussion, then Bradley exited the building followed by a second man.

By gosh. How could Dodds be here? Davis would have told me if he'd been released from prison.

Becca answered her cell in her car. "Gabe, I'm driving down from Staithes behind the caravan. Troy is in good hands in town, and the townsfolk are having a lark, with everyone in on the caper."

"I miss you, Becca. I'll text later with my plan for tonight."

Gabe then called Davis. "I'm at the farm and they just left for Portsmouth. Can I get an update?"

"Scotland Yard is in charge now in Portsmouth. Customs ID'd Bradley last month, and we've traced him to a black market dealer on the French coast, and a Chinese liaison. The financial transactions incriminate all of them—Jarvis, Bradley, Dodds and Hennie.

"We've given immunity to the customs officer, Mr. Soulani, for his testimony. He accepted a hundred pounds for their Marmite to bypass x-ray or a search, and Bradley now offered it again. Soulani will cooperate when Bradley arrives tonight."

"Mr. Davis, how secure is the transfer of the exhibit to London? I know you and Inspector Knight have Portsmouth well in hand, but I'm concerned about Becca en route."

"Two armed guards and several escort cars. Why?"

"If you don't mind, I'll pass on being at the Portsmouth takedown. I want to get to London to make sure the exhibit and Becca are safe."

"That's probably wise. I'll let you know how we do here," Davis said. "As soon as it wraps up, we'll return to London."

Gabe sped to the museum, and parked at a quiet lane to wait for Dodds' truck and the exhibit convoy with Becca.

Dodds had picked up Hennie, fresh out on bail. Fergus was already inside the museum, integrated in the security unit and setting the stage for the heist. Satisfied that Troy's kidnapping was complete, Dodds and Hennie had no reason not to be overconfident.

Dodds boasted, "If the coppers picked up anything from prison taps, it was that Jarvis and Bradley will smuggle gold through Portsmouth tonight. While the cat's away, the mice can play. Jarvis was intending to throw me under the bus to save his reputation and bank account."

"Fergus is ready at the receiving bay," Hennie said. "It'll be swifter than waiting for the exhibit to be set up, when Fort

Knox security would then come into play. But keep in mind that they're being escorted tonight with heavy guns."

"Does Fergus have backup?"

"Let's say he has friends . . . you know, down and out on their luck. He hired a skilled fellow to disable the alarm, down for five minutes, then rebooting. I have a laser gun to demagnetize the cameras, and a pair of sawed off shotguns in the boot."

Hennie slotted six bullets into the barrel, delighting at the clicking sounds as they eased into the chamber.

After midnight, the high beams of the first transport rounded the corner, followed by two more. Gabe watched each one pass, then saw Becca at the end of the convoy, and a security vehicle behind her. Gabe pulled out from the lane and tucked in at the end.

He called Inspector Knight. "Are there enough units in the vicinity? The caravan has arrived and I've tagged to the back. I haven't seen Hennie and Dodds yet."

"Significant precautions have been taken to protect the museum, including a tactical unit on the roof with snipers in position, and an inside swat crew in the corridors. They'll be watching the warehouse as we speak."

"Becca and I will go inside now, if you say we're covered. We don't know who Fergus has as his inside man. I still have Davis's rifle, and Becca has a revolver."

Simultaneously, Dodds was on the phone to Fergus. "We've arrived, and we're outside, watching from the street. Gabe just went in with the Becca woman. Wait until the complete load has been taken off, and keep your eyes on the crates with the arrow and the cache."

"I'll need a few minutes warning when you want the alarm disabled, if the door's not open," Fergus replied. "Everything is a go here. There's a swarm of warehouse workers, dollies and forklifts, so it's easy to blend in."

"Good news."

Hennie got out to sort their assault weapons, masks and gloves in the back of the truck.

In silence, Gabe and Becca moved through the staff entrance toward the security office with their weapons raised. "Becca, you take the office and I'll assess the loading dock."

The security office door was wide open with no one inside, and smelled to her of burnt coffee. A lunch box was open with a half-eaten sandwich and a lukewarm coffee. Becca found a uniform from the coat rack.

Easing into the empty corridor, she looked for Gabe. A click of her heels echoed on the marbled tiles and she froze. Then a dark figure loomed in front, dressed head to toe in black, with a padded bullet-proof vest.

"Ms. Clayburn," he whispered. "Stay behind me, it's not safe for you to go further without an agent."

Becca nodded and followed behind the officer.

Three security guards and two employees were outside, guiding the transport as it backed to the ramp.

Hearing voices at the loading dock, Gabe moved closer to identify if one were Fergus. An agent stepped in front of him.

"Mr. Farrow, my name's Miller. I'll be partnering with you on Inspector Knight's orders. He has authorized me to give you a stun gun for protection."

The agent's finger was to his lips, deferring to hand signals. Gabe and agent Miller stayed low behind a bin and watched as two men stood over a rolling dolly.

"When crate #14 and crate #23 come off, snap open the lids and place the contents in this cart," Fergus said to his accomplice. "Quick and clean, and we'll wheel it out."

Becca overheard it, and from the shipping room she found an identical cart and inched its rubber casters down the hall.

The external alarm was disabled by the museum while the doors remained open for unloading. The largest slabs were carried by forklift into the warehouse, then the crates, and two hours later, #14 and #23 were checked off the manifest.

Like cradling a babe, Fergus eased the Hardrada contents into his cart. Smiling, he snapped the lid tight.

"Show time!" Becca whispered, stashing her uniform. "Officer, my staff would expect that I take charge. Allow me leeway to engage the unloaders."

"I'll have my eyes on you."

Becca clicked her heels again as a distraction on the marble floor and approached the dispatcher first.

"Everything going smoothly, Reynolds?"

"Very well. We'll finish ahead of time."

As Becca made comments on the unloading, Gabe crept behind containers to retrieve her substitute cart. From the adjoining mechanics room, he loaded it with a weight of mixed parts.

Inhaling her deepest breath, she stepped up to Fergus.

"Has it been a long night for you . . . ? You must be new here, I don't recognize you."

"I've worked nights the last four months. Probably not the time of day you are here," he joked.

"Of course, that's true." She stretched out her small talk as Gabe made the exchange, then did a pirouette to the office doors.

Fergus messaged Hennie. "It's clear here. Come on in."

Hennie and Dodds entered through the loading door, and Hennie took the cart from Fergus. Dodds raised the lid to inspect the goods.

"What the heck!"

A barrage of tactical police appeared from nowhere, circling the two with guns drawn. Naïve to the switch, Fergus grabbed the cart and headed for the door.

"No you don't. You thief!" Hennie shouted, assuming a double-cross. Dodds got off a pair of gunshots—one to the wall but the other through Fergus's shoulder. Before he shot again, Miller downed him with a stun gun.

Jammed and stuck in traffic on the A3, Bradley's temper was boiling. He called to Jarvis, behind in the Mercedes. "It's an overturned car ahead!"

"Just pass it! I don't care how! If we miss midnight, the next is six in the morning. Soulani's our ticket through tonight!"

Bradley's face was red in panic. "Okay, here goes!" He screeched out of the lane, narrowly missing an emergency vehicle, and fishtailed back to the open road to Portsmouth.

Jarvis gripped his wheel and followed at high speed, toppling a barricade and traffic cones.

"Now speed up!" Jarvis said.

At 11:30 p.m., Bradley pulled to the ticket office with Jarvis two cars behind. He locked up and went inside to queue up for passage.

From a parking lot, Davis and Inspector Knight stood beside an entourage of vehicles—a car with Customs officials, two Interpol agents, and a van from Museum's Security.

Jarvis knew he'd been spotted and stared back.

"He knows something is up," Davis said. "He could be erratic to do whatever it takes to protect his son."

"The lead now is with Scotland Yard," Inspector Knight said. "It's under control. Soulani will be the clerk handling him."

At his turn, Bradley stepped up to the familiar clerk. "I'd like ferry passage to cross to Le Havre with my vehicle."

"What kind of vehicle is it?"

"A Ford 350 pickup truck. It's 2007." He watched Soulani's keyboard.

"Are you transporting any illegal goods, Mr. Turner?"

"No."

"What is the purpose of your visit?"

"I'm meeting with an acquaintance. I won't be staying long."

He looked up. "We'd like to examine your vehicle."

Bradley moved foot to foot. "Why? You don't usually do this, Mr. Soulani."

"No problem, Mr. Turner. We have an alert tonight so we are being extra vigilant."

"Of course. My truck's outside the door."

Confused and flustered, Bradley looked over his shoulder for anything out of order.

My Dad's outside, he'll take care of this.

Two customs agents stepped from the darkness with flashlights on Jarvis. The lead agent tapped on the driver's window. "Turn off the car and step outside."

Jarvis was seated in a waiting room, and watched Bradley pass him with an agent. Opening all the pickup doors, the officer removed luggage and anything loose.

A sniffer beagle leaped onto the driver's seat, then to the floor, announcing something under the seat.

Bradley remained confident. "If you're looking for drugs, you've got the wrong man."

"This box here, Mr. Turner. What are its contents?"

"English Marmite. It's a gift for a friend."

"Bring those three boxes into the office."

The clerk led Bradley to a closed door. "In here."

"I don't understand. What's going on?"

On the other side, another door opened, and Inspector Knight of Scotland Yard entered with two men.

Bradley knew he was caught red-handed if they tested the Marmite. From the connecting office, Jarvis Turner sat with an agent, viewing Bradley's interrogation in a two-way mirror.

"You're Mr. Bradley Turner, I presume?" Knight asked.

"So what if I am. Is it a crime not to be dead?"

Bradley's toque was removed, revealing a mass of ginger curls. Sweat glistened on his brow in the prolonged silence, as Knight slit the center fold of the cardboard box.

"Hmm . . . Marmite. I wouldn't mind a taste." The Inspector enjoyed toying with Bradley and watched him squirm.

A prod into the middle of the first jar encountered the obstacles, and with a small prong, he withdrew the first of the gold ingots.

"What do you have to say for yourself, Mr. Turner?" The detective leered at Bradley, while Jarvis sat red-faced and tight-lipped next door.

"I had no idea that was in there."

"Shall we bring Mr. Soulani back and ask his opinion? We have a taped phone call from this morning—it's your voice notifying him of your planned arrival for the ferry tonight, and offering a bribe to bypass detection."

"I'm sure it's not my voice. I didn't leave my home in Harrogate until this evening."

"Make this easy, Bradley. We have witnesses and video of your movements today."

"Your father is behind the two-way glass, Bradley. I'm sorry . . . but he gave you up. We know it all, including conspiracy for murder. It's much more than smuggling as you know."

Bradley's eyes flashed with anger. "My father wouldn't dare."

Knight knew the words would pierce and allowed a moment.

"Your acquaintance, Mr. Farrow, deceived your father into believing that he was a long lost son. In a moment of conscience, he had to make a decision—between you, the son who has everything, and the other who lost his name and his heritage. It's called balancing the scale."

"That's preposterous! You're saying Gabe Farrow is my half-brother?"

Davis looked at Inspector Knight, pleading for a reprieve.

"Inspector Knight, this line of attack on Bradley is premature. Whatever offspring Jarvis Turner has is irrelevant to the smuggling of gold ingots."

"Yes, you're right, Mr. Davis. Perhaps you could pursue that later."

Knight returned to Bradley. "Son, for starters today, you're under arrest for smuggling gold across the border illegally, and for conspiracy to defraud the British Museum of Hardrada's arrow and burial cache."

"What conspiracy?"

"Did you forget your scheme to steal Hardrada's burial wealth? Ravaging the Yorkshire Moors with theatrics to scare the curious away? Two accomplices murdered—John Darby and Axle Bing? Whether or not you did those deeds is irrelevant, as you're both accomplices after the fact.

"And just minutes ago, your partners Dodds and Henderson were apprehended at the British Museum in London."

Bradley glanced helplessly toward his father's mirrored window for intervention. Watching it all, Jarvis remained stoic but appalled by the thoroughness of the investigation.

"Then to clinch the theft of the golden arrow, you sent two known criminals, Sally Robbins and Ken Billington, to kidnap and endanger a ten year old boy, as bait in your con."

Inspector moved over to Jarvis Turner's room. "I knew nothing about the kidnapping, I assure you," Jarvis said.

"That will be sorted out in due course. Today, we are arresting you for profiting illegally from UK resources and historical artifacts, defacing their image, smuggling and selling fraudulent securities. Interpol has validated the transactions."

In a lapse of compassion, Jarvis asked. "Is the boy alright?"

"Indeed, Troy Duckworth is safe in Staithes, thanks to the town's vigilante group. Robbins and Billington are lucky they were rescued by police as the town didn't take kindly to outsiders harming one of their own. You see, Jarvis, they have this grapevine . . ."

Jarvis knew no stone was unturned and interrupted.

"Spare my boy, Inspector Knight. Dodds was attempting to put the entire blame on my son and me, and Bradley did whatever he did to defend me."

The sullen Jarvis pair were led handcuffed to separate cars to return to London.

20

THE LONDON MEDIA buzzed about the planned re-enactment of the burial chamber and ceremonial circle.
Gabe sat in the museum corridor. Finally, Davis's door opened and Dennis Merkle of the Evening Standard left from his privileged interview about the exhibit and its arrests.

"Come in, Gabe," Davis said.

Gabe removed the tattered clipping from his wallet.

Words between us are unsaid.

He breathed deeply to start. "I wasn't sure if it could be Jarvis Turner or you. I was six years old when my father left. My mother was heart-broken and I hated him for doing that to her . . . but I wanted every night for you to come back."

"I'm so sorry, Gabe. I didn't know until Inspector Knight showed me the DNA. The Inspector dug into your background wondering if you had a vendetta with Jarvis. When

I saw your birth name, Samuel Gabriel Hermes, I knew. I immigrated here twenty years ago. After a few years, I married a beautiful Irish girl and we raised a three boys and our youngest is a girl.

"I was tortured by my poor choice to leave the States, but over the years I made untraceable deposits into your mother's bank to be sure you were provided for and had the opportunity of an education."

"I wanted Jarvis Turner to pay."

"You have every reason to be angry with me, Gabe. I can't redeem myself in your eyes, but I will do my best. Consider staying in London for a few days. We have a guest house and you'll be comfortable. It allows time to decide how to go forward as father and son. I just ask that you trust me as I trust you."

"I'd like to check with Becca, but we can talk later. Perhaps we could have dinner." Gabe offered an olive branch. "I'm glad it wasn't Jarvis."

The lightness of his joke broke the tension.

Becca's re-creation of the burial vault would spare no expense, with animated theatrics of shadows and chants, taking the visitor to the shivers of a ceremony of Hardrada's time.

Construction of a room-sized model of a Viking longboat was underway in hardwood, on floor slabs within the stone circle. The Roxby crates were still unpacked, with ancient unseen treasures that would be displayed.

With the opening gala invitations in the mail, Gabe called his young lookout man.

"Can't wait to see you in London, Troy. A junior suite is booked for you and your Mum at the Chesterfield Mayfair. And a room for Niles too. While in London, I'll show you all the town."

"Gabe, my school will have a Troy Duckworth Day, and I will be making a speech."

"Just tell me when, and I'll be there."

Troy's hero status became a town celebration, with a worthy, sold-out reception at the masons lodge. Wisely, M.J. was protective, preventing media interviews without her presence or Niles Cobb's, but national attention to the young boy from Yorkshire Moors was sparking a craze among children to view the exhibit. For every age, it was fodder for the press, sparking new interest in the history of the moors.

While in London, Troy was scheduled by Davis for multiple opening week events and appearances with M.J., and back in Staithes, the theft and kidnapping news was on every lip.

Sentinal in the Moors, London Museum

SILVER TRAYS of champagne graced the entrance foyer waiting for the official receiving line. Gabe and Davis arrived together in tuxedos from the estate eager for the unveiling of the exhibit, *Sentinel in the Moors.*

Becca joined Gabe, with a gentle kiss and slipped her arm in his. Gabe was in awe at her elegance, in a silver grey gown beaded with baby pearls, and her hair gathered into an upsweep. He whispered something precious enough to cause her to blush and kiss him again. She squeezed her hand, visible to everyone.

"I've missed you, Gabe."

Photographers roamed the room and rallied around Sean Davis insisting on a picture of him with his two field agents, from Yorkshire, responsible for the discovery of the golden arrow.

After the photo session, Gabe took the tattered newspaper clipping from the back of his wallet and discarded it in the nearest trash can.

I need to find Troy.

Gabe rose on his toes to scan for Troy, and spotted Niles across the room with M.J.

Surely Troy is there too. He's just not tall enough to in the crowd.

With Becca, he eased his way over. Beaming, Troy stood between M.J. and a man that Gabe didn't recognize.

"So glad you're here Troy, M.J . . ." He waited for an introduction.

"Gabe, this is my Da. He came back to see us."

"I'm pleased to meet you, Sir."

Kyle Duckworth was a shy, tall man, lean and rugged from days at sea. After formalities, Gabe took him aside for a word.

"Mr. Duckworth, you have such a treasure in Troy. I grew up without my Dad and yearned always for him. I want you to remember this conversation every day of your life, when you wake up in the morning and go to bed at night. Your only job in life is to love your family. I've heard that you have a passion for the sea . . . but I also know a good man that could apprentice you as a glass blower right in Staithes. I hope you would consider that."

Within a few feet, Niles smirked. Troy moved close and pressed his hand into his father's, curious about their talk.

Kyle Duckworth looked into Troy's freckled face. "What would you think if I applied to Mr. Cobb here to be a glass blower?"

"Oh Da, that would be wonderful!" His young blue eyes pooled with water but his toothless smile beamed from ear to ear.

EPILOGUE – ONE YEAR LATER
(In order of Appearance)

Gabe Farrow:

Continued field assignments on Yorkshire in archaeology for the British Museum. He and Becca purchased a cobblestone cottage on Cow Bar Lane to spend every summer in the town of Staithes, with long walks on the beach and stories with local merchants and residents. He felt indebted to the townsfolk, to those who helped him generously.

Bradley Turner:

Faced numerous charges for his part in conspiracy to murder, smuggling, theft, and defrauding the Securities Commission. Serving a life sentence at Millbank. Was injured in a knife fight in the prison courtyard with Dwight Henderson and was removed to a different prison.

Maude Capp:

Gabe Farrow gifted Maude a share of his finder's fee. She went into a partnership with Vera Robbins and they remodeled the Blue Cove into a Bed & Breakfast. Regular Ladies Auxiliary meetings were held in the new parlor every Wednesday afternoon. She was invited to give a talk at the Cook Museum about her experiences during the heist of Yorkshire.

Troy Duckworth:

Received honors in History at school for his project on English history. He enjoyed summers at Cobbs' Mill as the honorary adopted grandson of Niles Cobb. Kyle Duckworth excelled as an apprentice as a glass blower and was the instigator bringing a Boy Scout troop to Staithes-Hinderwell. M.J. is now the owner of the Seadrift thanks to Troy's finder's fee.

Dwight Henderson:
Tried on numerous charges including murder, smuggling, theft, conspiracy to kidnap and smuggling. Serving a life time sentence in Millbank Penitentiary in London. Joined an in-house power gang with a vendetta against Jarvis Turner for evidence against him.

Fergus:
Provided evidence in trials against Hennie and Dodds. Serving a five year prison sentence he was assigned to a road crew, and managed to escape. Believed to be somewhere in Scotland.

Sean Davis:
Provided evidence against the Florida gold scam class action suit and contributed to Ian Dodds' conviction on smuggling and mail fraud. Frozen funds taken from Jarvis Turner and Ian Dodds were re-appropriated to victim claims from frauds over the years. Sean, with Vivian and his children, spend Victoria Day weekends with Gabe and Becca. Sean funded the building of a new community center in Staithes.

Niles Cobb:
Held in high esteem for his leadership to Staithes during the kidnap caper. His glass buoys were in demand all along the northern coast of the North Sea. He made a business plan with Kyle Duckworth to buy out the mill over the next ten years. On weekends, he volunteers at the Lifeboat Station of Seaton Garth.

Ian Dodds:
His co-conspirators threw him under the bus in court for a lengthy list of crimes over a twenty year period. Life sentence without chance of parole. He was featured in a magazine

article entitled 'One of the Most Despicable Criminals of England' written by Dennis Merkle.

Jarvis Turner:
Found guilty of mail fraud, smuggling and interference with the Securities Commission. He was not connected to the murders or kidnapping, and received a twenty year sentence in a medium security prison. Suffering failing health.

Stewart Arbuckle:
Pled guilty to conspiracy, however he was congratulated for his role in halting the kidnapping of Troy Duckworth. Townsfolk petitioned for leniency in his court hearing and he was given five years' probation in community service to Staithes.

The End.

For the latest on our upcoming books, see us at

shirleyburtonbooks.com

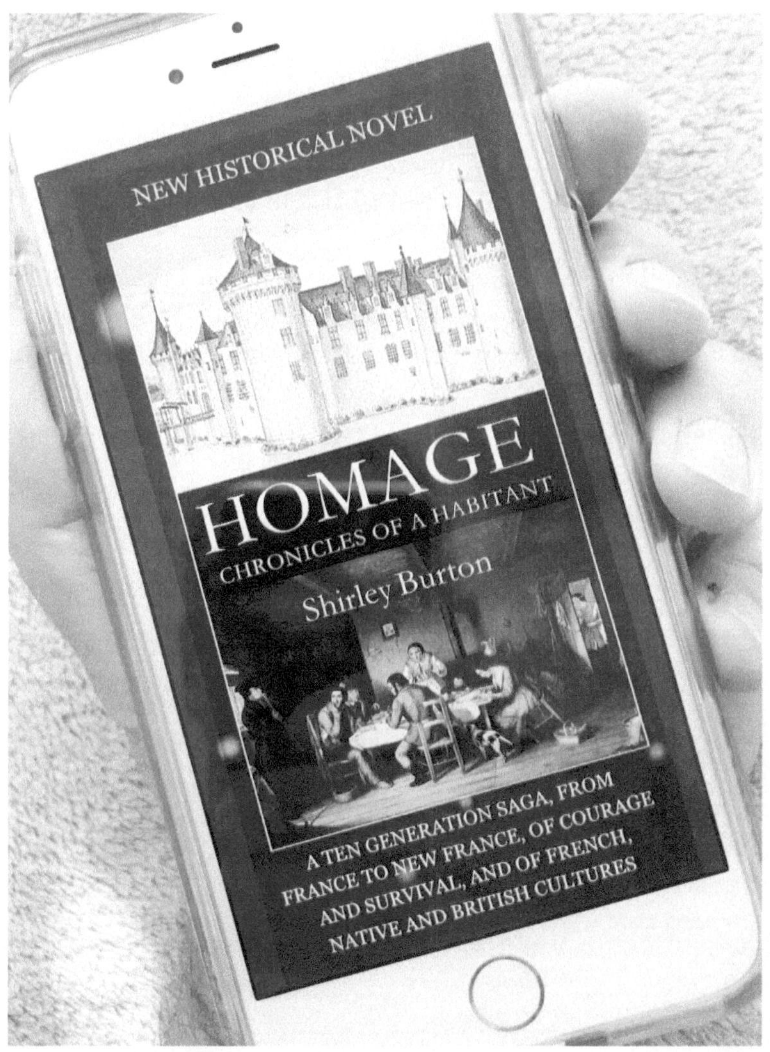

HOMAGE

CHRONICLES OF A HABITANT

622 Page HISTORICAL FICTION

Shirley Burton's ten generation historical fiction, beginning in France in the 1600s. A journey based on a family's lives, tragedies and immigration to North America. Experience typical life as early migrants travel from France to settle in Quebec, with generational conflicts and cultural clashes in the early centuries of the new land.

www.ingramcontent.com/pod-product-compliance
Lightning Source LLC
Chambersburg PA
CBHW020600310726
48979CB00008B/1279/J

* 9 7 8 1 9 2 7 8 3 9 1 1 9 *